She stood up and ran down the sand hill to the beach, stopping short of the incoming tide.... When the man appeared in front of her, she could not imagine, at first, where he had come from. It was as if he had appeared by magic from the sand.

"How did you get here?" she cried. "I didn't see you." And she began to run towards him, tears streaming down her face.

It was only when she saw the blade of the wide, triangular kitchen knife, shining in the moonlight, that she began to feel afraid. It was that and his failure to answer, his stillness and silence. She realized then that he had been waiting for her. He had known all the time where she was....

Also by Ann Cleeves
Published by Fawcett Gold Medal Books:

A BIRD IN THE HAND
COME DEATH AND HIGH WATER
MURDER IN PARADISE
A PREY TO MURDER
A LESSON IN DYING

MURDER IN MY BACKYARD

Ann Cleeves

FAWCETT GOLD MEDAL • NEW YORK

A Fawcett Gold Medal Book
Published by Ballantine Books
Copyright © 1991 by Ann Cleeves

All rights reserved under International and Pan-American Copyright Conventions. Published in the United States by Ballantine Books, a division of Random House, Inc., New York.

Library of Congress Catalog Card Number: 90-93578

ISBN 0-449-14720-7

Manufactured in the United States of America

First Edition: April 1991
Second Printing: August 1991

1

Stephen Ramsay moved into the cottage in Heppleburn on March 1. When the estate agent first sent him the property details, he dismissed the place out of hand. He did not want to live in Heppleburn. The village had been the scene of a disastrous period in his career and he thought he would always be reminded of failure. Then, on a cold Sunday afternoon in January, he went to look at the place just out of interest. It was at the end of a quiet road on the edge of the village. He drove past a small row of miners' houses with long front gardens dug over, ready for the spring, and then there was open countryside—except for the low, white cottage with the estate agent's sign outside. It was beginning to drizzle. Beyond the cottage the road dwindled into a farm track and then a public footpath, which led down Hepple Dene to the sea. Ramsay stood by his car in the rain and looked at the cottage. It was old, built before the miners' houses, before the Industrial Revolution. It was single-storeyed, whitewashed with a grey slate roof, and it was small. The front door was below the level of the road, and it seemed that the house had been built into the hill. From the back there would be views over the dene to the woods and the fields beyond. Now, when the trees were bare, it might be possible to glimpse the sea, slate-grey as the roof, between the hills. Ramsay had never been impulsive. In his relationship with Diana she had been the irresponsible one, laughing

1

at his desire for a conventional security. But now, standing, listening to the dripping trees, the decision was immediate and irreversible. It was late afternoon and very quiet. A red van loaded with turnips drove up the farm track towards the village. The driver stared at Ramsay as if he recognised him. He probably did. Everyone in Heppleburn knew Ramsay. But even that thought failed to deter him from his decision.

He crossed the road to the cottage and knocked at the door. Eventually it was opened slightly by a small, frail man who peered out nervously. The garden must have seemed almost dark to him. Ramsay could see nothing of the room inside.

"I want to buy your house," he said.

The old man looked around him, as if searching for help. He clearly thought Ramsay was dangerous or deranged.

"I don't know," he said. He had not understood. "My daughter told me I wasn't to show anyone around when I'm here by myself. We told the agent—appointment only."

He would have liked to shut the door in Ramsay's face but did not quite have the courage.

"That's all right," Ramsay shouted. He had decided the man was deaf. "I'll not disturb you now. I've seen enough. But I want to buy it. I'll tell the agent tomorrow."

He turned and left the old man gaping, still peering out from the crack of the door.

Ramsay hired a van and on March 1 he moved his belongings himself. It was not that he needed to save money. He had enough, and since his wife had left there was no-one to spend it on. He had offered, in his old-fashioned, gentlemanly way, to support her, but she had laughed at him. She wanted freedom, she had said extravagantly. Not cash. So he was motivated not by meanness but by a peculiar form of pride. It seemed wrong to him to pay someone to do a task that he could perform perfectly adequately for himself. He also felt distaste at the prospect of a stranger touching his personal belongings, especially those given to him by Diana. So he had tackled the job himself, with the help of a colleague, Gordon Hunter.

Ramsay realised that his request for help from Gordon

2

Hunter marked a change of attitude. He had never before met Hunter away from work. Even before his marriage he had found the male, beer-drinking evenings in the pub distasteful. Diana, he realised later, would have rather enjoyed them, and perhaps because of that he kept her away. He knew that at work he was thought of as distant, aloof. He married above him, they said, and now he thinks he's better than us. When he was still living with Diana, he caught whispered suggestions in the canteen that with all her money he ought to retire. When they separated, no-one offered sympathy or understanding. Perhaps they were rather pleased. It took him down a peg or two and showed he was mortal like the rest of them. So when he asked Hunter if he was free on Saturday morning to give him a hand to move some of the bigger items of furniture into the cottage, his colleague was shocked.

"Why, aye," he said. "Of course I'll help." Ramsay sensed that things between them would never be quite the same again.

They worked all morning, carrying the heavy furniture, most of it donated carelessly from the big house in Otterbridge by Diana, into the cottage. At midday Ramsay took Hunter to the Northumberland Arms and bought him several pints of beer and his lunch. The landlady recognised him and smiled but did not ask what he was doing there, so he thought the news of his move must already have reached the village. In the afternoon Gordon Hunter left—he would want to be in Newcastle on Saturday night and it took him time to prepare—so Ramsay was left to inspect the house alone.

Apart from a cursory glance when he was shown round by the estate agent, he saw the inside of the house for the first time when he moved in, and they were too busy at first for him to look properly. There had been surveys, of course. He was not such a fool that he did not care whether or not the place was falling down. But he had not wanted to inspect it in detail until the cottage was his. He wanted to see it stripped of the sad memorabilia of the old man's life: the photographs in heavy frames, the hand-embroidered chair backs, the plastic mug for holding false teeth in the bathroom.

3

From the front door there were two steps down into the living room. It was the biggest room in the house, the width of the cottage, with windows onto the road and at the back overlooking the dene. It had been a mild February and in the small back garden there were daffodils in the borders and a forsythia tree in bloom. The crocus were past their best. Inside the room there was a narrow brick fireplace. The windows were low and the sills two feet deep. At opposite ends of the room facing each other were two doors. One led along a narrow passage to two bedrooms and a tiny bathroom, the other to the kitchen, which had been built as an extension. Ramsay carried the last packing case down the steps into the house just as it was getting dark, and almost immediately after, as if he had been watched, the doorbell rang.

Outside stood a spry, white-haired old man. He was small and immaculately dressed with black shoes that gleamed in the light of the hall. He thrust out a hand towards Ramsay.

"Hello," he said, and his accent was as thick as any Ramsay had heard. "I'm your new neighbour. I'm a bit of a friend of Jack Robson, like, and he said you were moving in. Wor lass sent us round to see if there was anything you need."

"No," Ramsay said. "I'm all right. I think. But it was kind of you to call."

"I'll be away then. She'll have the scran on the table."

"No," Ramsay said, and that, too, was an indication that things were changing, that he had decided it was impossible after all to live in complete isolation. "Come in. I've a drink somewhere. You'll have one with me to welcome me in."

As the old man moved into the house, even Ramsay recognised that things were different. In the three years since Diana had left, no-one had crossed the threshold into the Otterbridge flat he had rented. Here, in a day, he had received two visitors. He went into the kitchen and unwrapped glasses from newspaper and rinsed them under the tap. He poured out whisky and took it to the living room, where the old man was staring out of the window into the dark.

"What made you buy this place then?" he asked.

4

Ramsay considered and followed his gaze to the window. "That probably," he said. "The view."

"We'll have to hope it'll still be there in five years' time," the man said. "I'd not bet on it myself."

"Why?" Ramsay asked. "What do you mean?"

"Do you not know who owns that land?"

"No," Ramsay said. "I'd presumed it belonged to the farm in the lane."

"Him!" The old man almost spat his disapproval. "He's nothing but an asset stripper."

"Who did he sell it to?"

"A man called Henshaw," the man said. "A builder from up the coast. He specialises in executive developments in rural situations. That's what his adverts say. I've heard them on the local radio."

"The council wouldn't allow building there," Ramsay said. "It's green belt. I checked before I bought the house."

"It'll not be up to the council, lad. Not anymore. And I don't think that bunch in Westminster know what green belt means."

They finished their drinks in silence and then the old man left.

At the time Ramsay considered the conversation as doom-laden scaremongering. The dene was a local beauty spot and it was inconceivable that development would be allowed there. Later he saw it as almost prophetic. It set the tone for his work over the next few weeks, and when he met Henshaw, he felt that his judgement had been corrupted.

Ramsay woke the next morning to a fresh southeasterly breeze that rattled the bedroom window and swept through the trees beyond the burn on the other side of the dene. He made a pot of real coffee and felt pleased with himself because he found mugs in the first packing case he tried, until it came to him that fresh coffee was a taste he had acquired from Diana. Diana had been on his mind more often this winter because she had sent him a Christmas card. It was the first approach she had made to him since the divorce came through. He saw her occasionally in Otterbridge, striding

5

down the centre of Front Street as if she owned the place. Her confidence still gave him a thrill of admiration and excitement, but he was too proud to let her see him watching. He wondered if the card meant she was already bored with her new husband, but the notion gave him no pleasure. He would like to think she was happy.

He took his coffee to the living room and sat on the windowsill, watching the clouds blow across the sky from the sea. He felt unusually content.

The sound of the phone shocked him and he answered it automatically without thinking who might be there. He should have known it would be work. Who else was there to phone him at home?

"Sorry to disturb you," the voice said, and he realized he must have sounded as if he had just woken up.

"That's all right," he said. It was Gordon Hunter, excited, breathless, urgent. But as Ramsay listened to the voice of the other policeman, he was still staring out of the window at the racing clouds. When he replaced the receiver, it took him longer than it usually did to prepare to leave.

2

Further north, along the coast, the east
wind pushed hard grey waves into Brinkbonnie Bay, blew
strands of dry seaweed around the legs of cattle grazing on
the dunes and sand into the road in drifts. It was March 1 but
still as cold as winter. The small boats kept on the beach for
fishing in the summer were still upturned in the carpark next
to the shop that sold ice-creams to day-trippers when the
weather was good. In the cottages that were so close to the
beach that the washing lines stretched out into the sand hills,
people listened to the wind and were glad that the tides were
low that week.

The bay spread for seven miles in an unbroken sweep of
beach and dunes, and Brinkbonnie at the southern point was
the only village. It was a straggling, ill-defined place. There
was the row of cottages along the water's edge with the post
office and the ice-cream shop as part of the terrace and Tom
Kerr's garage. Inland was the green, muddy and bare from
a winter of children's games, overlooked by the Castle Hotel,
some pleasant grey-stone houses, and the village hall. Then
the road continued west towards Otterbridge, and along it
were farms and an occasional monstrous surburban villa.

The Tower was to the north of the village on a rise in the
land backed by an old deciduous wood. It was older and more
impressive than the church that had been placed beside it.
The Tower had been built by a settlement of border reivers

7

who irritated the clansmen of Scotland by stealing their cattle and burning their houses. It stood, facing east, to withstand raiders from the sea. More recently it had been restored, almost rebuilt by an affluent Victorian, and turned into a comfortable house with views over the flat green fields and pools behind the dunes.

Alice Parry looked out of one of the upstairs Tower windows and briefly hoped that the rain would stay off until the family arrived that evening. Rain, she thought then, was the least of her troubles. She absorbed other people's problems and cared about them as if they were her own. She thought about Charlie Elliot, who had left the army and was such a worry to his father. She thought about Olive Kerr, who helped with the housework at the Tower and who had seemed so strained and nervous since her separated daughter had come to live with her. It was a compliment, she supposed, that they confided in her, and she wished she had answers for them. Then she thought of the proposed development in the village and her responsibility for it and decided that at least she could do something about that. She fetched her coat and outdoor shoes and then set off for the village, leaving the kitchen door unlocked, as she always did, until last thing at night. She walked quickly, ignoring a twinge of arthritis, which seemed to have got worse since her husband died.

The main entrance to the Tower was from the Otterbridge Road, but Alice took the footpath through the churchyard that brought her out by the village hall. She looked at her watch as she came out into the street and saw that it was already two o'clock but thought that it would not matter. Village meetings never started on time.

She was surprised by the number of cars parked in the street. She knew the controversy of the new houses had stirred up feelings in Brinkbonnie, but she had not expected people from the outlying farms to be so concerned. As she walked up the road she saw a few other latecomers enter the hall, but when she reached it the door was shut again. She stood outside for a moment to catch her breath and looked in through the smeared glass pane in the door. The hall was

8

packed with people sitting on uncomfortable wooden chairs. Behind a table on the stage sat Fred Elliot, postmaster and chairman of the parish council.

As she watched he stood up and began to speak. Even from outside she could sense his nervousness. He was used to meetings but would never have spoken in front of so many people before. Mrs. Parry felt awkward now about pushing open the door into the hall in case the interruption should put him off his stride. Before she could decide whether to go in and listen or go away, the door was suddenly opened from inside and she stumbled into the room. There was the sudden smell of damp, the gas fires they used to try to dry the place, and mice.

"What's this then?" said the big man who had opened the door. It was Charlie Elliot, the mechanic from Tom Kerr's garage, Fred Elliot's son. "It's a spy from the opposition."

There was a little embarrassed laughter and, encouraged, he went on.

"Come to gloat, have you, Mrs. Parry? Come to see how much money you're going to make?"

He looked round for admiration, like a child showing off.

Everyone in the hall was staring at her. She felt hot and angry.

"No," she said. "Not at all. I wanted to explain. I'm on your side."

But he would not listen.

"A development in the heart of the village, home for a couple of dozen yuppies. I suppose you think that's just fine."

"You don't understand," she said. "I'm on your side."

He seemed to hear her for the first time.

"How's that then, Mrs. Parry?" he said, still playing to the audience. "You're the one that sold the field behind the Tower to Henshaw. He couldn't build all those fancy houses on it without you."

"Away man, Charlie!" Fred Elliot called from the stage. "This is no way to run a meeting. Give Mrs. Parry a chance."

"Go on then," Charlie said sulkily, nodding towards the

9

stage. "You wanted to explain. Go up there and tell us all about it."

She walked to the front of the hall, her sense of outrage at the position Henshaw had put her in getting her through the awkwardness. She stood on the stage beside Fred. As she spoke she was acutely aware of her southern, middle-class accent. It's not my fault, she wanted to say. I was born in Northumberland, too. I didn't ask to be sent away to school.

"It's true that I sold the land to Henshaw," she said. "But he misled me about the sort of development he was planning for the Tower field. I suppose I was foolish to trust him, but he showed me professionally drawn-up plans. He said there would be twenty small, reasonably priced houses for local families and six retirement bungalows. I talked to members of the parish council and they approved of the idea. . . ."

She faltered. A strand of white hair had become unpinned from her untidy roll at the back of her head. She felt old and self-conscious.

"That's a bloody big field for twenty-six little houses," Charlie shouted from the back of the hall. "What did he tell you he was going to do with the rest of the land?"

Mrs. Parry blushed. "I know it sounds naïve," she said, "but he told me he was planning a children's play area and football field. I believed him." She looked round the hall. "I sold the land for well below the market price," she said helplessly, "because I wanted to so something to help the village. I've been so happy here. I'm sorry. Really. I'm sorry."

There was a sympathetic silence, but Charlie shouted: "It's all very well being sorry, isn't it, but that won't stop Colin Henshaw from building eighty executive detached dwellings, each with a double garage." He sneered as he quoted the exact wording on the planning application. "We'll be outnumbered. There'll be more incomers than there are of us. Of course, you're an incomer, so maybe you'll feel at home with them."

"Charlie!" Fred Elliot said sharply. He turned apologetically to Alice Parry. "Go on, pet," he said.

10

"The planning inspector has approved Henshaw's plans," she said, "but the council still has time to appeal against the inspector's decision. That's why I'm here. We must persuade the council to fight the case in the high court. I want to support your campaign. I don't want Brinkbonnie ruined any more than you do, and I'll fight to protect it."

She sat down to a spasmodic burst of applause and to more jeers and hisses from the back of the room.

Fred Elliot called for a vote on Alice Parry's idea that they should put pressure on the council to fight the planning inspector's decision. The motion was overwhelmingly carried and they settled down to form an action committee and to arrange a petition and letters to local councillors. When Alice left the hall to return to the Tower, it was four o'clock.

Outside the wind had strengthened and sand blew up from the street and stung her eyes. In the shelter of the high wall that surrounded the churchyard, she moved more quickly, almost running. She was glad to have attended the meeting—it was better, after all, than staying at home feeling guilty—but there would be a rush now to have everything ready before her visitors arrived and she felt overwhelmed by it all. Her nephews and their families always came to Brinkbonnie on St. David's Day. It was a tradition that had begun when her husband was alive. He was a Welshman and had demanded that they celebrate the day. She was never sure how much the boys valued the effort she made but kept the tradition for her husband's sake and because she knew the children enjoyed it. She especially enjoyed the company of the children, and as she grew older she thought she had more in common with them than she did with Max and James. She had never had a family.

She let herself in through the kitchen door at the back of the house and plugged in the kettle to make tea. Tea always had a calming effect. Then she began the preparations for dinner and was standing at the window, beating cream in a large glass bowl, when she saw a young woman walking down the drive. The woman, who was so young that to Alice she was a girl, had been in the village hall, though Alice did

11

not recognise her as a local. As she approached the house she hesitated, uncertain which door to try. Alice opened the kitchen door.

"Yes," she said. "Can I help you?"

"Mrs. Parry?" the woman said, though she must have known exactly who she was talking to. "I'm sorry to disturb you. Could I speak to you for a few minutes?"

There was, Alice thought, something of the Gypsy about her. She had very dark hair and her clothes were untidy but exotic and very brightly coloured.

"I'm very busy," Alice said, but something about the woman was familiar and she was curious. "You'll have to come into the kitchen."

"My name's Mary Raven," the woman said. "Could I talk to you? I'm a reporter with the *Otterbridge Express*."

Olive Kerr heard of the outcome of the meeting in the village hall from her daughter, Maggie, who was a barmaid at the Castle Hotel and heard all the gossip. People who had left the meeting early arrived at the pub just before closing time and were eager to talk. Charlie Elliot figured largely in the stories. Maggie passed on a carefully edited version of the events to her mother, but Olive was still indignant.

"He was always a troublemaker, that Charlie Elliot," she said. "I don't know why your father had to take him on." The words were like a refrain; she had spoken them so often before. "He's the last person you'd think Tom would want to work with."

Maggie said nothing. She knew the criticism was directed as much at her as at Tom. The two women were in the kitchen at the back of the house. Although it was only mid-afternoon it was almost dark and the wind blew sand onto the window so that it sounded like hail. Maggie's sons and her father were watching football on the television in another room.

"I'm sorry," Maggie said. "If I could find us somewhere to live, we'd move out. I'll phone the council again on Monday."

"You're welcome here as long as you want," Olive said,

12

but she was tight-lipped and angry, and Maggie knew it was not only the overcrowding that made her so tense.

The older woman began to put on a coat, punching out the sleeves with her fists, tearing at the zip with furious fingers.

"Where are you going?" Maggie asked.

"To the Tower," Olive said. "It's St. David's Day and the family are coming. I promised Mrs. Parry I'd do her a couple of extra hours before dinner."

"Shall I give you a lift up in the car?" Maggie asked. "It's going to rain any minute."

"No," Olive said. "The walk'll do me good."

"Take care then," Maggie said, but her mother had already gone and there was no reply.

Peter Laidlaw divided his year by the times spent at Brink-bonnie. When friends at school boasted about package tours to the Greek islands or Disneyland, he considered them with scorn. No place in the world had the magic of his visits to the Tower.

His father, Max, was a general practitioner in Otterbridge, and the family lived in a big Victorian terrace with tricycles in the hall and gerbils in the kitchen. Nine-year-old Peter was happy enough at home, but his parents were always busy and the house was often crowded with people he did not know. His parents promised him their attention, then found excuses for not fulfilling the promise. His latest campaign was for a tree house in the ash at the bottom of the garden. The excuse for not building it was a rusting tandem that had stood outside since the twins were born.

"There's enough rubbish in the garden already," his mother would say, "without making any more. When your father takes that thing to the tip, we'll think about it."

Max had bought the tandem when he and Judy were students and he was reluctant to get rid of it. It represented a time of great happiness: evenings in folk clubs, friendships, shared bottles of cheap wine. He had loved to ride with her around the Northumberland countryside. She had looked so striking—a frail Pre-Raphaelite beauty with red hair—and

13

people in the streets had stared at them as if they were celebrities. He had been proud to be seen with her. When Peter was born, Max had fitted a small seat on the back and they had still ridden out together on family outings. Then the twins had arrived and the tandem had been useless, pushed outside to make room for the rocking horse Alice had given them and all the other toys. Now Judy swore at it whenever she went into the garden to hang out the washing and nagged at Max to do something about it. The days of romantic bike rides seemed long past.

It seemed to Max that Judy could not be happy now unless she was part of a group of women. Whenever he came home from work, the house seemed full of them or of other people's children. But he never complained to Judy. That would be an uncharitable, unliberated thing to do. He had encouraged her to take part in the community activity and presumed she enjoyed it. She had been a nurse and she taught relaxation for the National Childbirth Trust. Sometimes he came home from running an antenatal clinic in the Health Centre to find rows of pregnant women lying on the living-room floor. She volunteered to run a crèche for the women writers' workshop and every Wednesday afternoon she was exhausted with the effort of entertaining a dozen precocious children, who ground Play-Doh into the carpet and tipped sand down the lavatory. She was a committee member of Amnesty International and Greenpeace and the groups met in their home. It occurred to him occasionally that he would not recognise her if she were not surrounded by a group of women, a coffee mug in one hand, leaning forward earnestly to listen or to make some point. He could hardly remember what she looked like when she was on her own. Even in bed she usually had one or the other of the twins beside her. She was always tired.

"Dad," Peter said, from the back of the car as they drove out of Otterbridge towards Brinkbonnie, "what do you get if you cross a sheep with a boiler?"

"I don't know," Max said automatically.

"Central Bleating."

Max groaned.

14

"That's very funny, Peter," Judy said. She looked at Max crossly.

Humour was an essential phase in a child's development.

"Will I be able to stay up for dinner tonight?"

"Perhaps. If Aunt Alice agrees."

"Will Sam and Tim? I expect they're still too small."

Sensing Max's irritation, Judy passed a copy of the *Beano* into the back seat, and for the rest of the trip to Brinkbonnie Peter was quiet.

From Otterbridge they drove east a long narrow lanes through farmland. To the south, on the horizon, was the winding wheel of a long-extinct pit and the chimneys of a newly built aluminium plant, but they seemed a long way off. It was late afternoon and the clouds were building for a storm. They drove straight into the wind, and in exposed places the car rocked and buffeted. In the valleys, where rows of trees lined the road, it was almost dark, and when they drove through the villages there were lights in cottage windows. When they drove into Brinkbonnie, it started to rain with slow, heavy drops and the clouds over the sea were so thick that they could not see beyond the first range of dunes. As Max turned into the Tower drive through the high walls covered with ivy, he had to switch on his leadlights to see, and it began to pour. As the car stopped behind the Tower, sheltered a little from the east wind, Alice came out of the kitchen door to meet them, under a huge golfing umbrella, followed by one of her cats. She wore a blue-and-white-striped apron over her clothes and there was flour in her hair.

"My dears," she said. "How nice to see you."

Peter was trying to open the car door to get out and kicked Sam in his eagerness to climb out. Sam began to cry. Max shouted at Peter for his clumsiness and it seemed there would be a horrible family scene until Alice scooped the baby from the back of the car and made him laugh, sent Peter into the house to wait for his cousin, and greeted the adults with a calm, slightly bemused smile.

"Come in," she said. "There should be some tea."

* * *

When he met his wife, James Laidlaw was thirty, already editor of the *Otterbridge Express* with ambitions of better things. He had interviewed Stella Rutherford in a small workshop in a converted barn on the outskirts of Otterbridge. He was preparing an article on local businesses and she was fresh from art school with plans to set up in knitwear design. He knew of her because her father was one of the biggest landowners in the district and he had expected someone loud and horsy. In fact, Stella was pale, fine-featured, and nervous. She chain-smoked and laughed at herself for being so anxious. It was her background, she said. Everyone expected so much of her. Her father had told her she would be a failure and she thought he was probably right.

James had left the interview feeling like a sixteen-year-old in love for the first time, and even now, thirteen years later, he was obsessed with her fragile beauty. She was right, the knitwear design idea had been a failure, and as soon as she had married she had given it up. She seemed not to have the strength to see anything through. Even motherhood, it seemed, was too much for her, and after the birth of Carolyn she had been so severely depressed that she had spent six months in hospital. Her father, an insensitive and self-centred man, had found her illness embarrassing and cowardly. He had never visited her in hospital and since then the family had had little to do with him. Stella claimed to hate him. James had seen her through the bad times, almost glad, it seemed, of an excuse to spoil and cherish her. Even now he considered her before anything. He had been offered a job in Fleet Street but turned it down without discussing it with Stella. He knew she would never survive the move.

He had been working and was home later than Stella had expected. He saw her waiting at the window and felt guilty for making her anxious.

"Do we have to go?" she asked as soon as he came into the house. "I'm not sure I can face it."

"Nonsense," he said gently. "You know you'll enjoy it once you're there."

16

"I won't," she said. "I don't know why we go. You don't even get on with Max particularly."

"Oh, well," he said easily. "It's always relaxing to be with Aunt Alice."

"She doesn't sound very relaxed at the moment." Stella was defensive. "She phoned not long ago and asked to speak to you. She's worried about the development on the land at the edge of the village. She wants your advice."

"That's not worry," James said. "It's guilt because she sold the land in the first place. There's nothing I can do about it now. We reported the Department of the Environment's decision in the paper."

The *Express* was a local paper with a limited circulation, but James Laidlaw took his journalism seriously. It was not all advertisements and wedding photographs. He had done a piece once about the poor standard of care in an old people's home, which had been taken up by the big Newcastle papers, and a feature about a county councillor's corruption had forced the subject of the article to resign.

Carolyn, who was twelve and their only child, appeared quite suddenly beside them. She was wearing a coat and carrying a holdall. She was slight and pale as a ghost, so quiet that they often hardly noticed she was there. Her mother dressed her in old-fashioned clothes, with skirts too long for her, so she looked younger than she was.

"Are we going?" she asked. The question surprised them, so seldom did she take any initiative. "Peter will want me to play with him. He'll miss me if I'm not there."

"Do you enjoy these trips to Brinkbonnie?" James asked. Sometimes he wished he had a son, someone noisy and robust to bring life to the house. Even now, when most of her friends had Walkman cassette players and bedroom walls covered with pop-star posters, the only sound to come from Carolyn's room was the practice scales of her violin.

"Oh, yes!" she said, her eyes gleaming. "It's the best place in the world."

When they arrived at the Tower, the front door was still open, but there was no sign of Alice. Max and Judy were in

17

the sitting room drinking tea, not speaking. In the wide, wood-panelled hall there was a pile of baby equipment.

"Look at this!" James murmured to Stella as he stepped over buggies, camping cots, packets of disposable nappies. "It's like a travelling circus."

Peter appeared at the top of the stairs on the first landing and called Carolyn to join him. She dropped her holdall with the rest of the luggage and ran to meet him, but by the time she reached the top he had disappeared into the small room where they kept their toys and were allowed to play. At the top of the stairs Carolyn paused. The house was very quiet. Her parents must have joined Max and Judy. The silence was broken by a muffled whimper. Carolyn moved quietly along the landing and listened again. The noise was coming from Aunt Alice's bedroom. Aunt Alice was crying. Carolyn stood quite still and felt her own eyes fill with tears. She felt betrayed. That was the sort of behavior she expected from her mother, not from her aunt. Now it seemed all adults were similarly unreliable. She turned her back on her aunt's room and looked for Peter.

3

Mary Raven sat in her car and dreamed of her secret lover. She had met him, one beautiful summer's evening, at a barbecue on the wild, uninhabited part of the Brinkbonnie dunes owned by the Northumberland Wildlife Trust. The party had been organised by the Trust, and she was there partly because she was sympathetic to the cause and partly to cover the event for the *Otterbridge Express*. At first it was a predictable evening. The fires took too long to light, the sausages were burnt on the outside and pink in the middle, and bossy women with jolly Girl Guide voices shouted to them as if they were children:

"Come *on*, everyone. There are hundreds more sausages."

Mary drank too much red wine from a plastic cup, then climbed over the dunes to look over the sea. It was late but still light, the sky's violet and gold reflected in the wet sand and ebbing sea. Behind her she heard the children complaining as they were rounded up for bed, the first chords of guitar music, the strains of a protest song. The empty beach stretched south for seven miles towards Brinkbonnie village.

When he climbed up the dune and sat beside her, she was not surprised. Perhaps she had wandered away from the crowd in the hope that she would be followed. It was that sort of night: hot, romantic. She was ready for excitement and some sort of sexual adventure. When she saw who it was, she was not surprised, though at the time almost anyone would have done. She had been aware of him all evening and had sensed as he prodded cindered sausages with a long fork that he was ready for rebellion, too.

"Hello," he said. "Are you all right?"

"Fine," she said. She smiled at him.

"You look a bit lonely."

"No," she said. "Just enjoying the evening."

She stood up suddenly and ran down the steep bank of sand, sliding and tumbling, sending up a rainbow of fine sand that gleamed in the last of the light. She was wearing loose, clown's trousers and a T-shirt in black and white stripes. When she reached the water, she looked back at him. Later she thought that if she had carried on up the beach without turning to see if he was still there, staring at her, none of it would have happened. He would have gone back to the fire, shaken the sand out of his trainers, and under the orders of the bossy women done his duty with black bin bags and rubber gloves. He would have gone straight home to his wife. But she did turn round, and he saw it as a challenge to follow her. He launched himself from the top of the dune and ran at full-tilt without stumbling. She was impressed by the run. She had expected a more cowardly descent, a sedate walk perhaps, with his hands behind him in case he fell. As he ran towards her she turned and walked away up the beach, just on the edge of the tide. He fell in beside her as if he were there by chance, as if in the whole vast expanse of the beach it was pure coincidence that he happened to be there.

Nothing extraordinary occurred that night. There was no wild passion in the marram grass. They walked almost the length of the beach until it got dark, acknowledging each other's presence in the end with brief bursts of conversation. Afterwards she could not remember exactly what had been said. She had talked, she thought, about her mother. Perhaps she had been more drunk than she realised. Halfway back they stopped. He put his arm around her and pointed out the shape of one of the constellations—she could not remember which. When they returned to the point on the beach where

20

the walk had started—she could see in the moonlight the skid marks of her slide down the dune—he kissed her.

"I must go," he said.

"Yes," she said. "Of course."

"I'll be in touch," he said. "I'll see you or phone you at home."

Yeah, she thought. Like hell you will.

The extraordinary thing happened the next day. She woke up with a sense of elation and joy she had not experienced since the uncomplicated happiness of childhood. She had more energy. She felt that for the last twenty years she had only been half alive. Inevitably the elation faded, though it lasted undiminished for almost a week, and then her craving to be alone with him again began. She dreamed about the walk on the beach, reliving it every night before she went to sleep, yet with every rerun its magic grew less potent.

What's the matter with me? she thought. I didn't go through all this when I was sixteen. I'm an independent woman.

The need to see him again was humiliating. She drank too much to try to forget him.

He's married, she thought. I mean, really. I don't need this hassle.

And all the time she knew it was not the man's company she wanted, but the elation and vitality that had followed it. She became desperate, like an addict, waiting for him to make an approach.

Then he phoned her at home late one Saturday afternoon.

"Mary," he said.

She recognised his voice immediately. "Yes."

"I was wondering if you were free this evening. We could go out for a drink, a meal. We could go into town."

Of course, she thought. Much less danger of being recognised in town.

"Mary," he repeated, and she realised that he was as desperate as she was.

"Yes," she said. "I'm free this evening." She felt a sudden panic in case he was disappointed with her.

That had been how it all started. They met in Newcastle in a poorly lit wine bar and she drank Perrier all evening because she wanted nothing to cloud her memory. Then she had taken him back to her flat and he had stayed all night.

"What will you tell your wife?" she asked. It was five in the morning, blackbirds were singing fit to burst outside, and he was shambling, naked, round the room retrieving his clothes.

"She'll blame herself," he said. "We've been through a bad time lately."

"So you only phoned me because you had a row with your wife?" Mary spoke carefully. If she made too many demands on him, he might not see her again.

"No," he said. "Of course not. It wasn't like that. You can't understand what she's like. I've been looking for an excuse since the night of the barbecue."

And that was true as well, he thought. She had haunted him. The phone call might have been an impulse, a way of escaping from his wife, a way of proving to himself that he was still attractive, but it was hard to forget Mary Raven.

After that they met every week, at least once, sometimes twice. Usually he came to Mary's flat. He never stayed the night again. She never introduced him to her other friends. They teased her about her secret lover, but she just smiled. That first joyous elation returned, but only occasionally, and she persisted with him in the hope that it would last.

Perhaps I should be satisfied with those moments, Mary thought, sitting in the car as the light faded and the wind blew stronger than ever. But she knew she wanted more than that.

In the Tower the dining room was decorated as it always was on March 1, with vases of daffodils. They were everywhere, on the polished wood table and on the windowsills and even standing on the floor. In the old days, when Anthony Parry was still alive, they would have been forced to listen to records of Max Boyce live at the Neath Rugby Club and even to male choirs singing the Welsh national anthem. Now the daffodils were enough to remind them of St. David's Day.

No-one except Carolyn noticed that Alice had been crying. If they saw that her eyes were red, it would never have occurred to them that she might be upset. She was not the sort to howl alone in her bedroom. She was made, they all thought, of sterner stuff. She stood at the head of the table ladling soup into bowls, an indomitable English lady, secretary of the WI, organiser of the village horticultural society, and now founding member of the Save Brinkbonnie campaign. She was wearing clothes she must have had for years: flared purple trousers that she had bought, in fact, when she had taken the boys for a trip to London in 1969 and a silk tunic her husband had brought home from a trip to Hong Kong.

It was Peter's first grown-up dinner at Brinkbonnie and for the first ten minutes he was so excited to be there, at the table between Aunt Alice and his mother, that nothing else mattered. The disappointment came slowly. He had expected a special attention from Alice, a conspiratorial joy in his achievement at persuading his parents to allow him to stay up. He had thought she would listen to his jokes. Bu throughout the meal she was distant and preoccupied and he wondered if he had offended her in some way. He became nervous and knocked over his mother's wine with his elbow.

"Peter," his mother said. "If you can't sit still, you'll have to go to bed like the twins."

Then he looked to Alice for her customary support, but she seemed hardly to have noticed the incident, and there was none of the laughter, the assurance that it was only an accident and really did not matter, which he might have expected.

At the end of the meal he sat sullen and silent. He had looked forward to this weekend for months and now it was all spoiled.

Immediately after the meal he was sent to bed. He had a room near the top of the Tower that he shared with the twins. His brothers were asleep in their cots snuffling and snoring.

23

The strong winds had blown the storm over and the rain had stopped, but the wind was still fierce and it was cold. The noise was deafening. The gale blew around the old stonework and through the trees behind the house. Night had come suddenly and it was dark. Peter thought it was very exciting. His mother pulled his sleeping bag around him and sat on the bed to kiss him. This attention was unusual. At home she was always in a hurry to clear up before going to a meeting or running a class and there was only time for a quick story. Now she sat close to him and waited in the dark and noisy room.

"Mum," he whispered, hoping to keep her there. "What's wrong with Aunt Alice?"

"Wrong?" she said. "Nothing's wrong. What do you mean?"

"She didn't talk to me," he said. "And she didn't say anything about the treasure hunt. She always does a treasure hunt on the first night."

Judy laughed. "She has more important things to think about than you children," she said. She began to stroke his forehead. "Besides, there might be a treasure hunt tomorrow."

"No," he said, quite certain. "It's always on the first night."

"Oh, well," she said easily. "I expect there'll be other treats." She stood up. "Will you be all right?" she asked. "With all this wind?"

"Yes," he said. "I like it. I'm never scared at Brinkbonnie."

When Judy returned to the dining room, they were all still sitting at the dining table. Alice had switched on the lights and drawn the curtains. They were drinking coffee, their elbows on the table, and as she entered the room she expected to hear the familiar family gossip, the old stories about Anthony, about other St. David's days, about James's and Max's childhoods.

But they were silent. She thought of Peter's whispered question, "What's wrong with Aunt Alice?," and realised

24

that Alice had always started the after-dinner conversations, bringing the others in until the whole family were included. Without Alice they had nothing to say to each other.

As Judy took her place at the table, Alice broke the silence.

"Carolyn," she said. "I realise it's not bedtime yet, pet, but would you mind going up to your room? I'm sure your mother will come up to see you later."

Carolyn got up and drifted out without a word, but the adults were surprised. Weekends at Brinkbonnie were informal, chaotic affairs with the children wandering around in their nightclothes until midnight and the parents complaining that it was impossible then to return them to a normal routine.

"I want to talk to you," Alice said, "about this development in the village. I feel strongly about it. I'm going to fight it."

They looked at each other, amused. Why was she taking herself so seriously? She was famous for her involvement with environmental issues, something of a joke even to Judy, who supported her. Alice the Green, James called her, secretly, to Stella.

"It's too late now," James said. "You've sold the land."

"It was in good faith," Alice said, "for small, cheap houses in the village. People like Fred Elliot's son who want to stay in the area. Not executive detached residences with double garages and two bathrooms." She looked at James sharply. "I expect your help," she told him.

"There was no proper contract," James said. "There's nothing I can do."

"You could run a story about it in the *Express*."

"Everyone knows you're my aunt. How seriously would that be taken?"

"You wouldn't have to comment," Alice raged. "Let me put my point of view and let the builder give his. The reader can make up his own mind who's right."

"You're too late," James said, so irritated that he lost his usual politeness. "The planning procedure's over. The decision has been taken."

25

"The council could appeal," Alice insisted stubbornly. "If they felt public opinion was against the development, they'd appeal against the planning inspector's decision."

"I'm sorry," he said. "It's no good. We carried the story when the plans first went before the council. I'm not going to do it again."

"Then why did you send a reporter to the action meeting this afternoon?" Alice demanded. "What was Mary Raven doing here?"

The name seemed to shock James, and for the first time he seemed uneasy.

"She came to the house after the meeting," Alice continued. "I found her a very pleasant woman, very committed. We had a long conversation. She was most sympathetic."

James shrugged. "She's young," he said. "No sense of proportion, no objectivity. She belongs to all those conservation groups. I've told her before that the *Express* isn't just a vehicle for her own propaganda."

"You don't understand!" For the first time they realised how upset Alice was. They were afraid she would cry. "You don't understand how important this is to me!"

There was a silence.

"Alice," Judy said at last. "What is this all about?"

The older woman got up suddenly and left the room. When she returned, she was carrying something that a child might have made at school, a collage of newspaper and magazine cuttings on a pink card. She set it on the table and they read the words, made up of letters from different sizes of prints and different sorts of typefaces.

"If you kill this village," it read, "we'll kill you."

"You're not taking this seriously," James cried. "Really. It's just some crank."

"I don't take the threat seriously," Alice said. "Of course I don't. But I take the sense of outrage seriously. This afternoon at the protest meeting I was accused of hypocrisy, of caring more about money than about the people who live in Brinkbonnie. But it's not true. This development is part of the greed and materialism that will ruin our countryside if we

26

let it. . . ." She paused dramatically, and Judy was reminded that Alice had made exactly the same speech at the county meeting of the WI with the tune of "Jerusalem" playing behind her. Judy pictured her aunt on the stage, articulate and ferocious, and remembered the cheers and applause that had followed her words.

But today there was no applause and Alice continued more quietly. "I love it here," she said. "When Anthony and I moved into the Tower, we were strangers, but people made us feel that we belonged. When he was ill, the house was always full of flowers—gifts from our friends. And when he died, there was always someone to talk to. The Tower and my friends in Brinkbonnie mean more to me, perhaps even more than my family. Now I feel I've betrayed them and I'm not going to let it happen." She looked directly at James. "The Tower will be yours one day," she told him. "Perhaps you should think that you have some responsibility for Brinkbonnie, too. Otherwise I might have to consider leaving the house to someone who's prepared to take the responsibility more seriously."

There was silence. The threat seemed so out of character that they could hardly believe they were understanding her properly. They stared at James.

"That's blackmail," he said at last. He spoke very quietly. "I don't give in to blackmail."

"Think about it," she said. "I told you that I was going to fight this development. I'm prepared to use everything I can to stop it."

She got up suddenly, went to a sideboard, and poured herself a drink. She brought the bottle of Scotch and some glasses back to the table. When she spoke again, they were reminded of the old Alice, of cheerful, eccentric good humour.

"I expect you all think I'm very silly," she said. "And I really don't want to offend anyone. But it's so important to me. You do understand, don't you, how important it is?" She looked around the table, inviting their sympathy, some response of support, but they were all too shocked to answer.

27

"Have a drink!" she said. "It's St. David's night. Anthony always got drunk on St. David's night. Don't you remember that time when it snowed and he insisted we all go sledging by moonlight?"

Then they joined in the conversation, glad to hide their awkwardness with the familiar words, but the stories soon trailed away and they were left again with silence. Stella stood up first. Throughout the discussion she had been blankly unresponsive, as if she had not even been listening to what was going on.

"I'll just go and check on Carolyn," she said. "Make sure she's asleep."

She spoke with a jerky abruptness, which did nothing to relieve the tension, and they were glad when Alice stood up, too.

"Come on, Max," she said. "I want a word with you. Come into the kitchen and help me with these dishes."

When the others offered halfheartedly to help, she turned them away. "No, no," she said. "I'm not going to do it all. Just tidy it up for Olive to see to in the morning. Besides, I want a private word with Max."

Carolyn had fallen asleep almost immediately, but Stella stayed in her bedroom, staring at the child without attempting to touch her. There was nothing to do. Carolyn scarcely moved in her sleep and the sheets and blankets were still firmly tucked around her. All of her clothes were neatly folded on the chair. But Stella did not feel ready yet to return downstairs. The confrontation between James and his aunt had disturbed her. She did not know what to make of it. More important, she was not sure yet how it would affect her. She had always seen the Tower as part of her future. As the old panic and insecurity returned, she felt that they all ought to be more considerate towards her. Didn't they know that stress was bad for her and that the sort of hostility they had both expressed was likely to make her ill again? She decided to wait in the bedroom until James realised she was missing. That way she would avoid the unpleasantness of any further

28

argument and it might frighten him into realising that he should treat her more carefully. She needed the reassurance that he still worried about her.

She knelt on the floor by the long window and looked out into the garden. She could hear the movement of the big yew trees in the churchyard beyond the wall. Occasionally the wind blew the clouds away from the moon and the garden was lit. Otherwise all she could see were a street light beyond the churchyard, where there was a gate onto the village green, and occasional headlights as cars moved slowly down the Otterbridge Road towards the sea.

It took her a while to realise that there was a woman in the churchyard, walking backwards and forwards along the path from the green to the small wrought-iron gate in the wall that marked the boundary with the Tower garden. Stella saw the woman first in a brief flash of moonlight, a small figure, half hidden by the gravestones, with long hair that streamed behind her in the wind. She saw her again when the woman paused under the street light, but she was then to far away for her to see the details of her face or her clothes, though something about the way she stood and walked seemed familiar. The church clock struck ten and the woman looked up at it, as if she could hardly believe the time. Then she moved away from the light to begin pacing once again up and down the path between the Tower and the green. Stella could not see her clearly after that but was aware of a movement in the moonlight, a shadow blown, it seemed, by the breeze between the white marble stones.

When James came to find her, Stella did not mention the figure. Perhaps she thought he would think it one of her old hallucinations and would return to the subject of hospital and the need for proper treatment. Perhaps Stella hoped to save the fact of the woman until she really needed it, until she was in a situation when she needed them all to take notice of her, like money saved for a rainy day.

"What are you still doing here?" he asked gently when he came into the room. "The others are wondering where you are."

She got up quickly and moved away from the window.

"It was all that fighting," she said. "It upset me. You know I shouldn't be upset."

"Yes," he said. "I know." He put his arm around her and led her out of the room and held her tight as they walked down the stairs. But as they approached the living room, it was clear that Alice was involved in an argument again.

"I must talk to him," she was saying. "I won't sleep until I've talked to him." She was wearing a parka with a fur-lined hood, one of the sort that boys of eight or nine wear, and was pulling a pair of Wellingtons over the purple flares.

"But it's late," Judy said. "Why don't you wait until morning? Or phone him, if you want to talk to him now."

"It's all so simple," Alice said. "It came to me when I was talking to Max. I don't know why I didn't think of it before. It's obvious I'll have to buy back the land."

"What are you doing, Aunt Alice?" James asked. He stood just inside the room, his arm still around Stella's shoulders, blocking the door.

"She's going to see Henshaw," Judy said helplessly, "to persuade him to sell her the land."

"That's ridiculous," James said. "He's spent thousands drawing up the plans. He'll not sell it back to you now."

Alice sat on the carpet, so she could pull more effectively on the Wellingtons. She looked up at James.

"That depends," she said, "what I offer to pay for it."

"At least let me come with you," James said. "I don't like the idea of your being out there on your own."

"I don't need a bodyguard," she said. "Not yet." She stood up and waited for James to move away from the door. "Don't stay up for me. This may take some time."

She went out into the garden, slamming the front door behind her.

Judy made more coffee and they sat in the small, square sitting room until the fire died to embers. There was some talk of going out to meet Alice to make sure that she got safely home, but they decided she was a grown woman who knew her own mind and they drifted eventually to bed.

* * *

Peter woke soon after it got light, while his parents and the twins were still asleep. He dressed quickly and quietly, then ran downstairs to the kitchen, where he expected to find his great-aunt. Aunt Alice seemed to need no sleep at all, his parents always said. She was always last to bed after a party and first up the next morning. She had the constitution of an ox. Usually, early in the morning, Peter would find her in the kitchen, sitting on the wooden rocking chair next to the Rayburn, wearing the old lab coat she used as a dressing gown, a cat on each knee. But today the kitchen was empty and the cats came up to him, rubbing against his legs, hoping for food. Peter felt the disappointment of the night before. Aunt Alice had let him down again. He liked the morning ritual at Brinkbonnie. His aunt would make tea in a brown earthenware pot and set out the cups on a tray—for her, a wide, shallow one, the size of a soup bowl, and for him, a small yellow one with poppies on the rim. Then they would drink the tea, eat digestive biscuits, and plan the day's events.

There was a tap on the kitchen door and he thought for a moment that it would be Aunt Alice. But what would she be doing outside? There was another knock, this time louder and more impatient. Peter went to open the door and was surprised when it was unlocked. Usually when his aunt let him out into the garden in the morning, she took a big brass key from a hook by the door to open it. Olive Kerr stood outside, stamping her feet with cold and anger at being kept waiting. She was a large-boned, aggressive woman. She ignored Peter and swept past him. Soon after there was the sound of the Hoover in the dining room.

The boy stood uncertainly in the kitchen, trapped by Mrs. Kerr's activity. He was frightened of her. She had a haughty, imperious manner, and reminded him of his headmistress. She returned to the kitchen to fetch polish and dusters and he slipped hurriedly outside into the garden.

It was a cold, raw day and he wished he had waited to put on a coat. The wind blew a smell of salt and seaweed. In the kitchen he heard his father shouting that it was cold because

31

some fool had left the door open, but Peter took no notice. He was even less eager to see his father than to see Mrs. Kerr. He wished he knew where his aunt was.

He zigzagged, the wind blowing him towards the churchyard wall. In the corner there was a swing, which his great-uncle had tied to one of the heftier trees when Carolyn was still a toddler. The ropes creaked as he sat on the wooden seat and moved himself forward. With every swing he kicked a pile of leaves swept up in the autumn so that the wind picked them up and scattered them away in a brown whirlwind across the garden.

At that moment his father came to the kitchen door and shouted to him. "Peter!" He sounded resigned rather than angry. "What *are* you doing out there? What will your mother say? You must be freezing. Have you seen Aunt Alice?"

Peter did not answer immediately. He had seen, under the pile of leaves, a black Wellington and a piece of purple fabric. He jumped from the swing and ran towards his father, chasing and stumbling towards the house, crying.

Max took over then. He sent Peter indoors and went to look under the leaves himself. It was only later that Peter was told by his mother that Alice was dead.

4

*A*s Ramsay drove into the village he saw a poster advertising the meeting to protest against the proposed housing development on the Tower field. How would I feel, he wondered, if the developer at Heppleburn decided to put up a new housing estate behind my cottage? He answered the question immediately. Murderous, he thought. I'd feel murderous.

When he drove between the high walls towards the Tower, the drive was crowded with familiar cars, and in a huddle in the corner of the garden, hands deep in Barbour jacket pockets so that they might have been landowners preparing for a day's shooting, were his superiors, who waited uneasily for him to take over the investigation. It was always the same. Formality dictated that they had to be there, but they would take little active part in the investigation and they preferred not to interfere. Then they could claim not to be responsible for any mistake. When Ramsay got out of the car and approached them, he felt they were more anxious than usual. The body was still there, wet, half covered with leaves. He bent and looked carefully for a moment. The woman was lying facedown on the grass. The wound was in her back and her clothes were soaked with blood.

"She was stabbed," he said, almost to himself. "And only once. The murderer was either very confident or he

33

knew what he was doing." He stood up and turned away to face the group who watched him.

"Who is it?" he asked.

The superintendent, young, able, lazy, who had recently returned from an exchange visit to Colorado, answered indirectly.

"Steve," he said. "We might have a difficult one here."

"Why? Who is it?"

"Her name's Alice Parry. Does that mean anything to you?"

Ramsay shook his head.

"She's a magistrate and a well-known lady. Her nephew's James Laidlaw, editor of the *Otterbridge Express*."

"Yes," Ramsay said. "I know James Laidlaw. Does that matter?"

"Steve! Does it matter? Remember Heppleburn. We need the press on our side."

"Yes," he said. "Of course."

This is all I need, he thought. The press will be here, watching every move we make.

"Has the murder weapon been found?" he asked.

"No, and we've no information yet on what we're looking for."

Then the superintendent went away, telling Ramsay to be careful, that he would deal with all press enquiries, and Ramsay was left alone with the smell of ivy and wet leaves.

By then it was eleven o'clock and the congregation for parish communion were coming out of the church. The vicar, his cassock billowing about him in the breeze, stood at the door to greet his parishioners. There had been a christening and the mother stood proudly, holding the baby in its long robe while admiring friends took photographs. Then there was the giving of the amice—the coal, bread, salt, and money wrapped up in a napkin that in Northumberland churches is given to the first child the baby meets—and more photographs. Ramsay wished they would all go, but some of the congregation must have heard about the murder because they

34

came up to the wrought-iron gate and stared at the policeman searching the garden.

He found his sergeant, Gordon Hunter, in the kitchen talking to Olive Kerr.

"Sorry to call you out," Hunter said cheerfully. "How are you settling in?"

Ramsay said nothing. He disapproved of Hunter's easy familiarity. Perhaps it had been a mistake after all to invite him into his home. A murder enquiry needed tact and gravity. Yet he noticed that even the straight-backed, straitlaced woman was responding to the sergeant's attention. Hunter would be making her feel special, playing the part of the attractive, rather wayward son who needed looking after. Soon she would be making him tea and telling him to wrap up warm before he went out because the wind was cold. Hunter whispered something to Olive, which made her smile, then stood up.

"We need screens," Ramsay said. "There are already people in the churchyard staring. They can't see the body from there, but it'll not be long before we have the press in the garden."

"The press is here already," Hunter said. "In the house. One of Mrs. Perry's nephews is the editor of the *Otterbridge Express*."

"I know," Ramsay said. He was already feeling depressed. "Tell me who else is here."

"Laidlaw's wife, Stella, and their daughter, Carolyn, and his brother and his family. They're all in here."

Hunter led him through the hall to the warm square room where the family had waited the night before for Alice's return. As soon as he saw them all, Ramsay knew that these were Diana's sort of people and the thought triggered a profound unease and an excitement. They could easily have been friends of Diana's, invited to her dinner parties, sharing evenings at the theatre, meals in dimly lit foreign restaurants. He recognised the style. Although the women wore jeans and hand-knitted sweaters, their wardrobes were probably full of clothes that Diana might have chosen to wear. It had always

35

surprised him that Diana would admit quite happily to having found a bargain in a charity shop or at a jumble sale—"a real silk shirt and only five pounds"—but refuse to go near the cut-price chain stores in the high street where his mother always shopped. It always seemed to him a strange sort of snobbishness, though Diana always said he had no taste and could not possibly understand. Throughout the interview with the Laidlaws he felt that, with Diana's arrogance, they were saying the same thing. You're different from us, they implied. You're from a different background. How can you possibly understand?

Yet he felt from the beginning that because they were Diana's sort of people, he did understand them. It was his secret weapon, that understanding. They would always underestimate him.

He stood just inside the door and looked around the room. James Laidlaw sat on a worn leather Chesterfield reading an old copy of the *Times*. He recognised Ramsay and stood up.

"Inspector," he said smoothly, "I'm glad it's you. It's always easier to work with a person one knows."

Ramsay nodded but said nothing. There seemed to have been no collective support or sympathy, no communication between them even. Max Laidlaw was sprawled on the floor. He was tall like his brother but younger, good-looking in a dark Celtic way. He seemed too inexperienced, Ramsay thought, to be a doctor. It was hard to imagine him taking responsibility. He was too careless of other people, too self-absorbed. He took no notice of Ramsay.

It was the women who held Ramsay's attention. Their sophistication stirred memories that disturbed him. A fair, fine-boned woman sat on a small chair close to the fire smoking a cigarette. Her wrists were so thin and long that it seemed as if they would snap as she moved the cigarette to her mouth. She wore a white mohair sweater with a huge collar, and in contrast her eyes were very dark. She was so pale that he wondered if she were ill or had taken some medication. He had seen addicts with the same drawn pallor. But perhaps she was only scared, he thought, moved by her beauty. James

36

Laidlaw saw Ramsay looking at the woman and introduced him.

"This is Stella," he said. "My wife." With the few words he gave the impression of great pride.

She turned towards Ramsay. Her neck was very long and the hair was tied back so tightly that her head seemed small. She smiled sadly. "Good morning," she said, and returned her gaze to the fire.

The other woman was quite different in colouring and stature. She had a round face like a child's and copper-coloured hair. He thought she would easily be raised to anger. When James introduced her as Judy Laidlaw, she did not speak but glared at him. Ramsay thought she was probably the sort of woman who disliked policemen as a matter of principle.

At a coffee table away from the fire two children were making a jigsaw. They worked in silence, in a dreamlike absorption.

"I'm sorry," Ramsay said. "You'll be upset. But you realise I'll have to ask some questions."

"Of course," James Laidlaw murmured. "Anything we can do to help."

Judy stood up and walked quickly to the playing children. "Carolyn," she said quietly. "Would you mind taking Peter into your bedroom to finish the puzzle? We want to talk."

Ramsay thought for a moment that the girl would object or cause a scene. She turned towards her parents, who seemed not to notice that she was pleading to stay. Then, with an adult resignation, she picked up the jigsaw and left the room. Peter obediently followed her.

Judy stared at Ramsay with a mixture of hostility and curiosity. "That is all right?" she said. "Peter found the body. He still seems terribly confused and I don't want to make things worse."

"Of course," Ramsay said. "I'll need to talk to him later, but it can wait."

He stood by the fireplace and looked at them, waiting for some response, for their questions. Judy was struck by his stillness. He must be very confident, she thought, to stand

37

there quite immobile, watching us, waiting for someone to break the silence. For the first time she considered the police not as despicable but as frightening. Suddenly the silence was too much for her.

"Max said Alice had been murdered," she said. "Is that true? I can't believe it."

"Yes," Ramsay said. "Mrs. Parry was murdered. She was stabbed. It probably happened quite close to where Dr. Laidlaw found her. The murderer must have covered her body with the leaves. He, or she, might have thought it would take longer for Mrs. Parry to be found. If Peter hadn't gone to play on the swing, it would have taken several hours, I should guess."

"She?" Judy cried. "You don't think a woman would do anything like that?"

Ramsay looked at her seriously. "Why not?" he said. "It wouldn't have taken any great strength, you know. Especially if the murderer was known to Mrs. Parry."

He realised he was trying to shock them and checked himself. It was time, for the moment, to stick to fact. He directed his questions to Max.

"When you found the body," he said, "was the wrought-iron gate between the garden and the churchyard open or shut?"

"Shut," Max said. "Definitely shut. When I saw that she was dead, I noticed the vicar coming from the green towards the church. I shouted to him for help, though I don't know exactly what I expected him to do. It was so windy that he didn't hear me. It was like one of those nightmares, you know, when you shout and no sound comes out. In the end I ran to fetch him. The catch on the gate is very stiff and it seemed to take hours to get it open. He didn't realise that anything was wrong and just stood on the path smiling."

When Max stopped talking, there was another silence. Ramsay looked at them all again. They were shocked, of course, but still very self-composed. If anyone was lying, it would be hard to find out. Yet if anything the shut gate indicated that the murderer was a member of the household.

38

Would someone who had just committed murder stop in his flight to fasten a difficult catch on the gate? Then he remembered Olive Kerr and made a mental note to ask which way she had come into the house.

"Now," Ramsay said. "Tell me what you're all doing here and what happened last night."

"We always stay with Alice on St. David's night," James Laidlaw said. "It's a family tradition. Her husband was Welsh, and she liked to entertain."

"You arrived yesterday?"

James nodded. "Late in the afternoon."

"Did your aunt seem concerned, worried?"

James hesitated. "Not really. She was angry about a new development planned for the edge of the village, but that was nothing unusual. She was always fighting for some cause or another. I'm afraid she was rather a crank."

"No," Judy said. "That's not true. She was well-read, intelligent, especially concerned about environmental problems." She turned to Ramsay. "Alice was a scientist," she told him, "a chemist. She met her husband at Newcastle University, where they both worked. He was a historian and quite famous. You might have seen him on television. Alice may have dressed rather strangely and been a bit eccentric, but she was no fool."

"Perhaps you could explain about the new houses and what they had to do with Mrs. Parry," Ramsay said.

"Alice originally owned the land where the housing development is proposed," Judy said. "She sold it to a builder on the understanding that it would be used for cheap starter homes for the village people. Then she found out that the development would be much bigger than she'd been led to believe and that he was going to build big executive homes for people prepared to commute into Newcastle. Of course the villagers are furious and think Alice sold out—though she let the land go to the builder for well under the market value."

"What is the name of the builder?" The interruption was gentle and she hardly paused.

"Henshaw," Judy said. "Colin Henshaw."

Ramsay recognised the name immediately as the builder who owned the land behind his cottage. He said nothing, and Judy continued:

"There was an action meeting in the hall yesterday afternoon. Alice went to it, and apparently it got very nasty. Later in the day she received a threatening letter. It really upset her."

"Were you at the meeting?" Ramsay interrupted again. "Can you tell me exactly what happened?"

"No," Judy said. "We didn't arrive until it was all over. But one of your reporters went, didn't she, James? She would be able to tell the inspector what went on."

"Yes," James said absently, "though I'm not sure how reliable she is."

"What is her name?" Ramsay asked.

"Raven," James said. "Mary Raven."

Ramsay turned to Judy. "You mentioned a letter," he said. "Could you tell me about that?"

"It was delivered here some time after the meeting," Judy said. "By hand, I suppose. But if Alice guessed who had made it, she didn't say. It was anonymous. There was no handwriting, only words cut out from newspaper. It was horrible, violent. It said something like 'If you kill our village, we'll kill you.'"

"How did Mrs. Parry respond to the letter?"

"She wasn't frightened," Judy said. "She was sad and upset but not frightened. She loved Brinkbonnie. She didn't want her friends to think she'd let them down." She looked at James and smiled a little maliciously. "She was angry, too. She thought James could do more to support her by making a fuss in the *Express*. She threatened to cut him out of her will if he didn't help her."

"Nonsense!" James said. "She said no such thing! This is preposterous."

"Come on, James," Max said, rolling onto an elbow. "She may not have spelled it out, but that's certainly what she implied."

It seemed to Ramsay that the couples did not like each

40

other very much. The brothers seemed to have little in common and the women had not acknowledged each other's presence since he had been in the room. Stella raised her swanlike neck and looked at them as if the bickering was beneath her. She had contributed nothing to the conversation, yet he thought that in some subtle way she was manipulating the direction it was taking.

"Tell me more about this letter," Ramsay said. "Do you know what happened to it? Where is it now?"

"I don't know," Judy said. "I didn't see it in the dining room this morning. Perhaps Alice took it out with her."

"Out?" Ramsay repeated. "Did Mrs. Parry go out after dinner last night?"

"Yes," Judy said awkwardly. "At about ten o'clock."

"Where on earth did she go at that time of night?"

"She went to see Henshaw," Judy said. "She wanted to persuade him to sell her back the land." Judy Laidlaw had become the family spokesperson. She was competent, articulate, and they seemed content to leave the responsibility to her. Yet occasionally, as she spoke, she glanced at Stella with undisguised spite, as if she were pleased to have the opportunity to put her and James in the wrong. "If James had promised her more support in the *Express*, she might never have felt it necessary to go."

"But you let her go?" Ramsay asked. "On her own?"

"She was a very independent woman," James said. "Of course we tried to dissuade her, but she wouldn't listen."

"What time did she come back?"

They looked at each other, ashamed and defensive.

"She told us not to wait up," Max said lamely.

Ramsay looked at each of them in turn.

"Did anyone see Mrs. Parry after she'd been to Henshaw's last night?" he demanded.

No-one answered.

"Who went to bed first?" he asked. "How long did you wait for her?"

"I went first," Judy said. "I didn't hear Max come in. I fell asleep very quickly."

"I was watching a late film on the television," Max said. "It didn't finish until midnight. James and Stella went up before me."

"And it didn't occur to you to worry about Mrs. Parry?" Ramsay looked at them all in astonishment. Why did they feel so little guilt? They were, in a way, responsible for their aunt's death. They should have taken more care of her.

Max shook his head. "I had a lot to think about," he said. "Problems at work, you know. I expect you'll find it hard to believe, but I'd even forgotten that she was still outside."

"You didn't lock any of the doors?"

Max shook his head again. "No," he said. "Alice saw to all that."

"And you didn't go outside?"

There was perhaps a momentary hesitation. "No," Max said. "Why should I have done?"

Ramsay paused, then the focus of his questions became more general. He could sense their relief but was unsure if it was because one of them had been implicated in the murder or because, after all, they felt some shame in having let an old lady wander about alone so late at night.

"Did any strangers come to the house yesterday evening?" he asked.

"Not while we were here," Judy said. "Olive Kerr was here until we sat down for dinner. Alice asked her to join us, but she said she wanted to go back to her own family. I suppose the letter must have been delivered by someone. And of course that reporter was here in the afternoon."

"The reporter from the *Otterbridge Express*? She came to the Tower as well as to the meeting in the hall?"

"I think so." Judy looked around at the family for confirmation. "Isn't that what Alice said? That she had a discussion with Mary Raven after the meeting?"

But the others, it seemed, could not remember.

"You didn't see any strangers at the house?" Ramsay persisted. "There was no-one hanging around the drive or in the churchyard?"

Stella Laidlaw smiled suddenly and spoke for the first time.

42

"Only those teenagers who hang around the bus stop on the green," she said. "They were there, I think."

"Can you see the green from the house?"

"Oh," she said, "you can see most of the village from our bedroom window." She remembered the moonlit figure pacing between the gravestones and smiled again, hugging the information to herself. Ramsay saw the smile and thought how heartless the woman was. She had nothing, after all, to be pleased about. All four Laidlaws would be under suspicion and subject to intrusion and prying questions until the investigation was over. Every family had secrets and he would know most of the Laidlaws' before the thing was finished. The thought gave him no pleasure.

"Will both Max and James benefit under Mrs. Parry's will?" he asked, and as he had expected the question provoked righteous indignation.

Could he really think, they asked, that they would hurt Alice? They all loved her.

"You do see why I have to ask?" Ramsay said mildly. "If you don't wish to discuss it with me, I can talk to Mrs. Parry's solicitor."

"The Tower comes to me with the understanding that it's to stay in the family," James said. "I'll respect her wishes, of course. She hadn't a lot of capital, but what there is goes to Max. Neither of us stands to make a fortune from her death."

"This is ludicrous," Max said. "You should be talking to Henshaw. He must have been the last person to see my aunt alive. And what about the maniacs in the village who called that meeting yesterday and want to stop the building? What about the lunatic who wrote that letter?"

Ramsay ignored the outburst and stood up abruptly. He felt he had spent enough time with them. In other circumstances he would have muttered something about leaving them alone with their grief. But grief seemed beyond them.

"Thank you for your attention," he said. "Please stay in

43

the Tower until one of my officers has taken statements from you. Then you'll be free to go.''

As he left the room he could sense their resentment.

In the playroom at the top of the stairs the children had finished the jigsaw puzzle and were talking with an earnest intensity that would have surprised their parents. It was a small cluttered room with a bare wooden floor and faded print wallpaper. The toys were mostly old, strange, unlike the bright plastic ones they had at home. There was a fort with carved soldiers and a large metal spinning top. On a trestle table along one wall there was a model railway with peeling papier-mâché hills and houses made of balsa wood. It had belonged to Peter's father and had been built by Anthony Parry, but Peter had been told that he was still too young to play with it unsupervised.

As Carolyn spoke to him he looked at the trains with longing. It seemed a terrible injustice that he could not touch them, and that thought on top of all his other misery made him cry suddenly. Carolyn watched in frustration as tears ran down his cheeks.

"It's no good crying," she said crossly. "I'm only trying to help you." She felt so much older than he and knew she would have to take all the responsibility. "We must sort out what we're going to tell them."

"I won't tell them anything!" he cried, looking up at her. "I promise." For the first time ever he was frightened of her. He had loved his cousin ever since he could remember, but the violence of her words made him wish she would leave him alone. Yet he still wanted to please her.

"Of course you'll have to tell them something," she said. "They won't ignore us just because we're children. Not this time. You found the body. The police will want to talk to you."

"Will they?" She seemed so clever. He knew he would trust her judgement. She had always protected him from unpleasantness. He stood up and wandered to the window. A pile of old annuals were stacked on the sill. Before he had started school Carolyn had read them all to him. Outside the

44

policeman who had spoken to his parents appeared on the grass. Frightened, Peter turned back to the room and his cousin.

"Answer all the questions about finding Aunt Alice," she said. "Tell them just what happened. That won't matter. But when they ask you about last night, this is what you must say. . . ."

She took his hand and pulled him close to her, so he could feel her fine hair on his cheek, then he listened carefully as she repeated her instructions.

5

*R*amsay had banned them all from the kitchen until it had been checked forensically. If Mrs. Parry had been stabbed, he said, the murderer might have gone into the kitchen to clean himself up. And the knife. They were to look for bloodstains on the floor and by the sink. Banished from the kitchen, Hunter took shelter in an open shed, which was attached to the house. Logs were stacked against one wall and there was a heavy saw hanging on a nail. Ramsay found him there, drinking tea from a flask with the civilian scene of crime officer. When the S.O.C.O. saw Ramsay, he melted into the garden and Hunter was left to explain.

"It's bloody cold outside, sir," he said. "You can't blame him. The village P.C. is keeping an eye on the site."

Ramsay said nothing and Hunter continued: "He's got a police house in the village. You'll be welcome to use it as a base, he says."

"Thank him," Ramsay said. "I'll see him later."

"Do you want some tea?"

Ramsay shook his head. "I've finished with the Laidlaws now," he said. "You can take their statements. Where's Olive Kerr?"

"Upstairs in the bathroom, washing her face. She was a bit upset."

Outside, the scene of crime officer was bending diligently over the body. Hunter had been right. It was very cold.

"Can you give me any information about the murder weapon yet?" Ramsay asked.

The man looked up, eager to be helpful.

"We're looking for a smooth, wide-bladed knife, I think," he said. "The sort you'd find in any kitchen for cutting meat. Something sturdy but not at all unusual."

"Anything else of use?"

The man shook his head. "Nothing yet."

Ramsay went back into the house and found Olive Kerr standing uncertainly in the hall. Her eyes were red from crying.

"Come on," he said. "I'll walk you home."

"I can't believe it," she cried. "I was here yesterday afternoon helping her get ready for the family. Now I'll never see her again."

Gently he helped her off with her apron and on with her coat. They went out through the front door and onto the drive. It was so cold that the bitter wind took his breath away, but Olive hardly seemed to notice it. There were more policemen in the garden now, searching along the line of the wall.

"What are they doing?" she asked.

"Searching for the murder weapon," he said. "Later I'll have to ask you to look in the kitchen and see if anything's missing. We're looking for a meat knife."

"I wouldn't know," she said. "Mrs. Parry was careless with her things. There's a pile of cutlery in the kitchen and more in the scullery."

They came to the wrought-iron gate to the churchyard. "Do you always come to work this way?" he asked, having to shout against the wind.

"Usually," she said. "It's quicker than going all the way up the Otterbridge Road and down the drive."

"Did you come this way today?"

"No," she said. "It was so wild Tom gave me a lift to the end of the drive."

47

So, Ramsay thought, you didn't shut the gate behind you this morning. Either the murderer was very careful or he left by the drive. Or, he thought, it was one of the family.

When they got to the green, they turned to face the weather. She walked very quickly, stiff, upright, and proud. The waves beyond the cottages were huge and relentless, and Ramsay could taste the spray where he stood.

"I'll be all right now," she said. "You can leave me here."

"I've some questions to ask," he said. "I'll have to come with you."

She nodded briefly and walked on.

In the house behind the garage there was the smell of meat cooking. Tom Kerr must have been looking out for her because he had the door open before they reached it. He was a tall man, bearded, rather serious. His hair was balding and he made Ramsay think of a monk.

"I heard in church," he said. "I was just thinking I should come and fetch you."

He put his arm around her and Ramsay felt excluded, a little jealous. They were obviously very close.

"I'm sorry," he said. "I'll have to come in. There are questions to ask. But I thought you'd be more comfortable here than in the Tower."

"Yes," she said. "Of course. Tom, this is Inspector Ramsay. He's in charge of the investigation."

Tom Kerr nodded and stood aside. "Maggie's at work," he said. "I told her she should stay here today, that you'd need us all around you, but you know what she's like at the minute. There's no talking to her."

"For goodness' sake, man, she's better at work. What good would she do here? Leave her alone. None of this is her fault."

The sharpness of her words shocked Ramsay and it occurred to him that there was a tension between them that had nothing to do with Alice Parry. He supposed that it was none of his business. Unless it had a bearing on the investigation.

Tom Kerr accepted the rebuke apologetically. "There's a

48

fire in the lounge," he said. "Why don't you go in there? The boys have been playing upstairs since they came back from Sunday school. They'll not disturb you. I'll make you some coffee and bring it in."

Olive nodded and led Ramsay into a small room with large, heavy furniture. She picked up a coal scuttle and rattled the fuel loose and thrust it onto the fire. The flames were damped briefly by the coal dust then burned again.

"Tell me about Mrs. Parry," Ramsay said. He settled comfortably into one of the armchairs. He wanted to show her that he was in no hurry, that he could listen to her all morning if she would talk to him. "How did she seem yesterday? You probably knew her as well as anyone."

She nodded, acknowledging the statement as a compliment before replying. "She was canny," Olive said. "Just like she always was. I never knew Alice Parry anything but thoughtful and kind. The meeting had upset her and she was angry about Henshaw and his houses, of course, but she was always in a state about something, and that had been rumbling on for days."

She paused. "I blame myself for that," she said. "I started it all off. My daughter's divorced and she and the bairns live with us. I was always complaining that there was nowhere in Brinkbonnie she could afford to buy and the council houses all sold off. I didn't know it then, but Mrs. Parry went off to talk to Henshaw about that land. I told them in the village she was only acting for the best, but they didn't belive me."

"Who didn't believe you?" Ramsay asked.

She looked at him stubbornly and shook her head. "I don't tell tales," she said.

"Alice Parry was murdered," Ramsay said. "Whoever killed her is dangerous and must be found before it happens again. Last night she had an anonymous letter from someone in the village threatening her because of her part in the new development. I have to know who felt strongly enough to send her that letter, even if it's only to eliminate them from our enquiries."

Olive Kerr sat up in her chair.

"You should talk to Fred Elliot," she said. "He's the postmaster and he's leading the campaign against Henshaw. He's a parish councillor. He'd not have sent any letter to Mrs. Parry. But his son, Charlie, is a difficult man. Likes an argument. You know the type. My man took him on as a mechanic when he came back from the army. I wasn't happy about it. I thought there'd be trouble. But Tom is a good man. He though it was his duty. . . ." Ramsay thought she was going to tell him something else, something personal, but she straightened her back and continued: "Charlie might have sent the letter just to stir up trouble."

"Does he live with his father?"

Olive laughed, a sharp, bitter laugh. "Charlie can't afford a house of his own either. Mrs. Parry's scheme would have helped him, too."

There was a knock on the door and Tom Kerr came in, carrying a tray with cups of coffee that rattled on their saucers as he set it on the table.

"I'll leave you to it," he said, and then directly to Olive: "I'll be in the kitchen if you need me."

Ramsay stood up and handed one of the cups to Olive.

"Tell me about the family," he said. "How did Mrs. Parry get on with them?"

Olive sniffed and spooned sugar into the thick brown liquid.

"Well enough," she said. "I suppose. She loved the bairns. Spoiled them silly. Not my way of bringing up children, but you couldn't blame her. She never had any of her own, though she practically looked after Carolyn single-handed until she was one. Stella was poorly—postnatal depression, they said, though she's always had trouble with her nerves. She was in hospital a lot and her family weren't much use. So James used to bring the baby there before he went to work and pick her up in the evening."

"What about the adults?" Ramsay asked. "Were they close to her?"

"Close enough when they wanted something," she said. "A nice weekend in the country, someone to mind the bairns

50

when they wanted to be out. They never bothered to see if Mrs. Parry needed them. She liked their company and she wasn't getting any younger. It wouldn't have hurt them to call in and spend more time with her. They say they're busy. We're all busy. She never complained. Said she had her own life to live, and that was true enough. But she would have liked to see more of them, all the same . . ."

She paused, but Ramsay said nothing. He was thinking it would be dangerous to take what Mrs. Kerr was saying too seriously. She was reinforcing his own prejudices about the Laidlaws and he needed to keep an open mind. Still, he hoped she would continue. At the beginning of an investigation he had endless patience.

"I suppose she was closer to Judy than to the others," Olive went on. "They had the same sort of interests and sometimes they went to meetings together, but I don't think Mrs. Parry liked her anymore. I don't know that she liked any of them, really."

"Are either of the nephews short of money?" Ramsay asked, then wondered if he had been tactless and too abrupt. But Olive Kerr's loyalty to Alice Parry did not extend to her nephews. She shook her head, disappointed almost that she had no positive information to give.

"No," she said. "James always seems well off. They've just bought a big new house in Otterbridge. Stella's got expensive tastes, but I expect her family sees her all right. She's a Rutherford, you know. From Rothbury." Ramsay nodded. Everyone in Northumberland had heard of the Rutherfords. Between them they owned half of the county. "Max and Judy were always moaning about money but only in the way those sort of people do. Doctors aren't badly paid. They bought that house in Otterbridge when Max first qualified, so there can't be much of a mortgage."

It occurred to Ramsay that Olive had said the same thing before, that she and Mrs. Parry had often discussed the nephews' financial and domestic arrangements. He imagined the women sharing coffee and moral superiority: "These young people don't know what hard work means. . . . Opportunity handed to them on a plate . . . It wasn't the same when we were young. You had to make your own way then.''

There was another pause. ''I didn't have to work there,'' she cried suddenly. ''It wasn't the money. She was a lovely woman.''

She started to cry and rubbed her eyes with a handkerchief clenched in a hard, red fist.

''Tell me about yesterday afternoon,'' Ramsay said. ''What time did you arrive at the Tower?''

''At about five o'clock,'' Olive Kerr said. ''I said I'd give Mrs. Parry a hand with the dinner. She was a good cook but messy. She needed someone to clear up after her.''

''Was she on her own then?''

''Yes. Max and Judy arrived about half an hour later.''

''Did she mention a reporter who had come to do an interview about the meeting?''

''Mary Raven, you mean. I saw her. She was walking back towards the village. I don't think Mrs. Parry would have said anything about her if I hadn't asked who she was. She was quite cagey about her and what they'd been talking about. It wasn't like her. She never usually minded publicity.''

''Did anyone else come to the house that evening? Apart from the Laidlaws.''

''I didn't see anyone, but then I wouldn't have done. I hardly moved from the sink. Mrs. Parry had used every pan in the kitchen and I wanted to leave the place straight before I went home.''

She looked at her watch. ''That beef'll be burnt to a cinder,'' she said. ''You'll have to let me go or we'll have no lunch today.''

''Yes,'' he said. ''I've nearly finished.'' She stood up in an attempt to persuade him to go, but he remained where he was for a moment.

''Mrs. Kerr,'' he said, ''why didn't you have dinner with the family last night? Wasn't it usual for you to join them?''

''Yes,'' she said. ''I usually had dinner with them on St. David's Day. Mrs. Parry always invited me. But I had my

52

own problems and I wouldn't have been very good company."

Then Ramsay did stand up and say that he would not take up any more of her time. As he left the house he saw Tom Kerr at the end of the corridor, peering out of the shadows to be sure that he had gone.

Ramsay walked back to the Tower slowly, his hands in his pockets, taking in every detail of his surroundings. He might have been a tourist. At first there was no-one else about. Even the Castle Hotel seemed almost empty. Inside, he supposed, Olive Kerr's daughter would be serving the customers who had no Sunday dinner to hurry home to. By the main gate into the churchyard was the bus shelter where Stella had seen the teenagers on the night of Alice Parry's death, and Ramsay stood there for a moment to shelter from the wind. As he waited, unnoticed, two boys dressed in black leather walked past. They seemed young, all the teenage bravado driven out of them by the cold, and they were whispering together, more like gossiping girls than boys. As they walked past he heard one of them say with the extravagance of the young: "If my dad finds out he'll *kill* him."

Then they were gone. Ramsay wondered if he should chase after them to find out if they had been in the bus shelter on the previous night, but he turned back towards the Tower. There was more to be done there and the boys would be easy enough to trace in a place the size of Brinkbonnie. He walked into the churchyard and followed the path Alice Parry would have used on the day of her death coming back from the village hall. Ramsay wished he had known her. He thought he would have liked her.

Olive Kerr lifted the heavy meat tray out of the oven and clucked over it before setting it on top of the cooker to keep warm. Tom had followed her back into the kitchen and stood, waiting for her to speak, prepared to offer any comfort or reassurance she needed. But when she turned to face him, she said nothing about Alice Parry.

"You shouldn't blame Maggie about that business with

53

Charlie Elliot," she said. "I've been thinking we haven't been fair to her. It's not her fault."

"She could have stayed with her husband," Tom said. "That would have provided a stable home for her boys and saved us all a lot of trouble."

"But she was unhappy!" Oliver Kerr said. "You could see how unhappy she was. And all those arguments weren't doing the boys any good."

"I know," he said. "I know I'm hard on her." He paused. "But don't you realise that her separation started it all? Charlie Elliot told me that he would never have left the army if he hadn't known she would be free. That's the only reason he came home."

"All the same," she said. "You can't blame her. She gave him no encouragement."

"I can't stand him hanging around the house," he said suddenly. "I see enough of him at work. Whenever I go out, he's there, waiting for her. If she wants nothing to do with him, she should tell him."

"She has told him," Olive Kerr shouted back. "She was engaged to Charlie Elliot when they were both eighteen. She broke it off after three months and she hasn't been interested in him since. She's told him so a dozen times. It's not her fault that the man's as daft as a ship's cat and won't listen to her."

"Then why doesn't he leave her alone?"

"I don't know," Olive said. "He's stubborn, lonely. Perhaps he's hoping that she'll change her mind. But pestering her will do no good. She's as stubborn as he is."

"It's not a joke anymore," Tom Kerr said. "A couple of nights ago I couldn't sleep. It was two o'clock in the morning. And he was still out there in the street staring up at her window."

"Why don't you talk to Fred?" she asked. "Perhaps he'd speak to him."

"No," Tom Kerr said. "He takes no more notice of his father than he does of me."

54

There was a silence. She took a heavy meat knife from a drawer and began to carve the beef.

"You know," she said, "you could do something about it if you want to."

"What do you mean?" he asked.

"If he had no work in Brinkbonnie, he'd have to leave. There'd be nothing to keep him here then."

"I've no grounds for sacking him," he said, shocked. "He's a good enough worker. What excuse could I use for sacking him? And you know why I took him on."

"You don't need an excuse," she cried. "You're the boss. Why should you feel guilty?"

But he shook his head. "No," he said. "I couldn't do that. It wouldn't be right."

"He's making your daughter's life a misery," she said. "Is that right?"

He did not reply.

She clattered plates from the top of the oven onto the table and began to serve the meal.

"I'll tell you something," she said. "If you don't sort out Charlie Elliot, Maggie will. And I'm frightened about what might happen. Alice Parry's death has made terrible things seem possible."

"You're upset," he said. He was relieved that she had returned to the subject of Alice Parry. He found that easier to deal with. "Of course you're upset."

She lost her grip on the knife she was holding and it slipped onto the table and then onto the floor, scratching a tile.

"Go and tell the boys to wash their hands," she said. "Their dinner's ready."

He picked up the knife and went slowly out of the room.

6

*A*t the Tower the Laidlaws were preparing to leave for home. There was a pile of suitcases at the foot of the stairs. One of the twins was crying in a monotonous, exhausted way that seemed to get on all their nerves. Stella Laidlaw sat on the bottom step, clutching a fat handbag to her stomach, like a child with a favourite toy, only her eyes showing over the white collar of her sweater. Peter was asleep with his head on Carolyn's knee, his face white and strained. They were waiting, it seemed, for Ramsay. Hunter had said that no-one could leave without his permission.

"We can't face spending another night here," James said. "I'm sure you can understand that, Inspector. The children need to be in their own homes."

Ramsay looked at them. They were irritated by the delay but showed no other emotion. Do you really have no feelings? he thought. Or have you spent all your lives learning how not to express them? He raised no objections to their leaving. He was glad to see them go.

Hunter helped the Laidlaws to load the cars. He even stood awkwardly for a while with a baby in each arm. The wind was even colder, carrying flurries of snow, blowing scraps of garden waste across the lawn. As they watched, a square pink card flapped and lifted with the leaves then came to rest against the bumper of James's car. Ramsay picked it up carefully by one corner and held it to show them. The card was

56

damp and the corners of the letters were unstuck, but it was clearly Alice Parry's anonymous letter.

"Where did this come from?" Ramsay turned on Hunter, aware as he spoke that his anger was unfair. It wasn't Hunter's fault. "I thought they'd searched the garden."

Hunter shrugged. He was thinking of the delights of the Bigg Market: the teenage girls dressed in tiny skirts, the disco music spilling onto the streets through open pub doors. Policing was only a job to him. The pleasures of his time off were more important to him. Ramsay's anger did not concern him. He had a date with a student nurse and he regretted that more.

"It's very blowy," he said. "It could have been dropped anywhere in the village."

"Quite a coincidence," Ramsay said. "Talk to them. See if there's anywhere they might have missed."

Hunter nodded, handed the twins back to their mother, and walked away without a word. The cars moved off down the drive. Ramsay stood outside for a moment watching them disappear through the trees. It was almost dark and Ramsay thought there would be more snow.

In the kitchen the forensic team were just finishing.

"Anything?" Ramsay asked.

The officer shook his head. "Sorry," he said. "It's spotless. That doesn't mean that the sink wasn't used, but there's no evidence. Nothing on the floor either."

Ramsay shrugged. It was the worst sort of information. It didn't eliminate or identify anyone. He was no further forward. He filled a kettle to make coffee.

"Did you look at the knives?" he asked.

"Yes. We'll take one or two of the more likely ones back to the lab to check, but I don't think your murder weapon's among them."

"That'll please them," Ramsay said. "They'll have to continue the search outside."

"You're a hard man," the officer said. "It's practically dark out there and it's freezing."

It was cold even in the kitchen. The family must have

switched off the heating. Ramsay shivered and made instant coffee in a mug. The forensic team left. He heard them calling to each other outside and the sound of their cars going up the drive.

When Hunter came in, he was wearing only denim jeans, a sweater, and a thin leather jacket. He never seemed to feel the cold.

"They say that card couldn't have been in the garden," he said. "They searched everywhere. They wouldn't have missed it. Is that tea?"

Ramsay shook his head. "You've drunk enough tea to sink a battleship. What do you think of all this?"

Hunter shrugged. "Attempted robbery?" he said. "If she was late coming back from Henshaw's, she might have surprised someone who saw the house in darkness. The back door hadn't been locked, so there'd be no sign of a break-in even if he managed to get inside. I can't see any of the family knocking her off for her money, and no-one's going to commit murder for the sake of a few houses."

Ramsay thought of the view from his cottage window. I might, he thought, if there was no other way. But only if I believed it would stop the houses being built. "Alice Parry's death makes no difference to the development," he said. "Henshaw owns the land anyway and can do what he likes with it. If someone in the village killed her, it was out of envy or hatred. It served no practical purpose."

"What about Henshaw?" Hunter asked. "Mrs. Parry could have made things awkward for him. Especially if she persuaded her nephew to make a fuss in his paper."

"Yes," Ramsay said. "I want to talk to Henshaw. But he'll be used to opposition to planning applications. I'll go and see him when I'm finished here. He was the last person to see her alive."

"Do we know that she reached him last night?"

"Yes," Ramsay said. "I sent someone to take a statement this morning. He claims they had a friendly discussion and she left about eleven. We'll have a house-to-house to see if anyone saw Mrs. Parry on her way home. The pub would have been emptying then. There should have been a few people about.''

Hunter stood throughout the conversation. He was restless. The inspector had made a fuss about him drinking tea, but he sat now, his hands clasped around the mug of coffee, uncertain, it seemed, what to do next. Ramsay had been promoted beyond his competence, Hunter thought. The words sounded good and he repeated them in his mind. The Heppleburn fiasco had almost finished him off. In Heppleburn Ramsay had arrested a women who had committed suicide in custody. The press had complained about police brutality and, on top of his divorce, the lads had all thought Ramsay's career was over. Yet here he was, still in charge, when there were younger officers to take his place.

While Ramsay finished the dregs from his mug, Hunter wandered to the window. It was snowing properly now, sharp, fine flakes against the grey sky. Hunter's anxiety for action increased. He did not want to be stuck all night in this sand-blasted village where the only entertainment was a game of dominoes in the pub. When he turned back to the room, Ramsay was on his feet.

"What are you waiting for?" Ramsay asked. "We can't spend all day in here. I'm going to Henshaw's. You go to the post office and talk to the Elliots. Nothing heavy. Just find out where they were last night and what they were doing. Olive Kerr thinks Charlie, the son, might have sent that letter. I'll follow it up tomorrow. Then you can go.''

Hunter said nothing and followed him out into the snow. Ramsay waited while the sergeant drove off angrily, then walked, as Alice Parry must have done the night before, down the drive towards the Otterbridge Road.

It was six o'clock and quite dark. As he reached the road the snow flurry ended and there was a thin, icy moon and a frost. Henshaw's place was harder to find than he had expected, because out of the village there were no street lights and the houses were hidden behind hedges. He went through the first gate and walked unexpectedly into a farmyard. He disturbed a dog lying in an outhouse. It barked loudly and an outside light was switched on. A woman came to the door and shouted out to know who was there.

Ramsay, embarrassed by his mistake and not wanting to frighten her further, waited until she returned into the house and went back to the road without being seen.

The next drive led to Henshaw's house. It curved pretentiously through borders of immature shrubs. There was a light outside the front door of the house and many of the windows were lit and uncurtained so Ramsay could see quite clearly how to approach. The bungalow was modern, the red brick unweathered, faced in places with local stone. In front there was a large, terraced garden, and set into one of the paved terraces was a swimming pool, empty, the blue tiles glazed with frost. In a typical Northumberland summer, Ramsay thought, it could hardly have been used. The garden must be exposed to the wind, cold even in sunshine. Attached to the house was a large garage built of the same violently coloured brick. The door was open and inside were two cars: a small Renault and a new and expensive Rover. Ramsay walked on, unnoticed, past the living-room window, the sound of his footsteps apparently muffled by the double-glazed panes. Inside a woman was setting bowls of nuts and crisps onto small tables. She was bent away from him to fill the bowls and Ramsay could not see her face, only her wide thighs covered by stretched blue silk. The Henshaws were expecting guests.

When he rang the doorbell, there was a two-tone noise, the same pitch as an ambulance siren from inside. Beyond the tinted glass he was aware of a bustle, a hurried preparation. They thought, perhaps, that he was an early guest and they wanted everything right before they let him in. At last a man opened the door to him. Henshaw was tall, heavily built, with a profile of a kangaroo. Despite his bulk and his age—he was in late middle age—his movements were decisive and self-confident. He spoke first before Ramsay could explain why he was there.

''Who are you?'' he demanded. He wore an open-necked
60

shirt and held a glass in his hand, but there was nothing relaxed about him.

"Mr. Henshaw," Ramsay said. "I'm sorry to disturb you. Perhaps I could come in for a while?" He showed the man his identity card. Henshaw studied it carefully, then stood aside.

"What do you want?" Henshaw said, not rudely, but making it clear he was not afraid of any policeman. "Someone came this morning to take a statement."

"A few questions," Ramsay said easily, carefully wiping his shoes on a mat just inside the door. A strip of transparent plastic matting led up the long hall. Mrs. Henshaw was obviously a house-proud woman and it would not do to antagonise her.

Without speaking, Henshaw led him through to the living room. Ramsay had expected Mrs. Henshaw to be there, but the room was empty. All of the large pieces of furniture had been pushed to the edge of the room against the walls, and the expanse of carpet, brightly patterned in swirling blues and greens, was broken only by several small coffee tables. At the time Ramsay thought the room had been arranged that way to accommodate the people the Henshaws were expecting, but when he visited again the room was just the same. It gave Ramsay the sense of a public building rather than a private home. It might have been the lounge of a smart, rather tasteless hotel.

The whole house was very hot. Along the wall was a stone fireplace and there was a gas fire, which simulated real flames. On the walls were several prints, chosen, it seemed, because their subjects were blue and green rather than because the Henshaws found them attractive. It was the sort of room Diana would have hated.

Again Ramsay was aware that he would have to conduct the interview with care. The fact that Henshaw owned the land behind his cottage coloured his attitude to the man. It was hard to remain objective.

"It's my wife's birthday," Henshaw said suddenly.

"We're expecting guests. I'm going to have another drink. Would you like one?"

Ramsay shook his head. "This won't take long," he said. "The policeman who came this morning told you that Alice Parry was murdered last light."

"Aye," Henshaw said, then added reluctantly, "They'll miss her in the village."

He might have said more, but they were interrupted by Mrs. Henshaw, who stood for a moment in the doorway to be admired. Ramsay guessed she must have disappeared when she heard the doorbell to put on makeup, because her face had a waxy, coloured glow. She wore a suit in blue silk with a bow at the neck and frills at the sleeves, and her fat, fleshy feet were squeezed into high-heeled blue shoes. She smiled kindly and walked forward, arms outstretched.

"I'm sorry," she said. "I don't think we've met. You must be one of Colin's friends."

She had been told, Ramsay thought, to be on her best behaviour.

"No, no, woman." Henshaw said impatiently. "He's a policeman. He's here to talk about Mrs. Parry. Though God knows what it's got to do with us."

To Ramsay's surprise Rosemary Henshaw's eyes filled with tears. Her emotion contrasted sharply with Henshaw's apparent indifference, and he wondered what significance that might have. She would be the sort, he thought, to cry easily.

"Poor soul," she said. "Such a shock to her family." And she seemed genuinely concerned by her neighbour's death.

"Did you know her well, Mrs. Henshaw?" Ramsay asked. Perhaps the women had been close friends and the awkwardness of the building dispute with her husband had come between them.

"No," she said. "Not well. But she was kind. When we first came to the village, she made us welcome. She took me to the WI. Not all the old families were so friendly. It's hard to settle in a new place, especially if you have no children."

"Yes," he said. "It must be."

Yet her sentimentality made him uneasy, and throughout the interview he treated her carefully, afraid of upsetting her again.

"Mrs. Parry came to see you last night," Ramsay said. "You were the last people we know of who saw her alive."

He looked at them, expecting some response, but there was none.

"She sold you some land," Ramsay said. "She came to see you to offer to buy it back."

"Yes," Henshaw said. "She sold me some land."

"Did you accept her offer to buy back the land?"

"No," he said. "Of course not."

"Did you argue about it?"

"I never argue," Henshaw said. "I explained to her the facts of business. I've already got prospective buyers for some of the houses. I've spent thousands drawing up the plans and putting them before the council. I couldn't sell it now."

"Is it true that Mrs. Parry only sold the land to you on the understanding that the houses you built would be small and inexpensive and available to local families?"

"No," Henshaw said firmly. "That was a misunderstanding. I never gave any such commitment. Even Mrs. Parry accepted she'd been mistaken by the end of the evening."

"Are you sure?" Ramsay asked. "There was a protest meeting in the village yesterday afternoon and Mrs. Parry was very angry."

"She was angry when she got here," Rosemary Henshaw said. "She was quite rude. I didn't want to let her in."

Ramsay looked directly at Henshaw. "What did you say to persuade her that she'd been mistaken about the houses?" he asked.

"There was nothing in writing," Henshaw said. "She was an old lady. Old ladies get muddled. Besides, it suited her purpose, didn't it, to let the village think I'd cheated her. Let me be the bad guy. I'm used to it. That way she'd get her money and they'd all still love her."

"Can you prove that's the way it happened?"

"No," Henshaw said. "I told you, there was nothing in writing."

"I see." Ramsay stood up and walked towards the window. The room was so stuffy that he felt he would fall asleep. He did not know what to make of the builder who stood before the gas fire with such confident certainty. "What time did Mrs. Parry leave here?"

"Quarter to eleven," Henshaw said.

"Are you sure?"

"I looked at the clock," Henshaw said. "I knew it was late. I offered to drive her home, but she said she'd rather walk."

"Did you go out after she went?"

"No," Henshaw said shortly. "I've told you. It was late. We went to bed."

There was a silence. Ramsay felt he was getting nowhere with the builder. Henshaw would have an answer whatever question was asked. Ramsay felt tired and incompetent. Hunter, he thought, would have bullied something out of him.

Rosemary Henshaw let Ramsay out of the house. Her husband, unmoved, stayed in the living room and barely looked up to say goodbye. In contrast she was too friendly to the policeman, almost gushing: "Do let us know if there's anything we can do to help. Call at any time."

Then he was gone. She watched him walk down the drive until the only sign of him was the sound of his shoes on the frosty gravel. She realised how cold she was and shut the door.

She was a plump woman, always had been. Built like a dairymaid, Colin had said when they first met. He was a city boy from the west end of Newcastle and he liked to think of her as a country girl, though there was nothing romantic about her childhood.

"We'll live in the country one day," he had said when they first moved into their flat in town. He had talked a lot about what he wanted in those days and she had thought he

64

was just dreaming. Now, wanting things had become a habit and he seemed unable to stop.

After seeing Ramsay out, Rosemary Henshaw paused in the hall before an ornate gilt-framed mirror and absent-mindedly studied her reflection. She wanted to confront Colin about the policeman's visit, but she had left the important things to him for so long that she did not know how to begin. He would accuse her of making a scene, as he did sometimes when she asked tentatively where he had been when he stayed out all night. She knew he had other women and had stopped asking. She did not want to cause a scene. She wanted to offer Colin her help, but even that seemed an impudent thing to do because he was so far above her in intelligence and understanding. She wanted, above all things, to know what was going on.

She looked with more purpose into the mirror, hoping to find there the confidence to persuade herself to face her husband. She was good-looking, she thought, for fifty. Her hair, carefully tinted and curled, suited her. She was a little over-weight, of course, but Colin liked his women big. She still had the soft, round dairymaid's face.

When she returned to the living room, he was sitting on the sofa with a fresh glass of whisky, staring at the fire.

"Colin," she said, sitting carefully beside him. "What was that all about?"

"You heard what the man said." Henshaw looked at her as if she were a complete fool, and when he continued, he emphasized every syllable. "Alice Parry was murdered. We were the last people to see her alive."

"I know that." She spoke calmly, trying to be patient, telling herself that he was very upset. "But what does it mean for us?"

"Nothing," he shouted. "It means nothing."

"I don't understand why the policeman asked all those questions."

"I don't know," he cried. "He'd heard we'd had a row over that land."

"But that was all sorted out," Rosemary said. "You told

me last week that you'd sorted that out. We'd hear no more about it, you said.''

"That's right," he said. "So it was."

He took a drink from his glass.

"Colin," she said. "Where were you last night?"

He looked at her sharply. "What do you mean?" he asked. "I was here. You know I was here with you."

"No," she said. "When Mrs. Parry left, I went to bed and watched the telly. But I heard the car go out. I stayed awake until I heard you come back. It was very late. Where did you go? Whatever it is, I don't mind. But I must know. I can't help you if I don't know."

He looked at her angrily. She thought for a moment that he was going to hit her. He had knocked her around a bit when they were first married, when he had not got on as quickly as he had wanted and he had taken it out on her. More recently, he had controlled his temper and there had been less to be angry about.

"Don't!" she said quietly. "Don't forget the guests will be here soon."

She was more concerned about his own position than for what he might do to her. He breathed deeply and leaned back in his chair.

"You shouldn't spy on me," he said.

"I wasn't," she said. "I was worried."

"I didn't kill her," he said. "There was no need."

"That's all right then," she said, like a mother forgiving the misdemeanour of a naughty boy even though she does not quite believe him.

"I do it all for you," he said suddenly. "All this." He looked around at the expensive carpet, the furniture, the real gas-flame fire. She moved closer to him on the sofa and put her arm around him, pulling his head onto her shoulder.

"I know," she said. "I know."

The front doorbell rang and the guests began to arrive.

7

Ramsay walked quickly down the hill towards the village. The interview with Henshaw had left him frustrated and undecided. He sensed that the builder was hiding something, but his prejudice against the man made him unsure of his own judgement. It was colder than ever and the air caught at the back of his throat. He passed the drive into the farmyard where earlier he had disturbed the dogs and was surprised by the incongruous sound of pop music coming from an upstairs window. At the entrance to the Tower drive he hesitated but continued down the hill, past the church and the green to the Castle Hotel. It was time to meet a wider section of Brinkbonnie's inhabitants.

At the pub the lights were on and a couple of cars were parked in the yard at the back. He went inside and pushed open the door that had "lounge" written on it in plastic letters. The room was separated into two by a step. On the raised section, tables were laid with cutlery and cruets and there, at lunchtime, microwaved meals were served. The lower section was carpeted, the furniture dark, imitation antique. There were beams and horse brasses, and the place was empty. Regulars obviously used the public bar.

In the bar the jukebox was playing an old Rolling Stones number, which brought back painful memories of his youth. The floor was stone and the place seemed to be unheated. There were a couple of high-backed settles; the wood was

67

dark and splintered where three old men were playing dominoes. Two teenagers were playing darts. In a corner by the window a squat, red-faced man with huge hands was reading a farming magazine and drinking steadily. On a stool by the bar a fat man, who turned out to be the landlord, seemed to be asleep. He woke up occasionally to drink brandy from a huge balloon glass. A pretty young woman in her late twenties was drying glasses behind the bar.

"Come on, Frank," one of the dart players said. "What about lighting a fire? It's bloody freezing in here."

The fat man stirred and stared at the boy with a cold, reptilian eye.

"The central heating's on," he said, speaking slowly, as if he needed to conserve all his energy. "It'll warm through soon."

"Mean bastard," one of the old men said, quite audibly. Frank took no notice and settled back on his stool, the hooded lids covering his eyes once again.

The woman behind the bar looked expectantly at Ramsay, waiting for him to order.

"Whisky," he said. Then, recognising a similarity of the features, "Aren't you Olive Kerr's daughter?"

She nodded, surprised, and he added, "My name's Ramsay. I'm a detective investigating Mrs. Parry's murder. I spoke to your mother this morning."

The darts game continued, the men muffled in scarves and coats still stared miserably at their hands of dominoes, and Frank sat in his stupor, but Ramsay was aware that the whole room was listening.

"Poor old Mrs. Parry," the barmaid was saying. "You'd never expect a thing like that to happen in Brinkbonnie. Mam loved going up to the Tower to work." She paused as she took the money he offered. "You know," she said. "I could tell something was wrong when she was in last night."

"Alice Parry was in here last night?" Ramsay was surprised, but his voice was smooth and unemotional. "What time would that have been, then?"

She was about to answer when Frank's left eyelid gave an

68

almost imperceptible flicker of warning. She paused awkwardly.

"If you're worried about closing time," Ramsay said, "there won't be any trouble. I can promise that."

She continued, relieved. "She came in at about eleven. We always draw the curtains at eleven so you can't see the lights from the road." She blushed and went on. "Then the people inside can finish their drinks. Without having to hurry."

"I see." He smiled to reassure her. "Was it usual for Mrs. Parry to come in that late at night?"

"No," she said. "Not that late. She was quite a regular customer. I think she got lonely on her own in the Tower and she came in here for the company. She didn't drink much."

"But last night she had a drink?"

"Yes," Maggie Kerr said. "She had two. She said she needed them. She seemed upset."

"Upset?" he asked. "Or angry?"

"Upset," she said. "She looked as if she'd been crying."

So, Ramsay thought, Henshaw hadn't been telling the truth. There hadn't been a reasonable exchange of views during Alice's visit. Something had happened to disturb her.

"Did she tell you what it was all about?" he asked.

Maggie shook her head. "There was a darts match in here last night. It was very busy. There wasn't time to talk."

One of the old men looked up from his dominoes and glared at the landlord. "If someone got up off his backside," he said, "and stood behind that bar occasionally, we wouldn't have to wait so long for our drinks when it's crowded in here."

Again Frank gave no acknowledgement that he had heard the comment. The red-faced man by the window stood up suddenly and brought his glass to the bar to be filled. While Maggie was pouring the beer, Ramsay turned round and addressed his next questions to the customers.

"Did she talk to anyone else last night?" he asked.

"No!" the old man said. "And that wasn't like her. She might live in that big house, but she's not one for sticking

69

her nose in the air." He turned towards the red-faced man, who had returned to his seat and his magazine. "Not like some of the women in this village. Mrs. Parry usually brings her Guinness down here and has a chat with us. Last night she sat up at the bar and didn't say a word to anyone. She was white as a ghost."

"Which locals were in?" Ramsay asked. "Colin Henshaw? Charlie Elliot?"

"Colin Henshaw doesn't come in here often," the barmaid said. "Charlie Elliot's on the darts team, but he went just before Mrs. Parry arrived."

"And that doesn't happen very often, does it?" one of the darts players shouted. "It's not often that Charlie leaves before you do, is it, Maggie? Doesn't he usually wait to walk you home?"

She looked suddenly angry and embarrassed, and Ramsay thought how difficult it was for an outsider to settle into a village like Brinkbonnie or Heppleburn. There was obviously some attachment or tension between Maggie and Charlie Elliot, and if he reacted wrongly, he would break the mood of the whole conversation. He decided to ignore the comment and continue with his questions. If the relationship between Charlie Elliot and Maggie was relevant to his investigation, it could be explored later.

"I was relieved Charlie went early," Maggie said.

"I bet you were," the darts player shouted again. "Been making a bit of a nuisance of himself lately, hasn't he? You should tell the inspector about it. Perhaps he'd be able to arrange police protection, or perhaps you enjoy it, really."

Again she ignored him. "I was relieved Charlie went early," Maggie said, "because I was afraid he might make a scene. After the way he treated Mrs. Parry at the meeting."

"Were you at the meeting in the hall yesterday afternoon?"

"No," she said. "I couldn't get there. But I heard what happened."

Of course, Ramsay thought, the whole of Brinkbonnie

70

would have heard about Charlie Elliot's rudeness to Alice Parry.

"Did Mrs. Parry walk back to the Tower on her own?"

She looked at the old men. "Did anyone go up the hill with Alice?"

"Aye." It was the old man with the almost unintelligible accent who regarded the landlord with such venom. "I took her home."

"But that's out of your way, Joe," the barmaid said.

"All the same," he said. "I think I'm enough of a gentleman to know what's right. I took her home."

"All the way?" Ramsay asked.

"To her drive."

"Did you see anyone else on the way?"

"No."

"You didn't see Charlie Elliot?"

"I've told you. We didn't see a soul. Besides, Charlie would have been long home by then."

"Was there anyone in the churchyard?"

"I wouldn't know," the old man said. "I didn't look."

"Did you see Mrs. Parry into the house?" Ramsay asked.

"Nah! You can't see the house for the trees. I'd seen her to her gate. I thought I'd done my duty." He glared at the landlord. "I'd spent an evening in here," he said. "I was perishing cold."

"Yes," Ramsay said. "I see."

He finished his drink, then went out into the street. He was almost at the church when he heard the sound of footsteps rattling on the frosty pavement. When he turned round, he saw Maggie running towards him, the tails of her scarf flying out behind her. When she reached him, she was breathless and her eyes were streaming with the cold.

"I wanted to talk to you," she said, "about Charlie Elliot."

He felt a moment of satisfaction when he realised that his approach in the pub had been the right one. If he had started asking questions in front of the customers, she would have said nothing.

"Come on," he said. "We'll walk back to my car. It'll be a bit warmer in there. Then I can drive you home."

"You'll be asking questions in the village," she said. "I know you have to do that. You'll hear about it anyway. You might as well have the truth. It's nothing to do with Alice Parry's death."

He said nothing. It was impossible to know what was relevant to the investigation at this stage.

"They said that I led him on," she cried suddenly, "that he lost his career in the army because of me. But it's not true. When I told him I was leaving David, I didn't expect him to be so silly."

Why do they talk to me like this? Ramsay thought. I have no real right to know.

"David was your husband?" he asked.

"Yes, and when I left him, I had to come back here. There was nowhere else to go. I couldn't stay in the house. David's a keeper on the Rutherford estate and it was a tied cottage."

"I don't quite understand," he said. "where Charlie Elliot comes in."

They turned into the churchyard, and the long grass was stiff with frost.

"Charlie and I grew up together," she said. "We were in the same class at school, got the bus together everyday. I liked him. He was a good friend. Then, when we were sixteen, he started taking me out. Into Otterbridge to the pictures, to youth-club dances. I thought it was just a bit of fun. Other girls had boyfriends. I had Charlie."

"But he took it more seriously?"

"Yes," she said. "On my eighteenth birthday when we were both still in school, he asked me to marry him."

They had come to the wrought-iron gate into the Tower garden. Ramsay lifted the latch and pulled it open to allow her to walk through. But she stood facing him, wanting him to understand.

"I was young," she said. "I was flattered. I liked him. I didn't think it would do any harm. When I agreed to get engaged, I never really thought it would end up in marriage.

72

It was an excuse for a party, for being the centre of attention for a while. You know what young girls are like. It made me special.''

Ramsay thought that he did not know at all what young girls were like and shut the gate behind her. He was not wearing gloves and the cold metal of the catch stung his hands as he struggled to fasten it.

"You changed your mind," he said.

"Yes," she said. "I changed my mind. Charlie became so serious and intense. He wanted me to spend all my time with him. He was only taking one A-level and some re-sits, but I was doing three A-levels. I wanted to go into nursing. He seemed to think that wasn't important. Not compared with spending time with him."

"How long did the engagement last?" he asked.

"Three months," she said. "Then one evening we had a furious argument and I broke it off. He left school and went to join the army." She paused. "I was quite proud of that," she said bitterly. "It seemed very romantic."

They reached the car. Ramsay opened the passenger door for her, then got in and started the engine so that he could switch on the heater. All of the windows were covered in ice.

"What did you do?" he asked.

"I passed my exams and started training to be a nurse," she said. "I saw Charlie sometimes when he was home on leave. He was always polite but very distant. I thought he'd made his gesture and the whole thing was over. I met David at a young farmers' dance and started going out with him. I got pregnant and we got married." She shrugged. "That time I thought I'd better see the thing through. On the day before the wedding I had a letter from Charlie saying I was making a terrible mistake and I'd never be happy."

"And were you?"

"Oh," she said. "For a while."

"When did you leave your husband?"

"About a year ago," she said. "Charlie was home on leave and I bumped into him in the Castle. It was good to have someone to talk to, flattering, I suppose, to have him so attentive. Towards the end of the marriage David had hardly noticed me. I told Charlie that I'd left David and that the boys and I were staying at Mum and Dad's. But that's all. I didn't give him any encouragement. He walked me home and gave me a good-night kiss, but I didn't mean anything by it. I was just pleased we were friends again.''

The heater was beginning to clear the ice from the windscreen and they could see the bulk of the Tower in the moonlight.

"What happened then?"

"Charlie left the army," she said. "It was awful. Like a nightmare. He wrote to his father to tell him and Fred Elliot turned up at our house accusing me of leading him on. "You've broken his heart once," he said. "Now you're meaning to do it again." His wife had recently died and everything seemed to upset him. I didn't know what to say or do. I wrote to Charlie telling him there was no point coming home, that I hadn't changed my mind, but it didn't do any good.''

"Did you persuade your father to give him a job?" Ramsay asked.

"No," she said quickly. "I didn't want to have anything to do with him. My father thought that if he offered Charlie a job, there would be a reconciliation between the families. You don't understand what it's like in a place like this. The village was split in two, with half supporting me and half supporting Charlie. My father's idea was to bring everyone together again.''

"But it didn't work?"

"It would have done," she said, "if Charlie hadn't been such a bloody fool." She began to cry. "He's worn me out. I don't know if I can stand it any longer. I think he's mad.''

"What does he do?" Ramsay asked.

"It started with presents—flowers and chocolates and bottles of wine. At first I took them back to him. But that only made him angry. He's got a terrible temper. So now I keep them and take them into the old Cottage Hospital in Otter-

74

bridge. Then he tried phoning me at home, sometimes dozens of times in an evening, begging me to see him and talk to him. More recently, he's taken to following me around the village. When I wake up he's out on the street looking up at me, and he waits outside the pub at closing time and follows me home. I don't know what to do. It's frightening. He's not normal now. He's completely obsessed." She paused. "It's affecting the whole family," she said. "My dad tried to talk to Charlie about it one night after work. There was a fight. Can you imagine it? My father brawling in the street. He must have caught Charlie off balance because Charlie hit his head on the pavement and knocked himself out. Then, of course, Dad felt guilty and that made things worse."

"But Charlie's still working at the garage. Even after the fight?"

"Yes," she said bitterly. "Dad's a great one for martyrdom. He wants to show the village he knows what's right even if he finds it hell."

"Have you talked to the police about this?"

"No," she said. "How could I? Dad assaulted Charlie. They might charge him. The village think it's all my fault that Charlie's in that state. How would it look if I reported him to the police, too? Besides, I'd started to hope that soon it would all be over. He'd become obsessed with the housing development on the Tower meadow. I thought if he became involved with that, he might forget about me. And it seemed to be working. The night Mrs. Parry died was the first evening for a month when he wasn't there to follow me home after work."

Ramsay looked at her sharply, wondering if the words were malicious, if she was accusing Elliot of having played a part in Mrs. Parry's murder. But she spoke quite innocently. She was simply relieved that she had been allowed to walk home alone.

"Have you seen Charlie today?" he asked.

"He was outside the house at lunchtime when I went to

75

work," she said. "But I've not seen him this evening. Do you think it might all be coming to an end?"

"I don't know," Ramsay said. "But I'd better take you home. Your parents will be wondering where you are."

He drove slowly down the drive towards the Otterbridge Road. At the junction he had to brake sharply, then skidded because a man stepped out suddenly into his headlights. The man stood for a moment in the road, shielding his eyes from the glare of the lamps with his hands, shocked, it seemed, to see a car coming down the Tower drive. It was only when he turned without apology and walked on up the road that Ramsay recognised him as the red-faced man from the pub.

"Who the hell is that?" he asked. "What on earth does he think he's playing at?"

"It's Robert Grey," Maggie said. "He farms the land behind the village. He lives just up the road, next door to the Henshaws'."

"Does he get as drunk as that every evening?"

"No," she said. "I don't know what was wrong with him tonight. He came in at opening time and must have just finished now."

At the house behind the garage the lights were still on and Ramsay imagined her father there, waiting anxiously. There was no sign of Charlie Elliot. She ran in without a word.

It was midnight when he arrived back at the cottage at Heppleburn. He assumed that the envelope stuck in his letter box would be a circular. It was Sunday and there was no post. Before looking at it, he lit the gas fire and made coffee. Only then did he see that it was a card, expensive and hand-delivered, from Diana welcoming him to his new home. He studied it, as if hoping for a clue in the pressed flowers and bland printed message to her motivation. But he did not find one, and when he got into bed he still was not sure whether he was pleased or sorry to have missed her.

8

The next day, Monday, the murder enquiry moved on like an unwieldy, poorly organised military exercise. At dawn the special patrol group began their search of the beech wood behind the house. Dressed in boots and anoraks, they moved in a single line through the trees, hindered by the frost and snow that covered the dead leaves, swearing about the cold. Some were sent to the churchyard. At first there was no communications equipment and they kept in touch by shouting. They complained, as they always did, of their superiors' inefficiency. They set up their base in the small police house on the edge of the village but found nothing there to help them. The only equipment provided was a wartime pamphlet showing the identification of German planes and a bucket of sand in case of fire. There had been little crime in Brinkbonnie.

They found the knife quite by chance soon after the search was started. The youngest member tripped on the edge of a flat gravestone and fell, facedown in the snow, accompanied by laughter and jeers. As he stumbled he knocked over a vase of dead daffodils that had been standing on the grave and the knife emerged with the rotting stalks of the flowers.

"You lucky bastard," someone shouted. "I suppose you'll take the credit for finding it now."

But they were all pleased that the murder weapon had been

77

found. It encouraged them that they might find something else of significance.

Ramsay was told about the discovery of the knife in Otterbridge. He was at the police station, supervising the setting up of the Incident Room, the arrival of computer terminals, extra phone lines, and piles of paper. Still no-one had found the screens to block off the corner of the Tower garden where the body had been found, and he, too, muttered about inefficiency. His superintendent was giving all his attention to the press and on every news broadcast there was a shot of him pleading earnestly for information about any unfamiliar cars seen in Brinkbonnie on Saturday night.

A group of detectives from Newcastle had been drafted to help and they milled around the Incident Room until Ramsay sent them off to Brinkbonnie to begin the house-to-house enquiry.

Hunter arrived at work elated and energetic after his night in Newcastle, wanting action, immediate results.

"Did you see the Elliots last night?" Ramsay asked.

Hunter nodded.

"Anything?"

"Not much. They weren't very communicative." I bet you weren't either, Ramsay thought. You'd want to get the interview finished as soon as possible so you'd be in Newcastle before your date walked out on you.

"Did Charlie Elliot tell you he'd been to the pub?" Ramsay asked.

"Yes." If Hunter was impressed by Ramsay's knowledge, he did not show it.

"What time was he home?"

"About eleven. His father confirmed it."

"How did he strike you?" Ramsay asked. "Apparently he's been making a nuisance of himself with Maggie Kerr, the barmaid in the Castle. They were engaged when they were teenagers and he never got over it. Did he seem unbalanced to you?"

"Not unbalanced," Hunter said. "Moody perhaps."

"Well," Ramsay said, "if he was home by eleven, he

can't have murdered Mrs. Parry. She was still in the Castle then. She definitely left Henshaw's and went straight to the pub. The barmaid said she was upset, but Henshaw won't admit that there was any unpleasantness. Perhaps you could make some enquiries in the village. Find out all you can about him. He drives a Rover. See if anyone saw it late Saturday night."

"Are you coming to Brinkbonnie?"

"Later. I've an appointment with the council's planning officer. I want to find out about these houses."

Despite Hunter's scepticism he was convinced that Henshaw's development had in some way triggered the series of events that had resulted in Alice Parry's death. Henshaw's version of the confrontation with Alice Parry was false. Something had happened to distress her, and almost immediately after she had died. The man's lying must be significant.

The council offices were in a shabby building that always reminded Ramsay of a large working-men's club. The planning officer was a small, solid man with a thin grey moustache. He had Henshaw's plans laid out on his desk.

"I don't understand the planning procedure," Ramsay said. "It might be relevant in this case. Perhaps you could explain."

"Mr. Henshaw made his original application for Brinkbonnie late last summer," the officer said. He had a brisk, clipped voice and spoke with the formality of a man used to local politics. "Previously the land had been of marginal agricultural use—occasionally leased to a local farmer for grazing cattle. After being purchased by Mr. Henshaw, I believe that arrangement stopped. The council felt that the plans were inappropriate for a village of Brinkbonnie's size and refused permission to build."

"Was there a lot of publicity at that time?"

"Not a great deal. We put a notice in the local paper and received several objections, but no-one seriously believed the development would be approved."

"Would a smaller scheme have been more favourably received?"

"I can't speak for the council, of course, but yes, I would have thought so."

"What happened then?"

"The developer, Mr. Henshaw, appealed to the Department of the Environment's inspector. The case was heard at the beginning of February."

"And the result of the appeal came through last week?"

"Yes. I received the inspector's report on Monday."

"And he found in Mr. Henshaw's favour?"

The planning officer sighed. "Unfortunately, yes. The inspector does seem to be taking a less restrictive view of planning rules now. And there is a move to release less valuable agricultural land for building."

"So what was the point of the Brinkbonnie residents holding their protest meeting on Saturday afternoon? Surely the planning procedure had been exhausted."

"No," the planning officer said sadly. "Not quite. There really is very little likelihood that the inspector's decision could be overturned at this point, but there is a faint possibility. I don't think the council would want to take the action any further because of the cost, but if there was sufficient public pressure, I suppose they might feel they had to make the gesture. I'd advise them against it, but they don't always take my advice."

"And what action could the council take?"

"They could appeal to the high court."

"And could Henshaw proceed with the building while the appeal was being heard?"

"Oh, no!" The officer seemed almost offended at the notion. "It would mean another delay."

"What would it take to persuade the council to appeal to the high court?" Ramsay asked.

The officer shrugged. "A widespread press campaign. A number of well-attended meetings, a petition, noise, demonstrations." He gave a little smile. "There are county council elections in May," he said. "I think the councillors would be prepared to listen."

"How long have the villagers got to persuade the council to appeal?"

"A month," the officer said. "They have until the end of the month."

"I don't understand," Ramsay said, "why there wasn't more fuss when the plans were originally proposed."

"Well I believe there was some confusion in the community about the exact nature of the development. And, of course, there are people who don't bother to read the planning notices in the local paper."

"Is Henshaw involved in other developments in the county?"

"Oh, yes," the officer said. "There have been half a dozen applications in the past two years."

"Have most of them been successful?"

"Yes," the officer said. "I believe five out of six were allowed. The most recently completed was at Wytham."

"Henshaw built those, did he?"

Ramsay drove through Wytham on his way from Heppleburn to Otterbridge and had seen the buildings grow. The estate was surrounded by a stone wall with pillars, which made him think of a decorative prison. Each house had a mock-Victorian conservatory. They had seemed to him ridiculously expensive, but all had been sold.

"Is that sort of success rate usual?" he asked.

The officer paused. "There may have been a couple of surprising decisions," he said, "but Henshaw is very clever, you know. His developments are relatively small and not designed to upset existing communities, so it's hard for objectors to get the level of support they need."

"You never suspected corruption?" Ramsay asked. "Henshaw doesn't have any special friends on the planning committee?"

"Oh, no," the officer said. "There's never been any question of that sort of dishonesty."

But Ramsay would have believed anything of Henshaw, and the planning officer was a loyal civil servant. He would hardly pass on rumours of fraud. Ramsay needed other, less partial information.

The council offices were stuffy, overheated, with waves of warm air from the open doors into the corridor where Ramsay was walking, and he reached the street with relief. Outside it was still cold and grey. There had been an inch of snow overnight and in the market square people stood in groups and talked about the weather. He collected his car from the police station, then was stuck for twenty minutes in crawling traffic.

When at last he was out of the town, he drove first not to Brinkbonnie but to Heppleburn. When he had worked on an enquiry in Heppleburn he had met Jack Robson, a county councillor, and it occurred to him now that Jack might be willing to help with information about Henshaw. Jack would have no affection for land speculators and Ramsay was convinced of his integrity.

Robson lived in a small estate in 1930s council houses. The move to smokeless fuel had not yet reached the village and clouds of smoke hung over the chimneys. There were neat paths through the snow cleared from the pavements to the front doors. Two elderly women in long coats and furry ankle boots gossiped on the corner. As he drove past they looked at him, wondering who he was. Whenever he came to this estate Ramsay had the impression of going back in time. It was preserved in an atmosphere of fifties' boredom and decency.

Through the living-room window of Robson's house Ramsay saw the old man sitting by the fire. He was eating an early lunch. His feet were straight ahead of him on the hearth; there was a book on his knee and a plate of bread and cheese on the arm of the chair.

When Robson opened the door to the policeman, he was brushing crumbs of bread from the front of his jersey.

"Inspector Ramsay!" he said. He seemed more pleased

to see the policeman than he ever had in the earlier investigation. "Why, man, it's good to see you. Come in, come in. I'll put the kettle on. Or perhaps you'd rather have a beer."

Ramsay was touched by the welcome. It was not that Robson was lonely and needed visitors whoever they were. He was a busy man.

"Sit here," he said. "By the fire."

Ramsay allowed himself to be brought tea. He refused the offer of food.

"Now," Robson said. "What can I do for you? You're not just here to say hello. Do you need any help with moving into the cottage?"

"No," Ramsay said. "It's not that. I'm here for information. Does the name Colin Henshaw mean anything to you?"

Robson looked at him carefully. "Aye," he said. "You know he owns that land behind you?"

"Yes," Ramsay said. "So I understand. But it's not about that. Not directly. He lives in Brinkbonnie."

"That's where Alice Parry lived," Robson said. "You're working on that case?"

Ramsay nodded.

"I knew her," Robson said. "Through the council, you know. She was a great one for charity projects. I liked her."

"She sold some land to Henshaw," Ramsay said, "on the understanding that it would be used for cheap starter homes for local people. When the plans were drawn up, she discovered that he meant to build bigger, more expensive houses there."

"That sounds the sort of trick Henshaw would play," Robson said.

"Alice Parry was leading the campaign against the development," Ramsay said. "There was a protest meeting in the village on Saturday afternoon and on Saturday night she was killed."

"Henshaw's a powerful man," Robson said doubtfully. "He can get his own way without violence. At least he can these days."

"What do you mean?"

"Well," Robson said. "You'll have checked his record. I don't know whether he was ever convicted, but when he first started out he had a bit of a reputation as a hard man."

"No," Ramsay said. "He was never convicted."

"He must have been a clever bugger even then," Robson said.

"As he's not got a record," Ramsay said, "you'll have to tell me what he got up to."

"He always liked a fight," Robson said. "So I understand. I never knew him then. He was still operating out of Newcastle. The story goes that he hired himself out to local businessmen who wanted to collect debts without the trouble of going through the courts. He was a big man. If he turned up on your doorstep, you'd soon pay up."

"How did he start up in legitimate business?"

"He bought in to an existing building firm," Robson said. "George Saunders and he were partners for a while, but Henshaw was soon running the business single-handed. Saunders was too much of a gentleman to survive against him."

"You say Henshaw's a powerful man," Ramsay said. "Has he any influence over the planning committee? I understand he has an unusual success rate with his applications."

Robson did not answer immediately. He chose his words carefully. "I don't know," he said. "I wouldn't have said so. I wouldn't put it past most of them, and it is surprising how he's managed to push his plans through the system, but in most of the cases the plans were rejected by the council and only approved on appeal by the inspector."

"I suppose," Ramsay said, "that the Department of the Environment inspector is incorruptible."

"I don't know about that," Robson said, "but I wouldn't have thought Henshaw would have had any influence there."

There was a silence.

"So how does he do it?" Ramsay asked, frustrated. "Is he just lucky?"

"Henshaw's always made his own luck," Robson said.

84

"I doubt whether he's changed now. Do you want me to find out for you? I'll talk to a few people. See what I can come up with. I'll get in touch."

Again Ramsay was touched by Robson's eagerness to help.

"Yes," he said. "Do that."

But he left with no hope that the conversation with Robson had achieved anything.

9

In Brinkbonnie Ramsay drove past the police house, with the communications van parked outside, stopped on the green, and then walked to the post office. Outside of Tom Kerr's garage there were half a dozen old and rather scruffy cars with hand-painted signs advertising them for sale, but the workshop was empty. From the street Ramsay could hear the waves on the beach beyond the row of cottages. It was almost high tide. He pushed at the post office door before he saw the sign in the window saying it was closed for lunch. He stood on the pavement for a moment rattling at the door, but no-one came to open it.

Fred Elliot's living accommodation was behind the post office and above it. Ramsay walked through an arch in the terrace of houses into a flagged yard with the sand hills beyond. There was a door from the yard into the house and Ramsay knocked there. It was opened almost immediately by a tense, upright man in his early sixties. His sleeves were rolled up to the elbows and his hands were wet and soapy.

"Yes?" he said. "The post office is closed. We don't open at dinnertime. Not until the summer."

"I'm a policeman," Ramsay said. "I've come about Alice Parry."

"But someone was here last night," Elliot said quickly. "I talked to him."

"I know," Ramsay said, "but perhaps I could come in."

Reluctantly Elliot stood aside and watched anxiously while he stamped snow and sand off his shoes. The door led straight into a kitchen, and the floor was spotlessly clean. There were painted wooden cupboards on the walls and a square table, covered in oilcloth, against one wall. A clotheshorse, held together at the corners with binder twine, was propped in front of a solid-fuel boiler and a pair of navy working overalls steamed. The small window was covered in condensation, so it was impossible to see out.

"I was washing up," Elliot said, as if there was something to be ashamed of in the activity. "Since my wife died . . . you know." He nodded to the chairs pushed under the leaf of the table. "Sit down," he told Ramsay. He was still holding the towel and scrubbed at his hands, although by now they were quite dry. From the other room came the sound of a television signature tune.

"Are you on your own?" Ramsay asked.

Elliot hesitated, though the noise of the television in the next room made it obvious that someone else was in the house. "No," he said. "It's my son, Charlie. He works next door at the garage and comes in for his dinner."

"Perhaps I could speak to him, too," Ramsay said.

Elliot looked unhappy. "I don't know that he'll want to speak to you," he said. "He was in late and he's just started his dinner."

Ramsay looked at his watch. "That's all right," he said easily. "There's no hurry. I can wait. I'll have a few words with you first."

There was a silence.

"You musn't mind Charlie," Elliot said. "He had a bad time in the army. He doesn't like the police."

Ramsay said nothing. Elliot stood by the boiler, arms by his side, a veteran at a British Legion parade showing his grief by respect.

"I'll miss Alice Parry," he said. "She was a good woman."

"Was she a friend?" Ramsay asked.

Elliot seemed surprised by the question. "Aye," he said

at last. "I suppose she was. We were different, of course. Her folks had a big estate up on the border and she went away to some smart school in the south, but I think she would have thought me her friend. I hope she would."

There was another pause, then he continued: "She was very kind to me when my wife died. Charlie wasn't here then and I was on my own. Mrs. Parry saw to everything. I couldn't have managed without her. That's why the business with Henshaw was so upsetting."

"Did you believe her," Ramsay asked, "when she said she'd sold the land to be used for a small development of starter homes?"

"Of course," Elliot said angrily. "Everyone who knew Mrs. Parry believed her. She was an honest woman."

"What about your son?" Ramsay asked quietly. "Did he believe her, too?"

Elliot stared at him. "Why do you want to know?" he demanded. "What have people been telling you?"

Ramsay shrugged. "That he was angry about the housing development," he said, "and that he blamed Alice Parry for it."

Elliot looked tired and confused. "He hasn't settled since he left the army," he muttered. "I was proud when he joined up, and perhaps it was a mistake. It changed him. Then when he came home there was trouble with a woman."

"I know," Ramsay said. "I've spoken to Maggie Kerr."

Elliot looked up. "Have you?" he said. "I try to tell myself it wasn't her fault, but I can't help thinking she led him on. He came home thinking she would marry him, then she wouldn't have him. It's made him a bitter man. It affects everything he does. If he hadn't blamed Mrs. Parry for upsetting him, it would have been someone else. He's a good mechanic, but he doesn't get on with his boss. Tom Kerr's choirmaster up at the church and he's well respected, but there's something hard about him. He's not as flexible as he might be! Charlie needs careful handling at the moment. He was well trained in the army and thinks he knows best."

88

"I'm surprised Mr. Kerr took him on," Ramsay said, "in the circumstances."

"Perhaps he thought he had a responsibility," Elliot said sharply. "Charlie packed up the army because of that girl."

"All the same . . ." Ramsay said.

"I told you," Fred Elliot said. "Tom Kerr's a good church man. He will have seen it as his duty. But he'll never let Charlie forget that he's done him a favor by taking him on."

"Is Charlie happy living here?" Ramsay asked.

"He's happy with nothing at the moment. He thinks he deserves better than living with me. He'd like his own house. I don't recognise him anymore. He's not the boy who went away."

The words poured out in an incoherent stream, released by shock and sadness. He looked towards the door that led into the rest of the house and Ramsay realised he was frightened of his son.

"What's he like in the house?" Ramsay asked. He spoke gently, but he had the man's attention. His eyes moved away from the door.

"He's angry," Elliot said. "All the time."

"Do you think he needs a doctor?"

"I don't know what he needs." The words were sharp and unhappy, then he reconsidered. "Perhaps he should see a doctor," he said, "but I'd never persuade him to go."

"Is he violent? I heard there was a fight with Tom Kerr."

"No!" Elliot seemed frustrated because Ramsay could not understand immediately. "Tom Kerr started that business. He's got a wicked temper. Charlie wouldn't hurt anyone. Especially not Maggie Kerr. But he talks loud. He talks big. He doesn't make the effort to be polite anymore."

There was a silence. "He misses his mother," he said. "His mother understood him. I could never handle him. I never had the patience. I always lost my temper. My wife said we were too alike, but I never saw it myself."

"Does he have any friends?" Ramsay asked.

"Not really," Elliot said. "He goes to the Castle and buys drinks all round. They say he's a grand lad then, but they're laughing behind his back. They think he's made a fool of himself over Maggie Kerr. Then Henshaw's never been popular and they like it when Charlie's rude about him. They haven't the guts to say the things he says, but they cheer him on. They set him up.''

"Does he drink too much?''

"Aye,'' Elliot said. "Probably.'' He hesitated again, then went on in a rush. "I talked to Mrs. Parry about him. I thought she might understand. She was a magistrate.''

"What did she say?'' Ramsay asked.

"To give him time,'' Elliot said. "And encouragement. She said he was bright. 'He's wasted at the garage,' she said. 'He should have a business of his own.' I even thought of selling the post office to set him up. But then where would I live? It would have been different if Henshaw had decided to build the cheap houses. Mrs. Parry offered to talk to him, but when I told him he just laughed at me.''

From the other room there was a sudden, loud burst of music, then silence.

"Dad!'' Charlie Elliot called. They heard his footsteps approaching the door. "What about some tea then?''

He pushed open the door and stood, just inside the kitchen, staring at Ramsay. His rudeness was deliberate and contrived, but it was the result, Ramsay thought, of insecurity. Throughout the interview the bravado hid considerable stress.

"Who are you?'' he asked.

"I'm a detective,'' Ramsay said formally. "I'm enquiring into the death of Alice Parry.''

"You're wasting your time,'' Charlie Elliot said. "Someone's been here already.'' It was hard to tell that he had once been a soldier. He was overweight, unshaven. Ramsay was not surprised that Maggie found him unattractive.

"I know.''

"What are you doing here then?''

"Just a few more questions,'' Ramsay said easily. "Routine.''

Fred Elliot had turned to the sink and was filling a kettle as his son had ordered. He clearly found the exchange em-

90

barrassing. Charlie sat on one of the chairs. "You'll have to be quick," he said. "I'll have to be back at work soon. Tom Kerr's a real slave driver."

"Mrs. Parry received a threatening letter on the afternoon of her death," Ramsay said. "Did that have anything to do with you?"

"No," Charlie Elliot said. "I had my say at the meeting. What was in the letter?" He grinned unpleasantly and spread his stockinged feet towards the fire.

"It threatened to kill her."

"She got what was coming to her then, didn't she?"

"Charles!" Fred Elliot turned on his son. He was white-faced with anger. "I'll not have that talk in my house. It's indecent."

The outburst shocked Charlie. He was unused to contradiction. He seemed confused and offended, like a spoilt child reprimanded in front of strangers.

"Where were you on Saturday evening?" Ramsay asked.

"I've already told that Hunter."

"Tell me."

"I was in the pub," Charlie said. "I always go to the pub on Saturday night. There was a darts match."

"What time did you leave?"

"I don't know. About quarter to eleven."

"Wasn't that unusual?" Ramsay asked.

"What do you mean?"

"Didn't you usually wait until Maggie had finished work?"

Charlie looked at Ramsay with deep hostility. "That's none of your business."

"I'm sorry," Ramsay said. "I'm afraid it is. Usually you waited until Maggie finished work and followed her home. What made that night different?"

"I don't know," Charlie muttered. "Perhaps I realised she wasn't worth it. I'd had a lot to drink."

Ramsay said nothing, waiting for Charlie to expand his explanation.

"Look!" Charlie cried. "Perhaps I'd come to my senses,

realised I couldn't carry on like that. I'd decided to leave the village. I'm going to look for work in the south.''

Ramsay nodded his understanding but gave no indication of whether he believed Charlie. He continued impassively: "What time did you get home?''

"About eleven o'clock, I suppose.''

Ramsay turned to Elliot, who was stirring tea in the pot. "Is that right?''

Elliot hesitated, then nodded. "Aye,'' he said. "I always wait up for him. I know it's daft.''

Ramsay returned his attention to Charlie. "Did you see Mrs. Parry on your way home?''

"No.'' Charlie had recovered some of his composure and was showing off. "I didn't see her, but then I'd had eight pints of Scotch. I might not have noticed.''

Ramsay stared out of the misted window. "So you can't remember what you did,'' he said. "You were drunk.''

"I can remember fine.''

"Did you stop on the way?''

"No,'' Charlie said. "Why should I stop? It was cold.''

"Did you meet anyone in the street?'' He spoke in a flat, courteous civil-servant's voice.

"No.'' Charlie was sneering. "Most of Brinkbonnie's in bed by ten o'clock. It was dead quiet.''

Then his triumph at remembering despite the alcoholic haze overcame his resentment of the policeman. For the first time he contributed freely to the conversation. "There was a girl! In the churchyard. I saw her when I came out of the Castle.''

"Who was it?''

"I don't know. I didn't recognise her. She was all right. Young, you know.''

Ramsay gave no sign that the information was of any importance to him. He turned back to the window. "Did you speak to her?'' he asked.

"I might have shouted to her,'' Charlie said. "Something about it being a cold night.''

"Did she answer?''

92

"No, snooty cow. She walked through the gravestones towards the Tower. She looked like a bloody ghost."

"Did she go through the gate into the Tower garden?"

"I didn't see. I wanted to get home. I needed to piss."

"What did the woman look like?"

Charlie shrugged. "It was hard to tell in that light," he said. "Small, dark. I think she had long hair."

"And what was she wearing?"

"How should I know? She was on the other side of the wall. I couldn't see much more than her head."

"You are sure," Ramsay said slowly, "that there *was* a woman? This isn't a game to annoy the police."

"Oh," said Charlie. "Think what you like." He swore under his breath.

Ramsay ignored him. "Did you notice a car near the green?" he asked. "One not usually parked there?"

"No," Charlie said. "I didn't notice anything." But he spoke too quickly to have considered the matter and it seemed that the childish resentment had returned. "Look!" he said. "How much longer are you going to keep me here? I'll lose my job."

"You're free to go at any time," Ramsay said. "We know where to find you."

He rubbed a clear patch in the condensation on the window and looked out into the yard. Charlie Elliot went to a cupboard in the corner and pulled out a jacket. They watched while he laced shoes and fastened buttons and then Ramsay saw him go out into the yard. Fred Elliot was standing helplessly in the middle of the room with a teapot in his hand. "I've made this now," he said. "Do you want some?"

"No," Ramsay said. "I expect you want to open the post office."

"Yes," Elliot said. He seemed miserable and lost. "I suppose I should." He seemed afraid to be left on his own. "There's no hurry."

"Is it just a post office or is it a shop, too?"

"Yes," Elliot said. "It's a newsagent. We sell magazines, stationery, confectionery. The post office counter is at

93

the back. It's a canny little business. Especially in the summer.''

"Where do you keep the stock you don't sell?''

"What do you mean?''

"There must be out-of-date newspapers, magazines. You can't keep them on the shelves. What do you do with them?''

"I save them,'' Elliot said proudly. "Then sell them to a wastepaper merchant. For charity. I give the money to the hospital where my wife died. I can show you it if you like.'' He had no suspicion, it seemed, of Ramsay's motive for asking. Still in his slippers, he led the policeman across the yard to a large, well-built shed in one corner.

The collection of wastepaper had become a hobby, it seemed, almost an obsession. "I collect the neighbours' papers as well,'' he said. "And the church helps. It's surprising how it mounts up. You can make pounds.'' He unbolted the shed door and switched on a light. Inside, against one wall, in neatly stacked and wrapped bundles, were piles of newspapers. Ramsay could imagine Elliot in there, escaping from his rude and unpredictable son, soothing his nerves by counting the papers and calculating their worth. In comparison to the general tidiness, the floor was a mess of paper scraps, as if a child had been playing at cutting out. There was a pair of round-ended scissors and a tube of glue. Elliot stood, betrayed and horrified, realising for the first time what the questions had been leading up to.

"I take it,'' Ramsay said, "that these have nothing to do with you.''

Elliot shook his head.

"You do realise that we'll have to take these pieces of newspaper to compare with the print on the anonymous letter to Mrs. Parry?''

"Yes,'' Elliot said. He looked at Ramsay desperately. "He might have sent the letter,'' he pleaded, "but that doesn't mean that he killed her.''

"No,'' Ramsay said gently. "It doesn't mean that he killed her.''

"What will you do with him now?''

94

"I'll talk to him," Ramsay said. "Probably take him to the police station and ask him some questions. You mustn't worry too much. He can see a solicitor."

"He wouldn't have killed her," Elliot said, as if he were trying to convince himself. "He wouldn't have killed her."

Ramsay left him in the shed, surrounded by his beloved wastepaper, standing by the open door and looking out at the whirlwind of sand funnelled by the wind into the yard.

Out in the street little had changed. An old woman stood on the pavement patiently waiting for the post office to open. Two detective constables moved slowly along the terrace on the other side of the green, knocking on doors, asking questions. In the garage workshop Tom Kerr stood before the open bonnet of a car. Ramsay stood by the open door and looked in.

Kerr straightened slowly. "Inspector Ramsay," he said. "How can I help you? Olive's in the house." He looked slightly ridiculous in his boiler suit still wearing the heavy-framed glasses. He would be more at home, Ramsay thought, in his choirmaster's cassock.

"I'd like to speak to Charlie Elliot," Ramsay said.

"Aye," Kerr said with a trace of anger. "You and me both."

He wiped his hands on a cloth and moved to the front of the garage to meet Ramsay. "He's not here," he said. "He came in from his dinner about half an hour ago. We had a car with a timing problem and he said he'd take it up the road to see what was wrong. He's not back yet. It doesn't take a ten-mile drive to check a timing problem."

"Where do you think he's gone?"

"I don't know," Kerr said. "He doesn't talk to me. He's very moody. This had made my mind up for me. I've been thinking of telling him to leave for a while."

"He was talking of looking for work in the south," Ramsay said.

"Was he?" Kerr seemed relieved. "He's not said anything to me."

"If Charlie comes back, will you tell him to get in touch? I'll be up at the police house."

But Ramsay knew that Charlie was unlikely to return and realised with a depressing certainty that he had allowed a major murder suspect to run away. In the street outside the garage a Radio Newcastle reporter stopped him and asked for an interview, but Ramsay said he had no comment to make and hurried up the hill to the police house. He sent cars up each of the roads out of Brinkbonnie, but by then it was too late. Charlie Elliot had disappeared.

10

H_{unter} seized on the disappearance of Charlie Elliot as an excuse for activity. While the communications centre at Otterbridge put out a general description of Charlie Elliot and of the car he was driving, Hunter drove at great speed around the country lanes, hoping to make an immediate arrest. He returned to the police house in the middle of the afternoon, disappointed, but still convinced that Charlie Elliot was a murderer. Ramsay knew the danger of jumping to conclusions too quickly and cautioned patience, an open mind.

"Charlie Elliot had an alibi for the time of the murder," he said reasonably. "His father confirmed that he was in the house by eleven. And then there was the girl he saw in the churchyard. We should be looking for her."

"What girl?" Hunter demanded. "Man, that was just Elliot making up stories to throw us off the scent. No-one in the Tower saw a girl. And the old man was lying to protect his son."

"What about motive?" Ramsay said quietly. "I thought you said no-one would commit murder for the sake of a few houses."

"No-one sane," Hunter said. "We know Elliot was unbalanced, unpredictable. Look at his obsession with that girl in the pub. He's our man. He can't have got far. We'll have him tonight."

But as the afternoon wore on there was no information about Elliot. No-one had seen the car. The men waiting in the police house became irritable and impatient, and to make things worse Fred Elliot was on the phone every half-hour wanting to know if his son had been found and claiming that Charlie, too, had been murdered.

At half-past six Ramsay had waited long enough.

"I'm going to Otterbridge," he said to Hunter, "to talk to the Laidlaws. Go and sit with old man Elliot. There's a chance Charlie will come home when he's cold and hungry. And you'll need to break that alibi if you're to prove Charlie guilty. Elliot might talk while he's so upset."

They walked together down the street to the green, where Ramsay's car was parked. Despite the cold, two teenage boys in black leather stood by the bus stop, smoking a cigarette, passing it between them.

Poor sods, thought Hunter. What else is there for them to do in a place like this?

"Nip over and get their names and addresses," Ramsay said. "Stella Laidlaw saw some lads at the bus stop on Saturday night. Find out if it was them."

Hunter went, sauntering towards them, indirectly over the grass. Ramsay thought Hunter had more in common with the boys than he did with him. The sky was clear and there would be another frost. Ramsay shivered as he watched the three figures by the bus shelter. He saw Hunter take a packet of cigarettes from his pocket and hand it around, then the three of them huddled together around the lighter, sheltering the flame from the breeze. He imagined the three in conspiracy against him. "That's my boss," he imagined Hunter saying. "But don't take any notice of him. If you've got any information, come straight to me."

That's ridiculous, he thought. Diana always said I was paranoid. But his suspicions about Diana had been justified and she had run away eventually with someone who produced television programmes for the BBC in Fenham.

Hunter returned, stubbing out the cigarette with the heel of his designer trainers before he reached the inspector.

"They're all right," he said. "Bored out of their brains, but who can blame them in a place like this? They weren't here Saturday night, but they've given me the names and addresses of a couple of other lads who might have been."

Ramsay nodded and walked on alone to his car. Hunter might be good at communicating with local teenagers, but he had other skills. He had been married to Diana. He knew how to talk to the civilised middle classes.

Max Laidlaw was on call that Monday morning but paid the deputising service to take the duty for him. Judy wanted him to take Peter to school, then spend some time with her and the twins. In the afternoon he had a surgery and by then he would be pleased to leave the house. He told himself he needed time to think. In a sense Alice Parry's death had changed nothing and there were still decisions to be made. In the chaotic house in Otterbridge he found decisions impossible.

Judy made things worse. All morning she seemed unable to leave the subject of his aunt's death alone. She followed him around the house demanding his attention, desperate, it seemed, for his opinion. Even while he was shaving she was shouting at him through the closed bathroom door.

"What did you think of Ramsay, the detective?" she asked. "I didn't know what to make of him. He seemed rather hostile, I thought." Then: "How did Alice seem to you that night? Was she even more upset than she said?"

"I don't know," he shouted, slamming out of the room, almost tripping over her on the landing. "And I don't bloody care."

"But you talked to her," Judy said, catching him up as he ran down the stairs to the kitchen. "You helped her clear up the dishes after supper and she wouldn't let anyone else into the kitchen. 'I want a private word with Max,' she said, and she sent us all away. So what was the great secret?"

"There wasn't any secret," he said. "You know what she was like."

"At one time you would have trusted me. Now you don't

share anything." She gave him one of her hurt and vulnerable looks.

"There was no secret," he said. "Really."

I'm too soft, he thought. When she looks at me like that, I'd promise her anything. He wanted to make some gesture of affection, but before he could show her how much he cared for her, one of the twins cried for her attention and she turned away.

Throughout the morning the children irritated him. On the way to school Peter was listless and tired, reacting to the smallest provocation with tears or temper, and in the house the twins whined with a mechanical, metallic sound that grated on his nerves.

"Of course they're demanding," Alice had said on the evening of her death when they were alone in the kitchen at the Tower. "But you wouldn't be without them, would you?"

And he had responded wholeheartedly: No, of course he wouldn't be without them. He loved them.

Now it did not seem so simple, and he longed for the old times, when he was a tandem-riding student, before guilt and responsibility.

When the time came to go to the surgery, Judy seemed to sense his unhappiness. She was concerned about him, she said. She put on boots and a sweater to help him clear the ice from the windscreen of the car and told him to take care when he was driving.

"Drive slowly," she said. "It's still very slippery. Perhaps you should walk."

"I'm only going into town," he said, though he was pleased that she was worrying about him. "The roads will be clear by now."

Before he drove off she stood close to him and kissed him. Her nose was cold and the unexpected gesture shocked and touched him.

"I'm sorry," she said. "It's been my fault. You will take care?"

He nodded and squeezed her arm, then got into the car.

100

The roads were a slushy mess, the thin layer of snow already melted by salt and regular traffic, but in a school playground a queue of running boys in grey uniforms slid down an icy run. Max braked too sharply at a traffic light and the car slid forward before stopping, harmlessly, against the kerb. The jolt made him think of Judy and her concern for him. She was wrong, he thought. It was not her fault, but he could think of nothing that would make things right. The lights changed and he drove on slowly.

The Health Centre was packed. Four buggies had been parked in the porch outside, and he had to push his way past them to get into the waiting room. Inside the room was hot and noisy with the damp acoustics of swimming baths. The place was full, it seemed, with feverish children and bronchitic grandmothers. The receptionist was flushed and fraught. She hardly acknowledged Max as he walked past because she was trying to answer the telephone and find a missing file at the same time. The ill-tempered chaos suited his mood and he called irritably for the first patient.

Stella Laidlaw phoned late in the afternoon when he was examining his last patient, a toddler with an ear infection. The receptionist spoke to him first.

"I'm sorry," the receptionist said. "I explained that you were busy, but the lady insisted. She wouldn't give her name. She said it was personal."

Max felt a sudden exhilaration. His promise to Alice was immediately forgotten.

"Give me two minutes," he said, "then put her through."

He wrote a hurried prescription for the child, then, as calmly as he could, saw him and the mother into the waiting room. He picked up the telephone again.

"Yes," he said. "Max Laidlaw."

Stella's voice surprised and disappointed him, and for a moment he could not place it. He had been expecting someone quite different.

"Max," she said. "I'm sorry, Max. I need your help again."

"No," he said angrily. "I told you before. That was the last time."

"You don't understand," she said. "I'm desperate."

"You should see your doctor."

"I can't. You know that. He's a friend of James."

There was a silence, then she continued spitefully: "I could tell James all about you, Max. I could phone Judy. I know she'd be interested. You wouldn't like that." She had the affected accent of minor royalty and always sounded to him like a lonely public-school girl, but it was impossible now to be sorry for her. "I know what happened, Max," she went on, "at the Tower. You wouldn't want me to tell Judy that."

"That's blackmail," he said, but even as he protested he knew he would do as she wanted, because he always took the easy way out. He was weaker than she was.

"You're ill," he said. "You need help. Real help. Not the kind that I can give you. You need someone to talk to, to share things with."

"I can talk to you," she said, her voice almost seductive, "when we meet."

"I'm so busy," he said, with a last flicker of resistance. "I've so little time."

"You've time enough for this."

"I can't come today," he said quickly, playing for time. "It's dark already and the roads are bad. If I'm late, Judy will worry and phone the practise."

"Tomorrow then," she said after a pause. "James is out all day. Come tomorrow."

She put the phone down quickly, so Max wondered if someone had disturbed her at the other end of the line. The conversation had upset him and he felt that he needed comfort, to feel good about himself again. He dialled the telephone number of the *Otterbridge Express* office, enjoying the sensation that he was taking a risk by calling her at work.

"Could I speak to Mary Raven?" he asked.

"I'm sorry." The woman's voice was bland, uncaring. "Miss Raven has just left the office. Can anyone else help you?"

102

"No," he said, and quickly replaced the receiver. He would have to plan some romantic gesture to make his peace with Mary. It was impossible, after all, to think he could do without her.

Judy spent the afternoon in desultory clearing-up. The twins grizzled themselves to sleep eventually, and after school Peter sat slumped close to the television watching a Walt Disney cartoon. His eyes were heavy and he refused to communicate with her. When she tried to hug him, he shrugged her away. All day the phone rang with friends offering their sympathy and help, wanting, she thought, a share of the drama. Finally she took the phone off the hook, and when people came to the door she sent them away. Only Max could reassure her and he was refusing to talk. She had known for months that he was worried about something but had been too busy, too exhausted, too engrossed in playing the part of a fulfilled and active woman to find out what was troubling him. Now perhaps it was too late.

She had longed to know what Alice had to say so urgently to her husband, yet this morning she had handled the whole thing badly. She had wanted to force him to honesty. Instead she had come across as a nagging shrew. She felt excluded and unimportant, a failure.

The television cartoon finished and she persuaded Peter to go to bed. He did not argue and allowed her to undress him, moving his limbs when she told him to but making no effort himself.

"Mum," he said. "When will the policeman come to see me?"

"When you're ready," she said. "Tomorrow, I expect."

She tucked the blankets around him, but he seemed unwilling to settle to sleep.

"Aunt Alice was murdered, wasn't she? Someone killed her?"

"Yes," Judy said. "The police think she was murdered."

"I saw her go out," he said. "She banged the door and went off down the drive."

"You can't have seen her," Judy said. "You were asleep."

"I wasn't," he said. "I was pretending."

"So you saw Aunt Alice walk down the drive to the road?"

He nodded.

"Did you see anything else later? Did you see your aunt coming back?"

Perhaps the urgency of her voice distressed him. He seemed suddenly frightened and pushed his head into the pillow. She held him and turned him gently to face her.

"You're quite safe here," she said. "You can tell me. Did you see anyone else that night?"

But his loyalty to Carolyn prevented him from sharing his fear.

"No!" he said, almost hysterical. "No!"

She held him tightly until he sobbed himself to sleep.

The kitchen was in the basement. It was the length of the house. At the front it was below the level of the street, but at the back there was a door into the garden. On one wall hung a red, cream, and black rug that they had brought home from a holiday in Portugal. There was a small sofa covered in an Indian bedspread bought in an Oxfam shop when Max was a student and a long oak table that had been made by a friend. There was a notice board made of cork tiles where the children's paintings and drawings were pinned, together with postcards, magazine articles, concert tickets. Max walked into the silent house and down the bare wooden stairs to the kitchen. He was later than usual and tried to think of some excuse if Judy should ask him where he had been.

The room was lit only by a spotlight over the table and another near to the cooker where Judy was standing. The mess of unironed clothes and half-completed models had become invisible in shadowy corners. The table was laid for dinner, with cutlery and a wooden bowl of salad. There were wineglasses. It was all quite different from what he expected. They seemed to live now on a children's diet of sausages and baked beans. He shut the door behind him and pulled across the heavy curtain that shut out the draughts from upstairs. He wanted to acknowledge the effort Judy had made.

"This looks nice," he said, realising at once how inadequate it sounded. Judy lifted a tray of baked potatoes from the oven and prodded one to make sure it was cooked.

"I put them to bed early," she said. "They were so tired."

He took off his coat and put it over a chair.

"There's some wine in the fridge," she said. "Would you like to open it?"

Why do we have to be so polite to each other? he thought. Do we have to start from the beginning again?

"Did you have a busy afternoon?" she asked.

"Hmm." He took white wine from the fridge, opened it, and poured her a glass. "Not too bad." He expected her then to ask why he was late, but she said nothing.

"Do you want to eat now?"

"If it's ready."

He sat at the table and she brought out the food. She had changed into a loose brown top and her hair was brushed out in chestnut curls. If only it were always like this, he thought. But he realised it could not be that easy. Now there were other complications, deeper anxieties, and he could not think clearly. They ate for a while in silence.

"Peter was very upset tonight," she said. "Did you realise he was still awake when Alice went out to see Colin Henshaw? He watched her from the window."

Max looked up sharply. "No," he said. "I didn't realise. How long was he awake? Did he see Alice come back?"

"No," she said uncertainly. "He says not. But he was so distressed it was hard to tell."

There was another period of silence. Judy's attempts to please had confused him. He supposed she would want something in return for her efforts—some reassurance that he still cared for her—but he no longer knew what he wanted.

Suddenly the doorbell, which was worked by an old-fashioned pull, jangled above them. Max jumped to his feet, glad of an excuse to leave the table.

He expected it to be one of Judy's friends. They turned up

regularly, often in tears, with tales of insensitive husbands, uncaring boyfriends. Sometimes he overheard the women talking together. "Of course," one of them had once said, "if I only had a husband like Max, things would be quite different!" He wondered what Judy could have told them about him. Was it loyalty that prevented her from sharing her dissatisfaction or pride that would not allow her to admit that she had made a mistake in her marriage? He was so certain that he would find a woman on the doorstep, probably a distraught woman with a child, that he greeted Ramsay almost with pleasure.

"Come in," he cried. "It must be cold out there."

"I wondered," Ramsay said, "if I could talk to your son. I thought it might be better to do it now, so he can return to normal as soon as possible."

"He's in bed," Max said. "He was worn out."

"Oh, well," Ramsay said. "Don't disturb him. I'll come back another day." But he did not move from the doorstep.

"Come in anyway now that you're here," Max said. "Judy's making coffee."

"Thank you," Ramsay said. "There are a few questions . . ." Through the door he had a glimpse of a warm, untidy house and he wondered how he could have found the Laidlaws so unappealing at the Tower. The cottage in Heppleburn was empty and uninviting in contrast. He was in no hurry to return home.

They walked down the stairs from the brightly lit hall and the kitchen seemed dark and gloomy.

"Let's have a bit more light in here," Max said, and switched on the central electric light. The muddle and dust were illuminated and the sense of intimacy was lost. Even Judy looked different. He could see the dark rings under her eyes and the sharp nose and pinched chin. The chestnut curls looked matted and untidy. He stood behind her with his arm on her shoulder, aware that they looked to Ramsay like a perfect, happily married couple.

"I came to talk to your son," Ramsay said, "but your husband says he's asleep."

106

"Yes," she said. "We don't have to wake him, do we?"

"No," Ramsay said. "It'll do another day."

He sat on the sofa, still wearing his overcoat, to show them that he did not intend to take up too much of their time. He was jealous of their companionship, their home, their children. If he sensed any tension between them, he put it down to the shock of their aunt's death.

"We've discovered that Mrs. Parry returned to the Tower at about midnight," Ramsay said. He turned towards Max. "You were the last person to go to bed. Were you still up at midnight?"

Max seemed uncertain and confused. "Yes," he said. "I think so. I told you I was watching the television."

"But you didn't hear Mrs. Parry come into the house?"

"No," he said. "I suppose she might have come in through the kitchen. I wouldn't have seen her then."

That was possible, Ramsay thought. If Alice Parry came back into the house after her meeting with Henshaw, she might have wanted to avoid the family. Especially if she was upset. But what had so distressed her about the meeting with Henshaw, a meeting he had described as a friendly discussion?

"She went to the pub on her way back from the Henshaws'," Ramsay said. "Did she go there regularly?"

"Almost every night," Max said. "She claimed she had to go to catch up with the village gossip, but I think she liked the company. She never had a lot to drink."

"A young woman was seen in the churchyard on the night of your aunt's death," Ramsay said. "Have you any idea who that might have been?"

"No," Max said. "I can't imagine." He looked at Judy. "What about you, love? Did you see anyone?"

She shook her head. "No," she said. She turned away to pour coffee into tall blue mugs. "I expect it was one of the girls from the village hanging round the bus shelter for the lads."

She handed coffee and sugar to Ramsay, and they waited for him to speak again.

"There was a discussion on Saturday night about Mrs. Parry's will," he said. "If she'd carried out her threat and refused to leave the Tower to James, presumably you would have benefited."

"Yes," Max said vaguely. "I suppose we would."

"That must have put some stress on your relationship with your brother."

"I don't know," Max said. "We've never been particularly close. He's ten years older than me. When you're a child, that's too big a gap for friendship. He was always like an uncle, a bit prim and pompous. I resented him rather. We used to go to the Tower together when Alice asked us because it pleased her, but we rarely meet each other socially otherwise."

"Can you explain his reluctance to help Mrs. Parry in her campaign against the new houses in Brinkbonnie?"

"Oh, yes," Max said. "It would have been a matter of principle to him, of ethics. He's a great one for editorial independence."

There was a moment's silence while Ramsay drank coffee, then set the mug carefully on the table.

"We've discovered who wrote the anonymous letter to Mrs. Parry," the inspector said. "It was Charlie Elliot. Do you know him?"

"I've met him in the pub a couple of times. Has he been arrested?"

"Not yet. We're having some difficulty in tracing him."

Judy was sitting on one of the wooden chairs and turned it to face the policeman. As the legs moved over the tiles, they made the harsh sound of chalk on a damp blackboard.

"Do you think he killed Aunt Alice?"

"We don't know," Ramsay said. "Not yet." He stood up. Judy saw that his coat was creased and crumpled from where he had been sitting. She thought that he probably lived on his own. He made his way up the stairs towards the front door and Max followed. At the doorstep he hesitated, as if reluctant to leave, then turned quickly and walked over the frozen path to his car.

In the kitchen Judy was stacking plates in the dishwasher. Max stood beside her and stroked a strand of hair from her neck.

"Leave that," he said. "I'll do it. You look exhausted. You should go to bed."

"All right," she said. She stood and faced him. "Are you coming, too?"

"Soon," he said. "I'll be up soon. I'll just do this."

She nodded and made her way slowly upstairs.

Max loaded the dishwasher, then sat at the kitchen table. He waited until Judy was out of earshot. He heard the gurgling in the old pipes, which meant she was running a bath, then went to the phone. Although he knew it was irrational and Judy could not possibly hear him, he conducted the conversation in a whisper. He would not take the risk that she would hear him. When she had finished in the bathroom, he was already upstairs, preparing for bed.

11

When Stella Laidlaw woke early that Monday morning, she knew it was going to be one of her bad days. A bullying father and a weak, overindulgent mother had left her with a great capacity for self-pity and an inflated idea of her own importance. She was special. She deserved attention, consideration, to be spoiled. When her family failed to live up to her expectations, she threw childish tantrums, swearing, shouting, and breaking crockery, or she punished them by retreating into herself. If she felt any guilt after these scenes, she reminded herself that she was ill and that excused everything. When she woke on that Monday morning, she felt unbearably tense. The skin on her face itched as if it had some allergic reaction to the air in the bedroom. Her hands were sweating. Her breath came in short, shallow gasps. When she had gone to her doctor with these symptoms, he talked of panic attacks, suggested that she might learn some useful relaxation techniques. But Stella knew what she needed to relax and it had nothing to do with lying on the floor taking deep breaths. Today the tension made her angry. She blamed her discomfort on Max, on James, and most venomously on Alice Parry.

At breakfast Stella was at her most imperious, demanding hot coffee and fresh orange juice, and when James provided these, they were rejected or ignored. She wore a white dressing gown with wide sleeves, and to Carolyn, who saw her

110

as if for the first time, she looked like the white witch from Narnia. Carolyn was as tense as her mother. She had found it impossible to sleep and her face was grey and strained. She felt as if she were under the weight of a terrible responsibility, as if she were the parent and these unhappy adults were her children. She stood up and began to pack her schoolbag with books.

"You're not going to school!" Stella cried. "Not today. You've had a terrible shock, darling. You must stay at home."

"No," Carolyn said, frightened. "I'd rather go to school."

"Why don't you stay with your mother today?" James said, and she returned to the table, unable to stand the thought of one of Stella's scenes.

Stella's swings of mood were unpredictable, savage, and cruel to a sensitive child. Carolyn hated it most when her mother made a fuss in public, but she knew that the times when Stella was silent and withdrawn caused her father the most pain. Yet whatever her mood James was gentle with his wife. He spoiled and petted her, bringing her presents, flowers, dresses. Then he was rewarded by her laughter and her tears of contrition and her protestations that she loved him more than anyone in the world had ever loved before.

After breakfast Stella went to her room. She sat in front of the mirror and stretched her long swan's neck so that the lines of tension in her face disappeared and she looked beautiful again.

Carolyn began to stack the breakfast plates on the draining board in the smart new kitchen that Stella had planned the summer before then lost all interest in. James hovered behind her, and she felt his misery so much that she turned round to face him. Now that Aunt Alice was dead, she had no-one else left to love.

"Look what she's doing to us!" Carolyn said.

"She's ill," he said.

"If she's ill she should go to hospital."

"She doesn't like hospital."

111

"I don't care," Carolyn said. "We can't go on like this. She's dangerous. She makes us all different. I can't stop being angry. The doctor thinks she should be in hospital."

Her father looked confused. "No," he said. "You don't understand. She would hate it."

Once, not when Stella was loud and dramatic, but when she was tired and childlike, James had sent for the doctor and asked for his help.

Carolyn had sat, unnoticed, at the other end of the room and listened to the conversation. She remembered quite clearly what the doctor had said.

"Can't you give her anything?" James had pleaded. "She seems desperate."

"It would only make her worse. That's part of the problem."

"What can I do?"

"Stand up to her. She knows she can manipulate you."

"But I want to help her."

"Then persuade her to go into hospital for a while. She needs time away from you both to sort herself out. You look after her too well. She needs to face up to her problems herself."

"I don't know," James had said. "It seems so hard. I'll think about it."

He had tried to take the doctor's advice, but whenever he did talk to Stella indirectly about going to the hospital, as if by magic she would improve. She would emerge from her bedroom and begin to play her part in the house again. She would help Carolyn with homework and encourage her in violin practice. She would make herself beautiful and go with James to civic functions or into Newcastle to the theatre. She would plan dinner parties and the house would be full of other well-dressed people.

For Carolyn the times of normality were almost worse than the periods of depression, because she knew with a helpless certainty that the relief was only temporary. Each day, when her mother was well, she would wake up wondering if this would be the day of crisis, when Stella would erupt in temper

112

or retreat into silence. At the same time she knew that this anxiety was wasteful and she should make the most of her mother's happiness while it lasted. There was no-one to talk to about this worry. When her mother was well, her father seemed able to convince himself that she would remain so for ever. Only Aunt Alice seemed to understand a little of Carolyn's insecurity, and now she was no longer there to provide comfort and sympathy.

Stella did not come downstairs until lunchtime and then she ate very little.

"I'll have to go out this afternoon," James said. "You don't mind? It's work. I'll not be long."

Stella looked at him incredulously. "But no-one will expect you to be there today," she said. "They'll have heard about Alice."

She was wearing black stretch leggings and a long black sweater, which reached almost to her knees. Her hair was tied back from her face. Her eyes were dark-rimmed and hollow. She wore vivid red lipstick.

"I'm sorry," James said. "Really, I have to go."

Carolyn was surprised. Usually he never stood up to her mother.

"But I hate being on my own." Stella slammed her coffee mug onto the table. "You know I hate it."

"You won't be on your own," James said mildly. "Carolyn will be here."

"But I don't want Carolyn," she screamed. "I want you."

Carolyn felt tears suddenly come into her eyes, as if she had been slapped. She knew her father was upset enough, so she turned away. She did not want him to see her crying.

"That's ridiculous," James said uncomfortably. "I'm sorry. I really have to go. There's this week's paper to put together. I can't leave it all to the others."

He put his arm round Carolyn's shoulder and squeezed it, then prepared to leave the house. As he went out through the front door, Stella shouted after him: "You care more about that paper than you do about me!"

When he had gone, the house was quiet. Stella wandered

into the sitting room and picked up a magazine. It was a long, narrow room with a window at the end overlooking the garden. There was a view down to the river. It was lit by the cold light of the remaining snow outside. There was a marble fireplace and the chairs were covered in marble-patterned fabric in a frosty blue. Carolyn followed her into the room. She never liked her mother's company when she was in this mood, but if Stella was left alone she worried. She laid out the pieces of a jigsaw on a low, white table and knelt on the carpet to do it.

"I'm sorry about that scene," Stella said suddenly. "I don't know what came over me. I was upset, I suppose, about Aunt Alice."

"That's all right," Carolyn said.

"Don't you want to watch television?" Stella asked. "There are some good children's programmes on this afternoon."

"I don't mind."

"If you want to go to your room to watch it, I'll be fine." Stella said. "I didn't mean what I said to Daddy. I was just upset. I don't mind being on my own."

"Well," Carolyn said, relieved to be released. "If you're sure. . . ."

Stella smiled. "Of course."

As Carolyn was on her way out of the room, Stella stretched out her hand, palm down, like a princess waiting to be kissed. Carolyn took it and held it for a moment, then she ran upstairs. When she came down a little later to fetch a drink from the kitchen, her mother was in the hall on the telephone. Carolyn could not hear what she was saying and as soon as Stella saw her coming down the stairs she hung up.

"Who was that?" Carolyn asked, curiosity overcoming the care that she usually took when she questioned her mother.

"Daddy," Stella said. She seemed, Carolyn thought, pleased with herself. "I phoned him to apologise for being so silly earlier."

114

"Will he be home soon?"

"I don't know," Stella said absently. "I don't expect he'll be long."

James Laidlaw walked to the office. As soon as he was out in the street he realised he was not properly dressed for the weather. The cold took his breath away and he thought he should have put on a warmer jacket. He could not return to the house to fetch one. Stella might not let him out so easily again. He followed the footpath along the river past the abbey. The river was frozen at the banks and a dirty-looking swan moved slowly along a channel in the middle. There might be a story in that, he thought: the effect of the cold weather so late in the spring on wildlife. He'd get one of the youngsters to look into it tomorrow. From the riverbank there were some steps onto the bridge that crossed the Otter and led into the town. The people James passed in the street seemed grey and unhappy, suffering, he supposed, from the unseasonable poor weather. He walked quickly, hoping the movement would fight off the cold.

He looked for Mary Raven's Mini in one of the spaces along the wide main street, but there was no sign of it. The *Express* had premises on two floors over the Blue Anchor Inn, and access was by a narrow door by the pub's entrance. There was a steep staircase, and another glass door at the top led to the office where the receptionist sat and he and the other reporters worked. The receptionist was the wife of the high school's headmaster, solid and sensible. She supervised the young staff with a motherly compassion.

"Is Mary in?" he asked.

"I haven't seen her," she said, "but I've just come in from lunch. I was sorry to hear about Mrs. Parry."

"Yes," he said. "It was a terrible shock."

He walked through into the big room where all the reporters worked, but most of the desks were empty, the computer screens blank. It was the quiet time of the week, despite what he had said to Stella. In a corner one telesales woman was trying to persuade an estate agent to buy advertising. She looked up as he went past and smiled sympathetically. He looked in the small kitchen, thinking Mary might be there making the dreadful instant coffee that she drank black and continuously and that had stained all of the mugs in the place, but there was no sign of her. His office seemed unnaturally cold. He shivered, fetched the electric fire they kept for emergencies, and plugged it in beside his desk. Then he made a cup of Mary's coffee and stirred in powdered milk and sugar to hide the taste. He began to work.

Mary Raven woke that morning with a hangover to the sound of the independent local radio station on her radio alarm. There was inane music and a breathy reporter talking about the "tragic death of Alice Parry." She had been out all the day before, drinking with her friends in Newcastle, and it was the first time she had heard the death reported. She switched radio channels for a more detailed review of the local news, then showered and dressed. The flat was a pit. There were unwashed pans in the kitchen and clothes all over the bedroom floor. She had to search through a drawer of laddered tights and single socks to find a clean pair of knickers. But the worst of the hangover seemed to have disappeared and she was left only with a dull, persistent headache.

When she was sitting in her car, trying to coax it to start, she decided not to go into the office immediately. She could not face James until her head was better. Besides, she needed time to work out for herself the implications of Alice Parry's death. It was the first Monday of the month and the magistrates court would be sitting in Otterbridge. James Laidlaw usually covered the court himself, but Mary thought it unlikely that he would remember it today. It would provide a reasonable excuse for her absence from the office.

The courthouse was a red-brick building between the police station and the cattle market, with the same air of depression as an urban social security office. The waiting room was thick with smoke. There was a queue at the tea bar run by the WRVS and by then she was desperate for coffee. In a corner a well-dressed solicitor was talking to his client for

116

the first time. Occasionally there were shouts of recognition as defendants waiting to go into court called to old friends.

Mary left her coat in the office of a friendly probation officer and slipped into the court, onto the press bench behind the prosecuting solicitor, just as three elderly magistrates came into the room. In the warm, calm, wood-panelled room Mary Raven listened to the cases and dozed until early afternoon. When the court finally rose at two-thirty, she felt she could not put off going to the office any longer. On the way out she was stopped by an anxious businessman who had been convicted of drunk driving and was convinced that he could persuade her to keep his name out of the *Express*, but she arrived at the High Street at three o'clock.

In the *Express* office James Laidlaw heard Mary's car from his desk and walked to the window to watch her arrive. The car's exhaust had been going for days and she claimed not to have the time or the money to get it mended. He wondered sometimes why he had ever employed her. Her lack of organisation was legendary. He watched her climb clumsily out of the small car and heard her come up the stairs. Then she burst into the office, dropping scarf, keys, files onto the floor.

"Don't look at me like that, Marg!" she said to the receptionist. "You've got to be kind to me. I've got a hangover."

"Where have you been?" James asked, standing in the doorway.

"Magistrates court," she said. "It's the first Monday of the month. I knew you wouldn't want to do it today. The flasher from Whittingham was up. Otherwise it was all motoring."

"Oh." James was momentarily distracted. "What did he get?"

"Remanded for social enquiry reports," she said. "There were a couple of drunk drivings and a strange thing happened—" She broke off, realising that legal gossip was inappropriate. "I'm so sorry about your aunt Alice, James," she said. "Isn't it awful? She was such a nice lady."

"Yes," he said. "She was."

117

"I met her, you know, on the afternoon before she died."

"Yes," he said. "She told me."

"She was so sympathetic. So easy to talk to."

"Have the police been to see you?" he asked.

"I don't know," she said. "They might have been to the flat. I haven't been in much. I went to a party in Newcastle on Saturday night and stayed with friends in town. I didn't get home until late last night. When exactly did she die?"

"Saturday night," he said. "At about midnight."

"So she died soon after I'd seen her," she said. "Do the police know who killed her?"

He shrugged. "They won't tell me," he said, "but there was a lot of ill feeling in the village about the new housing development."

"I know," she said. "I was at the residents' meeting on Saturday afternoon. They were really angry."

He looked at her sharply. "I wanted to talk to you about that," he said. "Why were you there? We'd decided not to cover the Brinkbonnie development because I couldn't be objective."

"I thought *I* could cover it objectively," she said. "And if you didn't want to run the story, someone else might."

"We don't work that way here," he said. "I intend to run a paper with standards."

"I've got standards!" she cried. Her face was flushed and he thought she looked like a moody teenager. He did not know how old she was. She had worked for him for five years and had seemed no younger then than she did now. He knew very little about what she did when she was on her own. She had kept her student friends and her social life seemed to consist of wild, alcoholic parties and evenings in smoky pubs.

"I thought it was a good story," she said.

"I'm sorry," he said. "I didn't mean to snap. I'm upset." He looked at her. "She didn't say anything that might help the police find out who killed her? They'll want to talk to you, anyway."

118

She shook her head. "We ended up talking about personal things," she said. "She was so easy to confide in."

"I'll miss her," he said, and returned to his desk to work.

They left the office together at five o'clock. He wondered if he should phone Stella to tell her that he was on his way home but decided against it. He had been half expecting her to ring him, to demand his presence back at the house, but there had been no call and that was a good sign. He pulled the glass door tightly shut behind them, then went down the stairs into the street. There was a smell of stale beer from the pub next door.

"Where are you off to tonight?" he asked, as he walked her to her car.

"Home," she said bitterly. "To an empty flat."

He waited until she got into the Mini and revved it into life, then with grating and erratic lurches drove it away up the street. By now it was very cold. With the darkness the temperature had dropped. He thought for a moment of the plight of the swan on the river, trapped as the ice spread, then started quickly home, resisting the temptation to go into the Blue Anchor for a drink to warm him up first.

12

As Mary Raven drove from the *Express* office to her flat, the depression that she had kept at bay with alcohol and frantic activity since Saturday night returned. Persistent and awkward questions repeated themselves in her mind, and she was very tired. She saw the lights of a large supermarket that stayed open late in the evening and realised she was hungry and that there was no food in the house. She turned sharply into the carpark. The motorist behind her hit his horn and she mouthed obscenities to him in her mirror.

She took a trolley and began to wander aimlessly down the aisles. The place was almost empty and the few shoppers she met intimidated her with their efficiency. They were well-dressed women on their way home from work with lists in their hands and a detailed map of the shop in their heads. They would have, she could tell, strong views on artificial additives, and she imagined that they looked at the contents of her trolley with disapproval. Defiantly she lifted pies, ready-cooked meals, and several tins of rice pudding from the shelves. What was the point in eating healthfully when you felt like dying? At the off-licence beyond the checkout she bought two bottles of wine and four cans of lager. Outside it was dark and the trolley had a wheel jammed. When she got into the car, she felt like crying.

She saw Max's car, empty, parked outside her flat when

she arrived there and read the licence plate by the street light with disbelief. She had been dreaming about Max for two days and had thought she would never see him again. The sight of the car, solid and familiar, made her think she had been a fool to be frightened. After all, she knew Max. He was a doctor, caring and gentle. He wouldn't hurt a fly. Her fears had been caused by lack of sleep and an overactive imagination.

One of the other tenants of the house had let him into the hall and he stood there by the ugly Victorian sideboard, clasping an armful of flowers. He looked worried and very serious and she thought he would put on a face like that when he was telling one of his patients that they had some dreadful illness.

"What are you doing here?" she asked roughly. She would not allow herself to seem pleased to see him. She could not forget the days of anxiety.

"I had to see you," he said. "Can't you let me in?"

She had a carrier bag in each hand and set them on the floor while she felt in her jacket pocket for her keys. A can of lager rolled out and he stopped it with his foot and picked it up. She opened the door and led him into her living room. It smelled damp and stale. He took both bags from her in one hand and carried them through to the kitchen while she lit the gas fire and drew the curtains. He still held the flowers carefully in the other hand.

"What happened to your aunt?" she asked. She was standing with her back to the fire, but she felt very cold. "I have to know."

He set the flowers carefully on the scratched wooden table.

"You can't think I had anything to do with that," he said.

She shrugged. "I don't know what to think. On Saturday night I thought it was all over. I'd come to terms with that, and now you're here. What the hell am I supposed to think?"

"That I can't do without you. I need you."

"Don't give me all that crap," she said, but as the fire warmed her feet and fingers, she felt her resistance melting, too. She longed for the old elation and felt that after all it

121

was still possible. Would it make any difference to her, she thought, if she found out he was a murderer? In her confusion and her pleasure in his company, she came to no conclusion.

"What about your wife?" she asked. "Can you do without her?"

"I don't know," he said. "It's not only that. I have responsibilities. There are the children, my work. And now there's the problem of Alice."

"So you've still not made a choice," she said. "You're here, but you've still not decided."

"How can I decide," he cried. "I care for you both."

"That's impossible," she said. "Really. It's impossible."

He moved away from the kitchen door and walked towards her. She knew she should be strong and tell him to go back to his bloody wife and his bloody kids, but she said nothing. He stood very close to her.

"I need more time," he said quietly. "You don't understand. Things have changed. Someone saw you in the churchyard on Saturday night. It could be dangerous. If the police find out . . . ."

"I know someone saw me," she said. "I recognised him. It was that man from the meeting, Charlie Elliot. But don't worry. He was drunk. He won't remember anything, and if he does the police won't believe him."

"He saw you?" Max demanded. He was shocked. "How could you let that happen?"

"I didn't know then," she said, "that it would be so important."

"How can you say that?" he said, then seeing the surprise on her face, wanting to reassure her, he continued more reasonably: "No, of course not. How could you?"

"You can't think I had anything to do with your aunt's murder?" she said. His reaction to learning she had been seen in the churchyard frightened her. "I liked her. I wouldn't have done anything to hurt her."

"No," he said flatly. "I know you had nothing to do with that." He reached out and stroked her face and neck, just

122

under her ear where he knew she liked it. She could not respond to the caress and turned away.

"Look," she said. "This business has made me feel really uptight. Why don't we open some wine?"

"I don't know," he said, tempted. "I don't think I should stay. Judy will be expecting me home. She's worried about the kids. Peter found the body. . . ."

"Oh, fine," she said, suddenly angry. "You were feeling guilty because you put me in such a bloody awkward position on Saturday night, so you bring me flowers and think everything's hunky-dory. Now you can go back to your wife and children and forget about me again."

"It's not like that," he said. "Really."

"It seemed like that on Saturday," she said, "while I was waiting for you."

"I'll phone you tonight," he said, "when Judy's in bed. Will you be in?"

"Yes," she said. "Of course I'll be in. Where the hell am I likely to go?"

But she allowed him to put his arms around her and kiss her, and it was only after he had gone and she was arranging the flowers haphazardly in water that she felt she had been deceived.

When James arrived home he found Stella calmer, returned almost to her normal self, though he could tell by her restlessness that she was still under considerable stress. She seemed to find it impossible to sit still. She had lit a fire in the living room and made him stand in front of it to thaw out, while she brought him whisky and slippers.

"You're losing all the heat into the garden," he said, nodding towards the window. "Why don't you draw the curtains?"

But she refused. The ice in the moonlight was so beautiful, she said, and lasted such a short time. They should make the most of it.

"Where's Carolyn?" he asked.

"In her bedroom, watching television."

123

"You should be more careful what you say in front of her," he said. "You hurt her at lunchtime."

"Nonsense," Stella said. "She didn't say anything. She's a tough little lady."

"No," he said. "She's not as tough as she makes out. She keeps all her feelings bottled up and that's dangerous. We expect too much of her."

He was genuinely worried about Carolyn. Since the weekend she had not mentioned Alice and he found her silence unhealthy, even if it was easier for him than tears or difficult questions. He wondered if he had gone too far in talking about the girl. Stella usually reacted to any implied criticism of her ability as a mother with tears. But now she seemed strong enough to cope with anything.

"I expect you're right," she said. "She's so grown up now. I forget sometimes how young she is."

Ramsay went to speak to the Laidlaws that night without any clear idea of what he hoped to achieve. He had nothing to ask them that would not wait until the following day. He was grasping for some shred of evidence that would move the investigation forward. From his car he contacted the communications centre. There was still no news of Charlie Elliot. He admitted to himself later that he also went because he had been so affected by the warmth of Max and Judy's home. He needed evidence that marriage was not always as happy as theirs seemed to be, that he was not really missing out on anything of value. Perhaps he hoped to find that evidence in the elegant house in Otterbridge. There was also an element of needing to propitiate James Laidlaw, of what Hunter would call "sucking up to the press."

When he first entered the tall Georgian house behind the abbey, it seemed to Ramsay that he would be disappointed. He was met with an image of domestic contentment. Stella was curled up in a large armchair in front of the fire reading a book and the little girl was playing with a jigsaw on the floor. James opened the door to him and showed Ramsay into the room, taking obvious pleasure in his family. Yet throughout the conversation Ramsay felt uneasy. Stella talked too much and too quickly, and this was odd in comparison with her silence of the previous day. James watched her protectively. He answered Ramsay's questions quickly, before Stella could come in, as if he were afraid of her making a fool of herself. More disturbing to Ramsay was the child, who watched him with an intense and unblinking stare, motivated, he thought, either by hatred or fear.

"Will you have a drink, Inspector?" Stella asked. "It's so cold. You must have a drink."

Ramsay said he would have a small one to keep out the cold. Stella returned to her chair with a drink for herself, and as she talked she twisted the stem of her glass between her fingers.

"This is all so upsetting," she said. "You can't imagine how upset we are."

Ramsay made no reply.

"How can we help you, Inspector?" James said.

"Just a few questions," Ramsay said. "And I wanted to keep you in touch with what's been going on. I've just come from your brother's house."

He paused, expecting some questions about how Max and Judy were, but James said nothing.

"They seem upset, too," Ramsay said. "I understand Judy and Mrs. Parry were very close. They shared a lot of interests."

But again, if he hoped to provoke a response from the Laidlaws, he was disappointed. Stella seemed about to speak, but James looked at her and she remained silent.

"I've been trying to get in touch with Mary Raven, your reporter," Ramsay said. "She wasn't at home yesterday. Do you know where she is? I phoned the paper earlier, but no-one had seen her."

"She was working in the magistrates court this morning," James said. "I usually cover it, but Alice's death made me forget all about it. She'll be in the office tomorrow, I expect, if you want to talk to her, though I'm not sure if she'll be able to help you."

125

That came as something of a relief to Ramsay. One disappearing witness was quite enough.

"We have a little more information about Mrs. Parry," he said. "She left Henshaw's quite safely and arrived home at midnight."

"We were both in bed by midnight," Stella said quickly. "Weren't we, darling? I was fast asleep. I always sleep so much better at Brinkbonnie than I do here."

"I was certainly in bed," James said, "though I was probably still reading then."

"You didn't hear anything?"

"Nothing."

"Where was your room?"

"In the northwest corner of the Tower."

"So you would have had a view of the churchyard and the drive?"

"I suppose so. Yes. But I didn't look out."

"What about you, Mrs. Laidlaw? Did you see anyone around the Tower or in the churchyard?"

She smiled a wide, feline smile. "No," she said. "I didn't see anything." She almost purred with satisfaction, stretched, and settled again into the chair.

"Surely the most important thing," James said, brusque and businesslike, "is to find out who wrote that anonymous letter."

"Oh," Ramsay said. "We know that. It was Charlie Elliot."

"He's your man then."

"Perhaps. We need to talk to him certainly."

"You mean you've let him go!"

Ramsay felt a familiar irritation. "It's important, you know, to keep an open mind," he said mildly.

"All the same, there'll be some serious questions about how this investigation's been handled!"

There was the sound then of a car pulling up on the drive outside the house and the front doorbell rang. James seemed frustrated to be disturbed in the middle of his indignation. He shut the door behind him as he went out, but from the

126

sitting room they heard raised voices, angry words. For a moment the other voice was vaguely familiar to Ramsay, but it subsided almost immediately and the impression was lost. The front door was opened and slammed shut and then the car drove away.

"Problems?" Ramsay asked when James returned to the room.

"Not really," James said. "We printed an uncomplimentary story about a local businessman who'd been prosecuted by the health and safety executive. He wanted to complain. Said we were biased. It's all nonsense, of course."

"Do people often come to your house?"

"No," James said shortly. "It's not something I encourage. It won't happen again."

They offered Ramsay another drink, but he refused and said he should go home. When he went outside, the air was milder and droplets of moisture hung in the air. All night there was the sound of melted snow dripping in the gutters, and in the morning the garden was green again and the sun was shining.

13

The car stolen by Charlie Elliot from Tom Kerr's garage was found late on Monday evening in the carpark of a Do-It-Yourself Superstore in the industrial estate just outside Otterbridge. No-one could remember how long it had been there. No-one had seen Charlie Elliot in the streets around the town, though a motorbike had been stolen from outside a house close to the estate and the police were working on the theory that he had taken it. His picture was on the front page of every local newspaper. The press had found an old army photograph with Charlie standing beside a friend, smiling, and because that did not look sufficiently sinister there was a police sketch, too, with staring eyes and stubble on his chin. It was evident from the pictures and from the tone of the newspapers' reporting that Charlie Elliot was a murderer.

Ramsay was under increasing pressure to limit the scope of his investigation to the arrest of Charlie Elliot. Early on Tuesday morning the superintendent had Ramsay in his office.

"Look," he said. "Steve."

Ramsay winced.

"I respect your integrity, but I think you're being unnecessarily cautious here. We have motive. We have opportunity. The chap's run away. That's almost as good as a confession. We really can't justify the time and cost of any wider investigation. It's a matter of following up sightings until he's caught. It's all a question of publicity now. He'll

128

be miles away. You're a good man. We must think about your career. After that unfortunate business at Heppleburn you should keep your head down for a while. Avoid controversy. Steve, I'm thinking of your future.''

"I don't think he did it," Ramsay said. "I believed him. There was a woman in the churchyard.''

"Find me the woman and we might have a different situation.''

"Look," Ramsay said. "I'm investigating a different angle on the development. Henshaw's got no record, but apparently he's been known to use violence to get what he wants. He's not the respectable builder he likes to be thought of. I want to follow that up, too. But I need time. And men.''

"Steve. Leave it alone. I'm sorry. This is an order. It's a matter of economics. If we had unlimited resources . . . .''

"Two more days," Ramsay said. "Give me two more days. Me and Hunter.''

"You think you can wrap it up in two days?''

"I'll have to," Ramsay said. "Won't I?''

The superintendent nodded.

In the Incident Room Hunter was on the telephone. Calls were coming in from all over the country. Elliot had been seen on a train between Cardiff and Swansea, hitching a lift down the M1, in a bus queue in south London.

"Fantasies!" Ramsay said, when Hunter showed him the reports. "Nothing worth bothering about there.''

He dialled Jack Robson's home number, but though he let it ring there was no reply. The lack of response made him irrationally angry.

"Come on," he said to Hunter. "You can't stay in here drinking tea all day. There's too much work to do. We're going to talk to Mary Raven.''

Mary Raven slept badly, and while it was still dark she got up and wandered about the flat drinking mug after mug of black coffee, trying to decide what she should do about Max. The sensible thing would be to stop the affair now. It had caused enough hurt. He had treated her abominably and had

129

appeared at the flat the night before because he wanted re-assurance and information. She was a fool to think he would leave his wife and his precious family for her. He did not care that much. Then the romantic excitement of his appearance at the flat, uninvited, shy, moved her almost to tears. She knew it was unreasonable to expect him to leave his wife, but she had never been one for logical thought.

She had always been attracted to danger and extremes. When other girls at school had misbehaved, they had kept open an avenue of retreat, of apology. In arguments with parents they had been prepared to compromise. Mary Raven had been expelled from school, and at sixteen she had left home to live in a squat until the life there had become too uncomfortable and she had returned, still defiant, to her parents. She had never been reasonable.

When it was light, she went to the kitchen and poured out a bowl of cornflakes. There was no milk and she padded, barefoot, through the entrance hall to the front door to fetch it. Outside it was warmer and the sky was clear. She felt restless and optimistic. Perhaps she should drive to the Health Centre, she thought, and wait for Max. It would be a pleasure just to see him, to exchange a few words with him. But she rejected the plan almost immediately. Max might be irritated by the attention and, besides, it would be dangerous. It was to distract her from doing anything foolish that she sat at the table to work. She began to write up the court proceedings of the day before, banging on her secondhand typewriter and waking up the student who had the bed-sit in the next room. Soon she became engrossed. When she paused to dress and make more coffee, she thought that while Max was making up his mind she still had her career to consider.

Mary Raven was not in the *Express* office when Ramsay and Hunter arrived. James Laidlaw was there, hostile and intimidating, still talking about the police mismanagement of the case and their incompetence in allowing Charlie Elliot to run away.

"I understand that he was interviewed twice," James said, "and still you let him go. I'll be making the point very clearly in this week's paper."

He could not tell them where to find Mary Raven, and it was Marjory, the receptionist, who suggested that they try the small café on Front Street.

"She came in very early," Marjory said, "before I arrived. She's rather a melodramatic young lady. She left me a note saying she was working on a story and she didn't know when she'd be back. But if she's in Otterbridge at this time, she usually has a coffee and a sandwich across the road." She returned to her typing.

The café was empty except for Mary Raven. It had print tablecloths, silk flowers in bowls, and an elderly lady in a black uniform to serve the customers. In the summer it would be full of day-trippers from Newcastle. Mary was drinking more black coffee, cupping her hands around the patterned china cup. She seemed lost in thought. Ramsay looked at her through the window and decided she might be the mysterious woman who had been in the churchyard. She was small, dark, with long hair. She fitted Charlie Elliot's description. If they could persuade her to admit that she was there, that night, walking through the gravestones, his superintendent might be inclined to believe the rest of Charlie's story. As they watched she set down the empty coffee cup and began to write in a shorthand notebook that was on the table in front of her. She wrote quickly and fluently, pausing occasionally as if searching for the right word. When they walked into the café, she looked up briefly but took no notice of them. She put them down as reps in town to collect goods from the agricultural suppliers near the market. She imagined them delivering dog food all around the region.

"Miss Raven?"

It was Hunter who approached her while Ramsay went to the counter to pay for tea.

"Yes," she said. "I'm Mary Raven. Who are you?"

"My name's Hunter," he said. "Gordon Hunter. I'm a policeman."

"What do you want?" They stared at each other with evident hostility. Ramsay thought they might have been brother and sister: too alike, always fighting. They were both

131

dark, aggressive, unruly. She was still holding the pen and seemed anxious to continue writing. As Ramsay approached with the tea she turned the notebook facedown so that they could not see what had been written.

"Just a few questions," Hunter said, "about Mrs. Parry."

"But I thought you were looking for someone in connection with that."

"We are," Hunter said angrily, "but there are always a few loose ends. You know how it is."

"No," she said, "I'm not sure that I do. But if you're going to disturb me anyway you can buy me another coffee." She waited while Ramsay bought coffee from the counter. "Who are you?" she asked. "His sidekick?"

"Something like that," Ramsay murmured. He sat back in his chair, out of her line of vision, and watched her, while Hunter asked his questions.

"You met Mrs. Parry on the afternoon of her death?"

"Yes," she said. She lit a cigarette. Ramsay thought she looked very tense, very tired. His optimism increased.

"Why did you go to Brinkbonnie?"

"You must know that already," she said. "To cover the residents' meeting about the proposed new development."

"But Mr. Laidlaw had made it clear that he did not want to follow the story any further."

"Yes," she said. "Well. Perhaps James has too many scruples." She spoke with a bitterness that surprised Ramsay. "Perhaps he could never had made it in Fleet Street, after all."

"What do you mean?"

"He once had an offer of a job in London on a daily," she said, "but he turned it down. He claimed it was because his wife wouldn't want to move, but I'm not so sure. I don't think he could have handled it. He's been a big fish in a little pond for too long." I must be tired, she thought, I'm just being bitchy.

"But you could handle it?" Hunter asked.

"Yes," she said. "Why not? I need a break. I don't want to stay on the *Otterbridge Express* for the rest of my career."

"And that's why you went to Brinkbonnie?"

132

"Partly," she said. "I do stuff sometimes for one of the Newcastle papers. Henshaw's got planning applications outstanding all over the county. I thought it might make a feature. And no-one had done an interview with Mrs. Parry."

"And she agreed to speak to you?"

"Yes. She was really nice."

"What did you talk about?"

"The development at first. The meeting had upset her. She wasn't the sort of rich outsider who moves into a village and takes no part in its affairs. She'd lived there for twenty years. Her husband died there. She thought they were all her friends, then they turned against her. That hurt her."

"What else did she talk about?"

"All sorts of things. Her family. She showed me photographs of her great-niece and nephews. Then I talked to her about my problems. She was dead easy to talk to."

"Oh." Hunter was all charm and flattery. "What problems could you possibly have?"

"I don't think," she said, "that's anything to do with you."

He shrugged and smiled. "She didn't say anything that you feel might have a bearing on her murder?"

"No," she said. "Nothing at all."

She looked at her notebook and Ramsay thought she wanted to be at work again.

"Do you know Max Laidlaw?" Hunter asked.

"Yes," she said. "He's a doctor at the Health Centre. I know his wife. We're both involved with the women writers workshop."

"Did you talk to Mrs. Parry about Max or Judy Laidlaw?"

"Only indirectly," she said. "She thought her family should have given her more support over the development issue."

"She wanted them behind the banners trying to stop the builder?" Hunter was sneering, trying to provoke a reaction.

"Something like that."

"Not very likely, is it?"

"I don't know," she said. "Probably not. James wants to keep his objectivity. Max might be more sympathetic."

"What time did you leave Mrs. Parry?"

"I don't know. About half-past four. She was expecting her family."

"Did anyone come to the house while you were there?"

"No," she said. "but as I was on my way into the village someone was coming across the green towards the Tower. When he saw me, he waited until I came out before he went into the churchyard. I was a bit worried. I wondered if I should go back and check that Mrs. Parry was all right, but I thought she was probably able to look after herself."

"Are you sure he went up to the house?"

"Yes," she said. "I saw him walk through the churchyard to the little gate into the garden."

"Who was it?"

"The fat man who was so rude to Mrs. Parry at the meeting."

Charlie Elliot, Ramsay thought, delivering the letter.

"Did you see him come out again?" Hunter asked.

"Yes," she said. "Just as I was getting into my car."

"Where had you parked your car?"

"By the green outside the church."

Hunter paused, drank tea. "Did you walk through the churchyard to get to your car?"

"No," she said. "I didn't like to wander through Mrs. Parry's garden. I went down the drive."

"Did you go into the churchyard later that evening?"

"No," she said. "It looked very interesting, but I didn't go in."

You're lying, Ramsay thought. But why? Hunter was continuing with his questions.

"When did you leave Brinkbonnie?"

"As soon as I got to my car," she said.

"Are you sure?"

She hesitated just for a moment. "Yes," she said. "What reason could I have for staying?"

Ramsay's head was full of questions, none of which was possible to ask her. If she was the woman in the churchyard, where had she left her car? No-one had seen any strange car on the green that night. And what on earth had she been doing there? Was there an angle on the planning story she was reluctant to talk about before her article was finished? Or was the reason more personal? He spoke for the first time since the interview had started and his soft voice surprised her.

"Tell me," he said. "What relationship do you have with your employer?"

"What do you mean?" she demanded angrily. "Relationship? Do you want to know if he is screwing me?"

He smiled, as if amused by her childishness, her lack of taste and sophistication.

"Let me tell you," she said. "James Laidlaw and I have no relationship at all outside the office. He's besotted with his wife."

"You don't meet him at all socially."

"Occasionally," she said vaguely. "We have some mutual friends."

Ramsay nodded and indicated to Hunter that he should continue the questions.

"Where were you on Saturday evening?" Hunter asked.

"In Newcastle," she said. "At a party." She looked at him defiantly. "I can give you the address if you like. I got drunk and stayed the night. I slept on the floor. On my own."

"That would be very helpful," he said.

"What time did you arrive at the party?" Ramsay asked.

"I don't know!" She was almost shouting. "How should I know? I went home to change first. I didn't want to get there until it had warmed up. What are all these questions about?"

"A woman answering your description was seen in the Brinkbonnie churchyard on Saturday night," Ramsay said formally. "We need to eliminate her from our enquiries."

"This is ridiculous," she said. "Who saw this woman, anyway?"

"A reliable witness," Ramsay lied.

"Why are you bothering with this?" Mary cried. "You know who killed her. Why aren't you out there looking for him? You're just wasting time, my time."

Ramsay said nothing. He knew Hunter agreed with Mary

135

Raven. He thought they were wasting time, too. Charlie Elliot had murdered Alice Parry and run away. If he was innocent, Hunter had said, he would have come forward by now. We'll find him. He might even have left the country, but we'll get him in the end. Ramsay sighed. He felt his options were closing. He could not afford another failure. It was easier, perhaps, to accept the general opinion that Charlie Elliot had killed Alice Parry in a drunken rage. It was not so unlikely, after all. He stood up and then, on impulse, wrote the number of the Incident Room on a scrap of paper.

"If you remember anything," he said, "or come across any information that might help, give me a ring. Inspector Ramsay."

She looked up briefly and nodded, but he saw her roll the paper into a ball and push it into her pocket before returning her attention to her notebook.

In the street the policemen paused in the sunshine. Hunter wanted to get back to the Incident Room, taking phone calls, tracking down Elliot, but Ramsay seemed gripped by an obsession, haunted, Hunter thought, by the woman in the churchyard.

"I didn't believe Miss Raven," the inspector said. "She was lying."

Hunter stood sullen and unresponsive. He thought Mary Raven was an irrelevance. He was afraid of their colleagues stealing the glory of Elliot's discovery.

"Go to Newcastle!" Ramsay said. "Check her story. Find out what time she arrived there and as much as you can about her."

Hunter nodded unenthusiastically.

"I'll go back to Brinkbonnie," Ramsay said, "and check the addresses of the lads in the bus shelter. They might have seen the woman in the churchyard."

He felt a renewed energy and hope. Mary Raven's denial became a challenge. He looked again through the café window. She was drinking more coffee and stared anxiously and absent-mindedly towards the wall.

Hunter found the house where Mary Raven claimed to have spent Saturday night in a quiet, scruffy street close to

136

the hospital. There was a Chinese take-away on the corner and rubbish in the small front gardens. Many of the houses were owned by the same landlord and let to students. From one house came the sound of rock music. Outside another group of young people sat on the front steps talking in loud southern voices. Hunter felt he had wandered into an alien land. The group on the steps stopped and stared at him, though by the time he reached the house where Mary's friends lived they had resumed their conversation. The house was near the end of the terrace, with a CND sticker in a bedroom window and a bicycle propped against the fence. He knocked at the door, hoping that he would find no-one there. Weren't students supposed to go to college after all? Didn't they have lectures and tutorials to attend?

The door was opened by a pretty blond girl wearing a kimono. She had a towel wrapped around her hair, bare feet, and pink toenails. She did not seem surprised by Hunter. Nothing surprised her.

"I didn't expect to find anyone in," Hunter said. "I thought you were all at the university." He would have liked to mention grants, taxpayers' money, but felt his disapproval would be lost on her.

"No," she said vaguely. "Not today. No lectures. I'll be going in to the library later."

She looked briefly at his identification card and stood aside to let him into a poorly lit hall. The plaster was peeling onto the floor, and as she walked ahead of him into the living room he saw the small white pieces stuck to the soles of her feet.

The living room was large and well proportioned but almost empty. A huge Japanese paper lampshade hung from the ceiling. There was a settee with a pine frame and brown cushions and an expensive stereo with a shelf of cassettes and a box of records. The carpet was threadbare and not very clean. Hunter sat gingerly on the settee. He could feel the wooden struts of the frame through the thin padding of the cushion.

"Sorry," she said. "It isn't very comfortable." She sat on the floor, her long, smooth legs straight before her, her ankles crossed. She began to dry her hair.

137

"What do you want?" she asked.

"You had a party on Saturday night," he said.

"Yes," she said, unbothered, unafraid. "It was my birthday on Sunday. Did the neighbours complain about the noise? I don't know why. We invited them all to come."

"No," he said. He was finding the interview very difficult. "It's not that. Was Mary Raven at the party?"

"Yes," she said. Her hair was long and fine. She pulled out the tangles with her fingers. "She was here. She stayed the night. She was too drunk to drive home."

"How did you meet her?"

"I can't remember exactly." She considered, frowning. "She was at university, I think, with some of my friends. I share the house with a couple of postgraduates. I probably met her through them. She always seems to be around. Of course, she's a lot older than me." She took the damp towel from her shoulders and folded it on the floor. "What's this all about?"

"Miss Raven was in Brinkbonnie on Saturday afternoon. We need to eliminate her from the Alice Parry murder. It's only a formality."

"Oh." For the first time she was shocked, even impressed. She looked at Hunter through long, fair eyelashes. "How exciting."

"What time did she arrive at the party?" he asked.

The girl shrugged. "She was late," she said. "We didn't get home ourselves until the pub shut and she turned up soon after, perhaps eleven-thirty, a quarter to twelve. She was definitely here by midnight. They all sang 'Happy Birthday' to me when the clock struck twelve and I remember Mary joining in. She's got a terrible voice."

"And she didn't leave the party after that?"

"No," the girl said. "I've already told you. She was too drunk. I think she'd been drinking before she got here."

"Was Miss Raven on her own at the party?"

"What do you mean?" She seemed already to have lost interest and was looking vacantly out of the window.

"Did she have a boyfriend with her?"

The girl smiled, her attention caught again. "Oh, no," she said. "We're never allowed to meet Mary's boyfriend. He's a deadly secret. She only talks about him when she's been drinking and then she starts to cry."

"Who is he?" Hunter asked.

"I've told you I don't know. None of us have ever seen him."

"But she must have told you something about him."

She smiled again. "Nothing useful," she said. "Only that he's handsome, stimulating, sensitive. And married."

"How long has she known him?"

"I think it all started last summer. She disappeared from the scene for a while then, and she's never gone out with anyone else since."

"And you have no idea who this man might be?"

"No," she said. "Sometimes I think Mary made him up. She can be quite strange at times, you know, a bit intense, and rude. I had thought he might be a figment of her imagination."

Hunter was reluctant to go. He sat on the low, uncomfortable sofa watching the pretty young woman brush her hair like a veil across her face, hoping that she might offer him coffee, allow him to prolong his stay. But she looked up at him and smiled.

"Is that it?" she asked. "Any more questions?"

He shook his head and she stood up to show him out into the street.

Outside Hunter felt elated. It was twelve o'clock and the smell of ginger and soy sauce lingered in the street, but he was no longer offended by it. If Mary Raven had arrived at the party in Newcastle by midnight, she could not have murdered Alice Parry. Now, perhaps, Ramsay would leave the case alone and admit that Charlie Elliot should be caught and brought to court. He would have to admit that Hunter was right.

14

All morning Ramsay was aware of time passing, of seconds and minutes slipping by. In Otterbridge on his way from the *Express* office to the café to interview Mary Raven, he had walked so quickly that Hunter had difficulty keeping up with him. On the way to Brinkbonnie he knew he was driving too fast. It was a mild spring day and the only remaining trace of snow was a white swathe under the hedges and trees and, as he drove past at speed, what might have been a carpet of snowdrops.

As he approached the village he reluctantly slowed the car. He passed Henshaw's palatial bungalow and turned briefly to see if Henshaw's Rover was parked in the drive. There was no sign of it. Then he came to the high, ivy-covered wall to the entrance of the Tower drive. From there he could see the sweep of Brinkbonnie Bay and the sunlight on the breaking waves. In the centre of the village he parked behind the Castle Hotel so that his car could not be seen from the street. He did not want to give the residents warning that he was there.

The first address on Hunter's list of lads who regularly hung around the bus shelter was a red-brick council house in a small crescent behind the smart houses that overlooked the green. The road was dark, in the shadow of the hill, and it was quiet. Ramsay knocked at the door, but there was no reply. A neighbour who must have been watching the inspector's approach from behind thick lace curtains hurtled out into the front garden, obviously afraid that he might leave before she could find out who he was and what he wanted.

"She's not there, pet," the elderly lady said, then, hopefully: "Can I take a message?"

Ramsay ignored the offer. "Where is she then?" he asked.

"At work, pet," the woman said. "She's a dinner nanny at the little school. She'll be home soon. You can wait in with me if you like."

"No," Ramsay said. "Thank you." She was so lonely that he knew it would take him hours to escape once he was in the house. "It was the lad I wanted to talk to."

"Oh," she said. "Well, he's not there. He's at school." She looked at him curiously. "At least he went off on the school bus this morning," she said. "Are you from the welfare?"

She had placed Ramsay as an education officer checking on truancy.

"No," he said. "it's nothing like that. I'll call back later when he's home from school."

Disappointed, she stood on the concrete path that divided her immaculate lawn into identical halves until he disappeared from the crescent and onto the green.

I suppose, he thought wryly, that was the neighbourhood watch in action.

The second address given to Hunter by the boys in the bus shelter was Grey's Farm. Ramsay recognised the name. Robert Grey was the man who had been drinking heavily in the Castle on the evening after Alice Parry's death, and Ramsay had turned into the farmyard by mistake, in the snow, when he was looking for Henshaw's bungalow. Ramsay came to a five-bar gate and swung it open a little nervously, expecting the dogs to bark again. The house was square, built of grey stone, and had a grey-slate roof. The cobbled yard was covered in mud. By the side of the house was a barn, and approached by a track to the side of the house was a cowshed and a large, open building containing farm machinery and an ancient tractor. An empty Land Rover with the engine still running stood in the yard. As Ramsay approached the house, Robert Grey appeared on the storm porch and almost ran to meet the policeman. He was shaking and Ramsay wondered if he had been drinking again. His behaviour was erratic and bizarre.

"Come with me!" he bellowed. "Where's your car? You can park in the farmyard and I'll take you up in the Land Rover. You'd not make it in a car. Man, you were quick. I'd just left Celia in the house phoning the police."

He sprinted towards the Land Rover and turned to Ramsay, expecting him to follow. Ramsay joined him, carefully trying to avoid the worst areas of muck.

"Mr. Grey," he said. "What is this all about?"

"Didn't they tell you then?" He had a broad accent, but he was not local. Ramsay, who had never travelled and did not have a good ear for these things, guessed that he came from Yorkshire or Cumbria. "I've found Charlie Elliot."

"Where is he?" Ramsay asked.

"In my barn up on the hill. I keep spare feed up there for when the weather's bad."

"Does he know you saw him?" Ramsay asked.

"No!" The man looked at him as if he were mad. "He knows nothing. How could he? He's dead."

He pushed a lever to put the Land Rover into four-wheel drive and turned the vehicle quickly. He followed the track between the house and the shed, through two enclosed fields and out onto the open hill beyond. The land rose steeply. On the hill there was heather and bare rock and the track petered out into a couple of tyre marks. As they climbed, the patches of snow spread into each other and the sunlight was reflected from it.

The barn was at the head of a small valley, sheltered from the east winds by a fold in the hill. It might have once been a shepherd's cottage. The solid stone walls had gaps for windows, but the slate roof had been replaced by corrugated iron. One wall had been taken down to allow a tractor inside and there was a roughly made wooden door in its place. The door had been opened as far as it would go.

"Was the door open when you found him?" Ramsay asked.

"No, I opened it to see how much hay was left."

"Did you touch anything else?"

"I don't think so. When I saw him, I went straight back to the house to phone you people."

"Yes," Ramsay said absent-mindedly. "Of course." He turned back to face the farmer and spoke more briskly.

"I'll not need you anymore now, Mr. Grey," he said. "I'd be grateful, though, if you could bring my colleagues up when they arrive. If your wife phoned Otterbridge, they'll be turning up soon. I'll need to speak to you and your family later, so it would be helpful if you could stay around the farm today."

He thought for a moment that Grey would argue and insist on staying, but he nodded and drove away.

Ramsay went back to the barn. There was still snow on the side of the roof that was in shadow, but it was beginning to melt and water dripped on his head and down his neck as he paused at the entrance to get an overall view of the scene inside. Most prominent was the powerful motorbike, stolen from the industrial estate in Otterbridge. The body was in a corner, poorly lit by a gap in one of the boarded-up windows. Ramsay took off his shoes and stepped carefully into the barn. He did not want to confuse the scene of crime team with the mud from his shoes or his prints, but he wanted a closer look at Charlie Elliot. He was lying, facedown, on a makeshift bed of a sleeping bag spread over paper fertiliser sacks half filled with hay. He had been stabbed in the back and the knife had been removed, so there was a lot of blood.

Had he been stabbed when he was sleeping? Ramsay wondered. If so, why was he lying on top of the sleeping bag instead of inside it?

He straightened and looked around the barn. Because it was the end of winter, most of the feed was gone. It had the domestic tidiness of a child's den. There was a Primus stove, a saucepan, a spoon, and a tin mug. On a rough shelf nailed to the wall were neatly stacked tins of beans, soup, and beer,

143

a box of tea bags, and small jars of coffee and powdered milk. There was even a small bucket and a bottle of washing-up liquid in one corner. He was expecting to stay there, Ramsay thought, for some time. On the floor, next to the bed, the only sign of disorder: an empty beer can. Ramsay looked more closely at the shelf and realised that most of the beer cans stacked there were empty, too. Had Charlie drunk them all himself? Or had he shared them with a guest?

Ramsay put on his shoes and walked out into the sunshine. He stood, leaning against the rough stone wall of the barn to wait for his colleagues. Above him the brown heather moor stretched to the distance, the skyline broken occasionally by a shooting butt where the gentry would come in the autumn to shoot grouse. Below was the improved land, grazed by sheep, the short, cropped grass sprouting in damp places with juncus grass and soft reed. Beyond that, down the line of the valley he could see the village. There was Henshaw's monstrous bungalow, Grey's Farm, and to the north, as much a part of the landscape as the rock and the moor, was the Tower. On the horizon, a thin line of reflected light, was the sea.

Ramsay could see that the Land Rover had arrived at the farm. Soon it would begin to climb the track again with Hunter and the scene of crime team. Before then, before the concentration on detail, he wanted to order his thoughts.

When Hunter arrived, he was driving the Land Rover himself. He had enjoyed the trip from the farm to the hill immensely. Action was what he had joined the police for. He had imagined high-speed car chases and midnight stakeouts. He had received the call about the discovery of Charlie Elliot's body on his return to his car after talking to Mary Raven's friend. He had driven straight to Brinkbonnie, jumping red lights, scaring old ladies on pedestrian crossings. Manoeuvring a Land Rover too fast up a slippery, occasionally dangerous track was action, too, and provided some compensation for the hours of boredom and routine.

When he got to the barn, Ramsay was still outside, deep

in thought, apparently surprised to see them though he must have heard the noise of the engine miles away.

"You were right then," Hunter said angrily. "Charlie Elliot didn't kill Mrs. Parry."

"I don't know!" Ramsay said. "I don't think we can be certain of anything at this stage." He saw that Hunter was wearing green Wellingtons that had remained miraculously clean.

"What do you mean?"

"That we must keep an open mind."

Hunter walked past him and stood at the entrance of the barn, looking inside. The scene of crime team had begun their work.

"He was stabbed then," Hunter said. "Just like Mrs. Parry."

"All the same," Ramsay said. "We shouldn't jump to conclusions. Charlie Elliot had enemies in his own right. It could be a copy-cat murder committed by someone with an alibi for the time of Mrs. Parry's death. The murderer might have thought we'd assume both were killed by the same person."

"It doesn't sound very likely," Hunter said.

"Perhaps not," Ramsay said. "But as I see it there are three possibilities. The first is the copy-cat theory—someone wanted to be rid of Charlie Elliot and saw Mrs. Parry's death as an excellent opportunity to cover it up.

"The second is that Charlie Elliot murdered Mrs. Parry and he was killed as an act of revenge. Mrs. Parry was popular. Her support for the Save Brinkbonnie campaign stirred a lot of emotion in the village." He remembered Olive Kerr, red-eyed and desolate, and Fred Elliot's moving description of his affection for Mrs. Parry. He could imagine a sense of outrage so ferocious that it led to murder.

Hunter yawned theatrically. He had never taken to being lectured.

"And the third possibility?" he asked.

"Obviously that Parry and Elliot were killed by the same person. That's probably the most likely theory. Elliot saw

145

something or discovered something, which made him dangerous to the murderer, so he was killed, too. As you say, both were stabbed with a wide-bladed knife."

"How did anyone know he was here?" Hunter demanded. "It's miles from anywhere. It's not the sort of place you'd come across by chance. Especially in this weather."

"No," Ramsay said absent-mindedly. "It's not the sort of place you'd come across by chance. But Charlie Elliot turned up here, I wonder why? We'll have to find out if he was friendly with the Greys." He remembered the noise made by the farm dogs when he had disturbed them. It was impossible to think that a noisy motorbike could have gone up the track without the Greys being aware of it. It would be important to check if there was another way onto the hill.

"He can't have brought all that stuff with him when he first came," Hunter said. "He left the village in too much of a hurry. He must have gone back for it."

"Perhaps," Ramsay said. "Or perhaps he had help. What do you think?"

"I don't know what to think," Hunter said. "Not yet. But your Mary Raven can't have killed Mrs. Parry. She was at that party in Newcastle by midnight on Saturday night."

"But she could have killed Charlie," Ramsay said, almost to himself. "He saw her in the churchyard."

Hunter did not reply and hardly seemed to be listening. He was eager to get down to practicalities, to see the blood, to discover if the scene of crime team had found anything to work on. Ideas always made him impatient. Why was Ramsay standing there, rambling away to himself, when there was so much to do?

The inspector seemed suddenly to come to a decision.

"Look," he said. "You look after things here. I want to talk to the Greys. There's something odd going on there. I'll send Grey back to fetch you later."

Hunter watched the Land Rover move over the hill and shook his head.

Promoted beyond his competence, he thought again, and turned with relish to the body in the barn.

15

R*amsay* stood on the storm porch at Grey's Farm and knocked on the door. He could see Robert Grey in the tractor shed, bent over the engine, but although the farmer must have seen the return of the Land Rover, he made no move to come into the house. Ramsay thought his feet were wet enough and refused to cross the muddy yard to fetch the man. The door was opened by the woman who had come into the yard when he had strayed into the drive by mistake. She was tall, attractive, rather grave. Her dark hair had a streak of grey along the centre parting. Behind her he saw a wide hall with uneven flags on the floor where eggs were stacked in trays.

"Yes?" she said, imperious, ready to send him away though she must have guessed who he was.

"I'm Inspector Ramsay," he said. "Northumbria police. I'll need to speak to you and your husband."

"We'll not be able to help you," she said.

"A man was murdered on your land," he said. "You can see it's important that I talk to you."

She opened the door wider to let him into the hall, then stood outside and called to her husband.

"Robert. Come here, please. The policeman wants to speak to you."

It was the voice of a woman speaking to a child or an employee, not to an equal. Ramsay wondered what sort of relationship they had. He presumed that the farm had been inherited from her family and thought she might have married Grey to do the work. The man walked to join them. He was shorter than she was, slightly bow-legged. At the door he stopped and took off his boots.

"We'll go into the kitchen," she said. "It's the only warm room in the house."

She must have been in the middle of baking. There were bowls and trays on the table and the smell of cooking in the air. On one chair there was a pile of unironed clothes, but the woman did not apologise for the mess.

"You'd better sit down," she said.

"I won't disturb you for long," Ramsay said.

"Well," she said. "You've done that already."

He ignored her and turned to Grey.

"What time did you find the body?" he asked.

In his wife's presence the man seemed even more awkward and inarticulate than he had before. It was not, Ramsay thought, that he was stupid. He had difficulty expressing himself as accurately as he wanted and that frustrated him.

"I don't know," Grey said. "Not exactly. I went up the hill to see how much feed was left. In case there's another cold spell. Quarter to twelve perhaps. It must have been about midday when I met you."

"Yes," Ramsay said. "When was the last time you went to the barn?"

Grey shrugged. "About a week ago," he said. He turned to his wife. "That would be right, wouldn't it, Celia? It was about a week ago."

"I can't remember," she said indifferently.

"You've not been up there since Charlie went missing?"

"No," Grey said. "Certainly not since then."

"Was Charlie Elliot a good friend of yours?"

"Not exactly a friend. I'd met him in the Castle, of course. He bought me a few drinks."

"Did he know you well enough to ask you a favour?"

"I don't understand," Grey said. "What sort of favour?"

"Did he ask you if he could camp out in your barn?"

148

"Of course not," Grey said. "I wouldn't have allowed that. He was wanted for murder."

"What were you doing on Monday evening?"

"I was in the Castle," Grey said. "Having a few drinks."

"Where were you, Mrs. Grey?"

"I was here," she said.

"Did you hear anything unusual?" he asked.

She shook her head.

"If Charlie Elliot had come through your farmyard you would surely have heard," he said.

"Not necessarily," she said.

"But what about the dogs? Wouldn't a stranger coming into the yard have disturbed them?"

"Perhaps," she said. "I don't know. Perhaps I was busy and didn't hear them. Or perhaps Charlie got onto the hill through the fields without coming past the house."

"Oh," Ramsay said. "He certainly came past the house. I stopped the Land Rover on the way down and there's a motorcycle track quite clear in the mud."

She said nothing.

Ramsay turned again to Robert Grey. "Where were you on Saturday night?" he asked. "On the evening of Mrs. Parry's death."

But before Grey could reply, Celia interrupted.

"He wasn't here," she said. "His mother lives in Penrith and she's been ill for a while. He went to the hospital to visit her. You can phone his sister if you like. She'll confirm it."

"And where were you, Mrs. Grey?"

"I was here," she said, then added bitterly, "I'm always here."

She got up to take scones out of the oven and to shake them onto a wire cooling tray.

"How well did you know Mrs. Parry?" Ramsay asked. The question was directed at them both, but again Celia answered.

"Quite well," Celia said. "We were both on the committee of the WI. She was a good woman. I liked her."

149

"Everyone seems to have liked her," Ramsay said, "but she was stabbed to death. Have you any idea why?"

For the first time Celia Grey's composure seemed shaken.

"No," she said. "Of course not. Unless it had anything to do with the development on Tower meadow."

"Have you never considered any of your land for building, Mr. Grey?"

And this time Grey did answer, stammering in his attempt to get the words out.

"I'd sell nothing to that bastard Henshaw," he said. "Nothing." He got to his feet. "Look, I'm busy. I've a lot to do. I'll be in the shed if you want me."

When Grey left the room, Celia turned back to the oven. She lifted a fruitcake onto the table and put a skewer into the centre, then replaced it at the bottom of the oven. Ramsay might not have been there.

"I wanted to talk to your son," he said, "but I expect he's still at school."

She looked at him seriously. "Why do you want to speak to Ian?" she asked. "He's got nothing to do with this."

"He's not in any trouble," Ramsay said. "He might just have seen something."

"He's not at school," she said. "He's upstairs. He's got the flu."

"Can I speak to him? It won't take long. You can be present if you want to."

She shrugged and disappeared from the room. She came back sometime later followed by a teenage boy. He was pale and seemed genuinely unwell. Ramsay recognised him as one of the boys who had passed him while he was standing at the bus shelter on the first night of the investigation. He sat next to the big, old-fashioned range and huddled into his polo-neck sweater.

"I'll get on with this washing up," Celia said, "while you talk to him. You won't mind that?"

"No," Ramsay said. "Of course not."

She moved to the sink with her pile of bowls and spoons, and as she passed him she turned to her son with a look that was half threat and half entreaty. The boy took out a large handkerchief and blew his nose. Ramsay could not tell whether or not he had received whatever message the mother was trying to send.

"It's about Saturday night," Ramsay said. "Were you at home?"

The boy glanced over at his mother, but she did not turn to face them. Ramsay thought she was concentrating on not showing a reaction. She lifted a soapy mixing bowl from the sink and placed it upside down on the draining board.

"No," he said at last. "I went out with a mate."

"Which mate?"

He gave the name of the boy who lived in the council house Ramsay had visited earlier that day.

"Where did you go?"

Ian shrugged. "Just about the village."

"Where in the village?"

"We were at Dave's house for a bit, playing records," Ian said, "but his mam and dad wanted to watch television, so we went out."

He began to cough. His eyes were streaming and he spoke with a hoarse croak.

"Where did you go then?" Ramsay asked. "Did you come back here?"

"No," the boy said quickly. "We didn't come here."

"Oh?" Ramsay said. "Why was that then?"

The boy looked embarrassed. "It was Saturday night," he said. "I wanted to be out of the house."

"If you didn't come home, where did you go?" Ramsay realised he sounded impatient and added: "It really might be important."

"Just around," the boy said infuriatingly.

"Perhaps you could be more specific."

"We met a friend," Ian said.

"Where did you meet him?"

"In the bus shelter on the green. It was too windy to hang around."

At last, Ramsay thought. At last.

"Was anyone else around in the village?"

"I don't know," Ian said automatically. He sneezed into his handkerchief.

"Look!" his mother cried. "Can't you see how ill he is? Is all this necessary?"

"I'm sorry," Ramsay said. He turned back to the boy. "Please think. As you say, it was very windy. You would have noticed. Did you see anyone in·the square or outside the church?"

"There was the woman," the boy said.

"Which woman?" It was impossible to tell from Ramsay's voice how excited he was.

"I don't know who she was," Ian said. "I'd never seen her before. She was hanging around the churchyard."

"What time was that?"

"I don't know. About nine o'clock."

"What did she look like?"

"Small," Ian said. "Dark-haired. Scruffy. I don't remember properly."

The thing was a matter of complete indifference to him, but Ramsay waited, willing him to recall more details.

"She had a bright red jacket," the boy said at last. "I'm sure she did. Dave made a joke about it."

Mary Raven, Ramsay thought. It must have been Mary Raven.

"If you saw her again would you recognise her?"

"Probably."

"What was she doing?"

"Nothing," Ian said. "Just hanging around. Sometimes she walked over to the gate to the Tower. We thought she must be waiting for someone."

But what a wait! Ramsay thought. From nine o'clock until eleven when Charlie Elliot saw her. Who could she have been waiting for? Alice Parry? Surely no story could be so important to a reporter on a local paper. What had she discovered?

"How long did you stay in the bus shelter?"

"Ten minutes," he said. "No more. It was cold."

"What did you do then?"

"We went to Dave's house," Ian said. "His mam and dad had gone out to the pub."

"What time did you leave Dave's house to go home?" Ramsay asked.

"Just after midnight."

"You must have walked across the green on your way home," Ramsay said. "Was the woman still in the churchyard?"

"No," the boy said. "I looked. She had gone. No-one was there."

"Did you see anyone else?"

"A couple of old men on their way home from the pub."

"What about Charlie Elliot?"

"No," Ian said. "I didn't see him."

"Did any cars go past?"

"Not that I remember."

"You didn't see a blue Rover that night?"

At the sink the woman put the last wooden spoon on the draining board, wiped her hands on a towel by the range, and turned to face the policeman. He was aware of her immense control.

"I don't understand where all these questions are leading, Inspector," she said. "I don't want Ian mixed up in all this."

"Oh," Ramsay said easily, "I'm sure Ian will have heard the rumours in the village. He'll know what's been going on. He'll know that Charlie Elliot was suspected of killing Alice Parry. And now your husband's found his body in your barn on the hill. In my experience teenagers aren't easily upset." He turned back to the boy. "What were you doing on Monday evening? Did you hear anything unusual?"

But it seemed that Ian had supplied all the useful information he had. On Monday the cold had already started and he had come straight home from school. He had been in his bedroom doing homework for most of the evening. He had not heard anything unusual. He'd been listening to records. Through earphones. His dad always complained if there was noise.

Celia Grey saw Ramsay out of the house with obvious relief. There was tension and unhappiness in the family, he thought, but as always in a serious investigation it was impossible to tell if they were the result of unrelated domestic problems or connected to the case. He paused for a moment in the yard, expecting Robert Grey to come, but the farmer had disappeared. As he walked back towards the Otterbridge Road, two Land Rovers filled with policemen drove past on their way to the hill. Hunter must have organised that, he thought. Hunter will be in his element now. He imagined the crowd of them working together, the banter, the shared drinks at the end of the day in Otterbridge, and felt lonely and left out.

But I was right about Mary Raven, he thought. She was in the churchyard that night and Charlie Elliot saw her. I was right about that. Mary Raven was the link between the village and the Laidlaws. She worked for James and had been haunting the village all that day. He knew she must be involved.

Ramsay walked down the Otterbridge Road, intending to collect his car, but he saw Colin Henshaw in his uniform of waxed jacket and Wellingtons ahead of him and followed him on, past the Castle Hotel towards the sea. A group of women was standing on the pavement, some with pushchairs and children, waiting for the school bus to bring the older children back from Otterbridge. Ramsay became aware that they were excited, angry. There were raised voices. As he walked on down the hill behind Henshaw, he saw the object of their hostility. In the Tower meadow, between the house and the dunes, a surveyor and two assistants were working with a theodolite and a tape. The women saw Henshaw and surrounded him, blocking his path to the field.

"You can't start building," one of them said. "Not until the council's come to a decision about taking an appeal to the high court."

"I'm not building," he said.

"What are you doing then?" She was a farmer's daughter, fearless, unintimidated.

"That's my business," he said.

154

"No," she said. She was redheaded. "It's our business. Village business."

He pushed past the women and climbed the stile into the field. He stood, calf-deep in mud, separated from the farmer's daughter by the fence.

"If you don't like my plans for the village," he said quietly, "what are you going to do about it? Murder me to keep your precious village intact? That's what Charlie Elliot did to Alice Parry after all."

"You don't know that," the woman cried. "It's your greed that was responsible for her death!"

"Greed!" he shouted back. "You're a fine one to talk about greed. Don't tell me that you're worried about scenic beauty. The only thing that bothers you is that a new development would bring your house prices down."

The redhead saw the school bus coming down the hill and controlled herself.

"I'm not going to descend to your level by having a public slanging match," she said. "But you'll not get away with it. I can promise you that."

The children spilled out of the bus and the mothers moved away.

Ramsay walked on down the street to the stile.

"Mr. Henshaw!" he called. "Could I have a word, please?"

The builder turned and scowled, but moved back towards the fence.

"What do you want?" he said. "I've had enough disruptions for one day. I've got to make a living. Not like those bloody women with their fancy talk."

"Have you heard that we've found Charlie Elliot?" Ramsay asked.

"No," Henshaw said. "Does that mean you're all going to go away and leave us in peace?"

"Not exactly," Ramsay said. "He was murdered. He was found by Mr. Grey on the land behind your house."

Henshaw said nothing.

"It might be considered a suspicious coincidence," Ramsay said. "The two people in the village who opposed your plans most vehemently are dead. I suppose that's convenient for you."

"Look," Henshaw said. "I'm a powerful man. I can get my own way without resorting to violence."

"But that wasn't the case in the past, was it?" Ramsay said. "I've been hearing rumours that you used to find violence rather useful."

"I've been convicted of nothing," Henshaw said. "You shouldn't listen to gossip."

"Perhaps not," Ramsay said. "I have some good news for you. Your story about Saturday night has been confirmed. We know Mrs. Parry was alive when she left you. She was seen in the pub late that night."

"There you are then," Henshaw said. "What did I tell you? This business has nothing to do with me." It seemed to Ramsay that he was too relieved. "Now perhaps you'll leave me and my wife alone."

"Of course," Ramsay said. "We don't intend to intrude." He paused. "Are you sure you didn't leave your house after Mrs. Parry went to the pub on Saturday night?"

Henshaw was suddenly furious. "What do you mean?" he cried. "What's she been saying?"

"Who?" Ramsay asked mildly. "What's who been saying?"

"Have you been to my house again," Henshaw demanded, "talking to my wife without my permission?"

"No," Ramsay said. "I've not been to your home. Do you think Mrs. Henshaw has some information that might be useful?"

"No," Henshaw said. "This is all a waste of time." He turned on Ramsay. "You should have stopped those women from bothering me. This is my land. That's what we pay you for."

"Oh," Ramsay said. "I should have thought you could handle them." He was about to return to the subject of Henshaw's movements on Saturday night, but the builder interrupted him.

"And it's not only them." He nodded towards the gaggle of women disappearing up the street. "That reporter from the *Express* phoned me up this morning. Could she come to see me? she asked. She's doing an article on local business-men. Like hell you are, I told her. Sod off and bother some other bugger. I'll get the police on you for harassment."

Ramsay knew Henshaw was trying to distract him, to stop him from following up the questions about Saturday night, but he was interested all the same.

"Which reporter?" he asked, though he knew the answer already.

"Raven," Henshaw said. "They call her Mary Raven."

Of course, Ramsay thought. It always comes back to her. She was the vital link between all of the major suspects in the case.

"If she gets in touch with you again," Ramsay said, "will you let me know?"

Henshaw nodded. He had recovered his composure and Ramsay allowed him to turn and walk away to the surveyors, then went back to the Castle to collect his car.

16

When it was dark, Hunter and Ramsay met in the police house. Outside was a glass-faced notice board with the faded photograph of a child who had been missing for five years and would look quite different now, even if she was still alive, and a poster about car theft. Every rural police house seemed to have the same notice board and to be built to the same design.

Ramsay had been to Otterbridge to face the anxieties of his superintendent.

"So you were right about Charlie Elliot," the man had said. "Well, well. You know I always trust your judgement."

"Elliot could still have murdered Alice Parry," Ramsay had said impatiently. His superior seemed incapable of logical thought and chose his theories according to convenience and what would provide maximum publicity.

"Do you think so?" The superintendent had seemed surprised. "Well, as I said, I'm prepared to trust your judgement on that. Just keep me posted, Steve. The door's always open, you know."

"We'll need a press release," Ramsay had said. "I've just been given a provisional time of death for Charlie Elliot as between five and six-thirty this morning. We'll need anyone who was out in Brinkbonnie to come forward."

"Of course, Steve." The man had relaxed. "You can leave that to me."

Hunter had just come back from the hill. He was flushed from the afternoon in the open air and full of good humour. Even the discovery that Ramsay had proof that Mary Raven had been in Brinkbonnie on the night of Mrs. Parry's murder could not suppress him.

"Why was she lying then?" he asked. "She can't have anything to do with the murder. I told you. She was at the party in Newcastle before midnight."

"I don't know," Ramsay said. He felt that he still knew very little. "Perhaps she knows who killed Mrs. Parry and she's trying to protect him. Perhaps she has reasons of her own. Did you find out anything else from the student in Newcastle?"

"Yes." Hunter was grinning. "Mary has a boyfriend."

Ramsay looked at him sharply. "Who?"

"She won't tell them. It's all a big secret."

"But they're her friends. They must know something about him."

"I don't think so." Hunter was eating a Mars bar. He screwed the wrapper into a ball and threw it towards a wastebasket in the corner of the room. "It seems that Mary's a bit of a loner. She goes to their parties and gets drunk with them, but she doesn't talk to them much."

"Is the boyfriend married?" Ramsay asked.

"The girl thought so."

"Perhaps she was waiting for him in the churchyard," Ramsay said. "But why Brinkbonnie? Because he lives here?"

"Or perhaps he was staying at the Tower," Hunter said. "It could be Max Laidlaw or James."

"We'll go to her flat later this evening, when she's likely to be in," Ramsay said. "She's approached Henshaw, too, and worried him. I'd like to know what that's about."

"Blackmail?"

"I don't know," Ramsay said. "If so, she's putting herself in a lot of danger."

159

"I've been thinking blackmail might have been the motive for the Elliot murder," Hunter said tentatively. "If Charlie saw something on Saturday night and worked out who killed Alice Parry, it might have occurred to him that he could put the information to his advantage. It would explain how the murderer found him in the barn on the hill. Perhaps they arranged to meet there."

Ramsay considered the idea carefully. "Why didn't he tell us? That way he could clear himself."

Hunter shrugged. "Perhaps he thought we wouldn't believe him. Perhaps he thought he could turn his knowledge to profit."

"Yes," Ramsay said. "It's possible. Dangerous. But I can see Charlie Elliot as a man who would enjoy taking risks. We've only his father's word that he stayed in after eleven. He could easily have gone out again and seen Alice Parry on her way home from the pub."

"Did you inform Fred Elliot of his son's death?" Hunter asked.

Ramsay shook his head. "I got the village policeman to do it," he said. "They've been friends for years. It seemed better." He stood up. "We'll go and see Fred now. Get it over with. Then I want a word with Maggie Kerr."

On the way to the post office Ramsay was tempted to send Hunter immediately to wait for Mary Raven. It was not only that he was afraid of missing Mary, but he was irritated by the other man's presence. He would have preferred to work alone. Hunter chatted about the conflicts and power struggles within the Otterbridge police station, turning the trivial gossip that comes out of any workplace into high drama. Ramsay wanted to concentrate.

The kitchen behind the post office was much as it had been when Ramsay had last visited. There was washing airing in front of the stove and clean pans on the table. Fred Elliot was tidily dressed, with black shoes immaculately polished. Yet there seemed to be no connection between the postmaster and the physical world around him. In his grief he had become clumsy, and when Ramsay walked into the room, he

160

seemed at first not to recognise who was there. The village policeman had opened the door and sat quietly in one corner while they talked. It seemed to Ramsay that he had been crying. Brinkbonnie was a close village.

"Oh," Elliot said. "It's you."

"I'm sorry," Ramsay said, "about everything that's happened."

"He didn't do it," Elliot said. "He wouldn't have murdered Alice Parry. You'll have to believe that now."

Ramsay did not answer directly. "When did you last see Charlie?" he asked.

"You know that," Elliot said defiantly. "You were here."

"Didn't he ask to meet you? Before he went up the hill. Didn't he ask you to bring food and a sleeping bag? He had no-one else to ask."

There was a silence and the old man struggled for control.

"I met him late yesterday evening," he said. "By the Otterbridge by-pass. I took everything he wanted."

"Did he telephone here to arrange the meeting?" Ramsay asked. "What exactly did he say?"

"Not much. He didn't have much change for the phone. He'd just made another phone call, he said, and used all his ten p's. He wouldn't wait for me to phone him back."

"Who else did he phone?" Ramsay asked. "Did he say?"

The old man shook his head. "I presumed it was Maggie Kerr," he said. "She was always on his mind."

"And when you met him by the Otterbridge by-pass," Ramsay said, "did he tell you where he was going?"

Elliot shook his head again. "He was waiting for me when I arrived," he said. "I was afraid you'd have me followed, so I drove miles out of my way round the lanes before I got there. I tried to persuade him to come back with me, to give himself up. I said you'd believe him, but he was too frightened. And he was wild, excited. There was nothing I could say that would persuade him. He just took the bag and drove away on that motorbike, laughing."

"Tell me what was in the bag," Ramsay said. "In detail."

Elliot began to list the equipment he had provided. "There was a knife," he said. "Not a bread knife. I've only one of those and I couldn't spare it. But there was a big, old kitchen knife at the back of the drawer. I gave him that."

"Would you recognise it again?" Ramsay asked. No knife had been found in the barn during the detailed examination. But it seemed that Elliot might have provided the means used to murder his son.

"I expect so," the old man said, unaware of the implication of the questions. "We've had it for years."

There was another silence and Ramsay could sense Hunter's impatience. He wanted to be out on the streets, knocking on doors, making things happen. He hated this waiting. But Ramsay could tell that Elliot had something else to say and that he wanted to say it in his own words.

At last the old man spoke. "There's something you don't know," Elliot said. "I didn't tell you. On Saturday night Charlie came in at eleven like he said, but he went out again. I heard the door slam while I was in bed. He wasn't gone long, not long enough to kill her, a quarter of an hour at the most."

Later Ramsay was to see this admission of Fred Elliot's as a turning point in the case. Everything else developed from it. Now Ramsay nodded sympathetically. There was no recrimination because Elliot had not told them before, though Hunter might have made threats about wasting police time.

"Where did he go?" he asked.

"Just out on the green," Elliot said. "I looked out of my window and saw him. He walked over towards the Castle." He paused. "I suppose he was waiting for Maggie Kerr."

"Did he meet Maggie?"

"I don't know. I didn't wait to see. I'd lost all patience with him. But I've told you he wasn't gone long. Just a quarter of an hour."

"And he didn't say anything the next day?"

"No," Elliot said. "Neither of us mentioned it."

Hunter, unable to sit any longer, got up and walked to the

162

kitchen window. There was nothing to see and he turned back to face the room.

"Mr. Elliot," he said. "What were you doing between five and half-past six this morning?"

Ramsay knew that the question had to be asked, but he thought Hunter brutal. He would have done it differently. But Elliot was so confused by unhappiness that he was not offended. He did not even ask why the question had been put to him.

"I was here," he said simply. "Putting up the papers for the delivery boys. The van from Newcastle comes at six and the first boy at half-past. There's never enough time." He shook his head, then repeated, as if it were a statement of profound belief, "There's never enough time."

Out in the street Hunter stamped his feet. "What did you make of all that then?" he asked.

Ramsay shrugged. "If Charlie Elliot was out on the green late on Saturday night or early Sunday morning, it adds weight to your theory that he was blackmailing Alice Parry's murderer," he said. "He might have seen something."

Then, just when Hunter was wondering if he would be able to claim the credit for making a breakthrough in the case, Ramsay added: "But it's still too early to be certain of anything at this stage. If Charlie did go back to the pub to walk Maggie Kerr home on Saturday night, why didn't she mention it to us?" He was talking almost to himself, and Hunter did not bother to reply.

Someone had put a bunch of daffodils on the pavement outside the post office. It was a form of apology. No-one believed that Charlie had murdered Alice.

In the house behind the garage the Kerrs were finishing a meal. As the policemen approached they heard Maggie shouting at one of the boys that it was rude to leave the table without asking to be excused. The snapping ill temper seemed out of character and her voice was strained. Olive Kerr let the policemen into the house. As she opened the door to them she realised she was still wearing a pinafore and took it off, apologising.

163

"We're not ourselves today," she said.

When Maggie saw Ramsay and Hunter, she turned on the boys again. "Go on and run the bath," she said. "You're big enough to do it yourselves now." Then, when she thought they were about to argue: "You can use some of my bubble bath. It's on the bathroom shelf." They leapt away up the stairs, whooping with glee.

Olive took the half-empty plates into the kitchen, and when she came back they were still standing, staring at each other. At the head of the table, his head bowed so that the bald patch gleamed in the electric light, stood Tom Kerr.

"I expect you've come about Charlie Elliot," she said. "We heard this afternoon. It's a terrible thing to have happened."

"Sit down," Olive Kerr said, and obediently they all sat around the dining table like delegates at some conference, or, Ramsay thought, very aware of Tom Kerr, like members of a church committee. He almost expected the man to suggest that they pray. It wouldn't do any harm, Ramsay thought. They didn't have much else to go on.

"How can we help you, Inspector?" Tom Kerr asked, and the normal quiet voice broke into Ramsay's fantasy and startled him.

"I need to ask your daughter some questions," Ramsay said. "If you feel you have any information to help us find out who killed Charlie Elliot, I'd like to hear from you and Mrs. Kerr, too. But I'm here to speak to Maggie."

"Would you like us to leave you alone with her?" Tom Kerr asked, but Ramsay shook his head. Something about Kerr's still, almost fanatical presence concentrated the mind. He turned to Maggie.

"What time did you get home on Saturday night?" he asked. "I spoke to the regulars at the pub, but you didn't tell me what time you got back."

"It was late," she said. "Gone one o'clock."

"Did you see Charlie Elliot as you came back from the Castle?"

"No," she said. "He'd left the pub much earlier. I think I told you. It was a relief."

"We know he arrived home at about eleven," Ramsay said. "But his father tells us that he went out again later. Fred presumes that he'd gone back over the green to walk you home."

"No," she said. "Really. I didn't see him."

"Did you see anyone else?"

"No," she said. "Not until I was almost home. Then I saw my father."

Tom Kerr looked up. "It was so late that I was beginning to worry about her," he said. "I'd gone out to see if I could see her coming. I could see that she had just left the pub, so I waited for her. I didn't see anyone else, either."

"You knew we were looking for witnesses who had been out on Saturday night," Ramsay said. "Why didn't you come forward before?"

"I wasn't out," Kerr said. "Not strictly speaking. I was only several yards from the front of the garage. And I've told you. I saw nothing."

"When I saw Dad waiting, I began to run," Maggie said. "It was very cold, although he was so wrapped up you'd have thought he was out on an Arctic expedition. I didn't see anything."

"Did you notice if there was a light on in Fred Elliot's cottage?" Ramsay asked.

She shook her head. "I was just so glad not to see Charlie," she said. "I didn't see anything else."

There was a silence.

"Did Charlie Elliot try to get in touch with you after he left Brinkbonnie on Monday afternoon?" Ramsay asked.

"No," she said. "Of course not."

"We know he made a phone call on Monday night," Ramsay said. "It wasn't to you?"

"No," she cried. "And anyway I wasn't here on Monday night. I was working."

Ramsay turned to Olive and Kerr.

"Was there a phone call here on Monday night?" he

asked. "Perhaps from someone who did not answer when you picked up the receiver?"

But they shook their heads. "We were here all evening," Olive Kerr said, "and the only call was for Tom from the vicar."

Then Ramsay began to share Hunter's impatience. This talk wasn't getting them anywhere, just leading them round in circles. He should have trusted his original instinct and concentrated on getting Mary Raven to talk to them. He knew that if he could persuade her to tell them why she was in the churchyard, at least some of the confusion would disappear. So they left the Kerrs in a hurry, almost rudely, refusing offers of tea and food, and they drove to Otterbridge. But when they arrived at Mary Raven's flat, it was dark and empty and the other tenants claimed not to have seen her all day. The policemen waited in the car for hours, with Hunter ranting about search warrants and, if that was impossible to arrange, breaking down the door and feigning a burglary. By midnight Ramsay was so desperate that he thought he might give in to this folly and knew it was time to go home.

17

O_n Wednesday morning Stella Laidlaw had still not seen Max. She had expected him to arrive the day before and had been prepared for him from early morning, as expectant and smartly dressed as a lover. She imagined that every car that approached the drive belonged to him, and by late afternoon she was in a frenzy of anxiety in case James came home from work before Max arrived. At four o'clock she phoned the surgery, but the receptionist said Dr. Laidlaw was out on an urgent call. Stella did not believe her and shouted and made a scene. Then she phoned Max at home, but Judy answered and Stella put the phone down without saying anything. There was a temptation to spite Max by telling Judy all she suspected, but secrecy, Stella knew, was her greatest source of power.

When James came in from work on Tuesday night, he found Stella more tense than he could remember. She was sobbing and shaking. She wished she was dead, she said. She wished it was all over for her, too. James tried to comfort her. He felt exhausted himself, but he put her to bed like a child and sat with her until she finally slept. In the morning the crisis seemed to be over and her confidence restored. She woke quite normally. He tried to insist on staying with her, or on fetching the doctor to be with her, but she sent him to work. She was at her most charming, apologising for making

167

so much fuss the night before. She was so much trouble to him, she said. She did not know how he put up with her.

Carolyn watched her mother's performance with a new, dull detachment. In the past, scenes like these would have upset her dreadfully. She would have hidden in her bedroom, her head under the blankets, trying to persuade herself that nothing out of the ordinary was happening. Now the hysteria hardly touched her. She wondered why she had ever considered her mother's moods of such importance.

She watched the weeping woman with curiosity, as if her mother were a strange child throwing a tantrum in the street. James and Stella were so wrapped up in each other that they did not notice the change in Carolyn. They did not realise that she had hardly slept for nights and that she had eaten little. When she made her way to school, she stumbled with tiredness.

James was relieved to leave the house, but all day he was thinking about Stella, remembering how she had been before Carolyn was born, wondering if she would ever be like that again. Wednesday was the day before publication, the busiest time for the *Express*, but he could not forget her.

When Ramsay came to the office in Otterbridge, it was late morning and James Laidlaw was holding an editorial meeting. His door was open on to the large, open-plan office to allow the cigarette smoke to escape and he was working through the list of news lines supplied by his reporters to decide which items should go on the front page.

"It'll be the Charlie Elliot murder, will it?" A large, elderly reporter with a peculiar crew-cut sat on the opposite side of the desk. He was looking at black and white photographs of the Tower, Charlie Elliot in army uniform, and Brinkbonnie village, squinting at them, trying to judge which picture had the most impact. "We'll need to cover the Alice Parry story, too. It's obviously related. I know the *Journal*'s done that in detail over several days, but we can run our own angle."

"Yes," James Laidlaw said. Worry about Stella made

168

him preoccupied, rather aloof. Even his aunt's death could not touch him. "What have we got so far?"

"A look at the facts as we know them, with details of Charlie Elliot's last movements and a map of the area. An interview with the father, Fred Elliot. You know the idea: 'I was convinced my son was never capable of murder.' I thought we might include a background piece on the planning issue. Something about the high feelings raised by new developments in small communities."

James looked up. "I'm not sure that would be relevant anymore," he said. "Not after Charlie Elliot's death. It looks more like the work of a lunatic now."

"We'll hold the planning piece for another week then," the reporter said. "We'll concentrate on the murders."

"What have we got from the police?" James asked.

"Not much. They're giving nothing away."

"There's nothing here from Mary Raven. What's she been doing this week?"

The report shrugged. "I don't know," he said. He had little time for Mary. He thought she was unreliable and disrespectful. "She said she was working on a special feature. I assumed she had your approval. She was in last night, but I've not seen her since."

"No," James said slowly. "She hasn't talked to me about any feature." There was a pause. "When she comes in again, tell her I want to speak to her."

He looked through the open door and across the large office and saw Ramsay standing at reception.

"Well," he said to the reporters. "We're organised now. That's all then."

Ramsay had climbed the narrow stairs and was standing with the receptionist.

"I was hoping to speak to Miss Raven," he said. "Is she here?"

Before the receptionist could answer, James Laidlaw had crossed the large office.

"Inspector!" he said. "Did you want to talk to me? Is there any news?"

169

"No," Ramsay said. "No news. Is Miss Raven here?"

"I'm afraid not," James said. "It seems that she's not been at work this morning. Perhaps she's ill. Have you heard from her, Marjory?"

"Yes," Marjory looked awkward. "She did phone in."

"Well," James said. "What's the matter with her?"

"I don't know," Marjory said. "Not exactly. I think she's going through some emotional problems. She didn't sound well. She told me she'd given up men and was going to throw herself into work. It was an important story. Something about a bankrupt businessman. The biggest story of her career, she said."

"That wouldn't be difficult," James said shortly.

"I need to talk to her," Ramsay said. "It's rather urgent. If she comes into the office today, will you ask her to get in touch with me at the Incident Room?"

"I can't help you, I'm afraid," the receptionist said. "I'm taking the afternoon off. It's my grandson's birthday and I'm having the children to tea. I was just going home."

She took a coat from the peg behind the door and tied a silk scarf round her hair, and picked up a large wicker basket. James Laidlaw listened to the exchange between Marjory and Ramsay without reaction. He nodded briefly and walked back to his office, apparently preoccupied with his own thoughts.

"You stay here," Ramsay said to Hunter. "Talk to Mary Raven's colleagues. See if you can find out what she's up to and where she might be."

He followed the receptionist, who was already halfway down the stairs.

"Can I give you a lift somewhere?" he called after her.

He held open the door to let her out and they stood together on the pavement. It was market day and in Front Street stalls were still set out with rails of cheap clothing and trays of vegetables. Now, at lunchtime, the stall-holders were shouting their special offers to clear the goods that would not keep for another day and the pavement was littered with old cabbage leaves.

"Are you sure?" She smiled, easily, motherly, used to

respect. "You must be very busy. I don't want to put you out."

"No," he said. "I'd like to take you."

He had reached a stage in the investigation when there were too many leads to follow, too much to do. He would welcome a break in the confusion, a breathing space. Besides, he wanted to find out more about Mary Raven.

He lifted her basket into the boot and opened the car door for her. She directed him out of the town towards a small modern estate with big houses and gardens full of trees. It was not sufficiently ostentatious, Ramsay thought, to have been built by Henshaw.

"Perhaps I shouldn't have mentioned where Mary was going in front of James," Marjory said, suddenly guilty. "She likes to keep her leads secret until the story's finished. I think she's afraid he'll cramp her style."

"Would he do that?"

"No," she said. "I shouldn't think so. He just likes to keep a tight rein on the newspaper. He's very proud of it."

"Mary didn't go home last night," Ramsay said. "She didn't say where she'd been staying, did she?"

"No," Marjory said. "She said she had a hangover. I didn't like to tell James that. He disapproves of her drinking."

"What sort of relationship do Mary and James have?" Ramsay asked.

"Oh," Marjory said. "Very prickly. They're both rather strong-willed. But I think there's an element of mutual respect, too. She's a good reporter, you know. James would miss her if she left."

She pointed to the entrance of a cul-de-sac, where two toddlers played on the pavement with dolls and prams.

"Could you drop me here?" she said. "Thank you very much for the lift. It's a long walk and there's a lot to do this afternoon before the grandchildren come to tea."

He felt jealous of her calm domesticity. He wanted to invite himself to tea, too. He knew there would be home-made cakes and chocolate biscuits. He was forty. Soon he would be old enough to have grandchildren of his own, but even when he and Diana were very close she had made it clear that children were out of the question. Perhaps she had been right. It would never have worked. Marjory climbed out of the car and declined his offer to carry her bags to the house. He acknowledged her thanks and drove smoothly away.

The decision to talk to Stella Laidlaw was an impulse, like the impulse to drive the receptionist home. James had made it clear that he would be working all afternoon on the *Express* and Ramsay had never talked to Stella alone. The discovery that Mary Raven had a secret lover made it important to check James Laidlaw's movements. He was the most likely candidate, and if James were having an affair with the young reporter, Stella might have guessed. That might explain the woman's nervousness, her lapses into silence, her brittle bursts of conversation.

He drove through the affluent suburbs of the town towards the river. The houses here were older, mock-Tudor mansions with long, sloping gardens and high walls to ensure privacy. Here the children would not be allowed into the street to play. Diana's sister lived in one of these houses, close to the Otterbridge Lawn Tennis Club, and even approaching the area made him uneasy. He was reminded of awkward, tedious evenings of conversation when his main objective was to say as little as possible and Diana, as bored as he was, became increasingly more outrageous. Diana had always laughed at his discomfort. She had told him to relax and be himself. She loved him, she had said. Her family would, too, if he allowed them to get to know him. Besides, they were too boring to bother about. He did not have her confidence and had never found it that easy.

Ramsay drove onto the gravel drive and waited in the car for a moment, collecting his thoughts, deciding the most important questions to ask. When he walked towards the front door, he saw Stella Laidlaw staring at him from an upstairs window. She must have recognised him, but even after he had rung the doorbell and stood back onto the drive

172

to wait, she did not move. Their eyes met and she stared at him with horror.

When at last she came to open the door, it might have been a different woman. She was smiling, gay, almost flirtatious, but managed just to miss the right tone. She asked him to sit by the fire, suggested that she make him coffee with an insistence that was embarrassing. She was trying too hard to make a good impression.

"Now, Inspector," she said. "How can I help you?" But as she spoke, she glanced at the small gilt clock on the mantelpiece, and he thought that despite her hospitality she wanted him gone as soon as possible.

"You will have heard that Charlie Elliot was murdered," he said.

"Yes," she said, and giggled nervously. "And we all blamed poor Charlie for Alice Parry's murder. You must feel rather foolish, Inspector, to have allowed another tragedy to occur."

Ramsay ignored the comment and continued. "We must assume that there was some connection between both murders," he said. "So I'm talking again to everyone who was in Brinkbonnie on Saturday night. How well did you know Charlie Elliot?"

"Not at all," she said. "I'm not even sure that I ever met him, though I go to Kerr's garage for petrol sometimes and he might have served me there."

"But you knew of him?"

"Oh," she said. "I knew of him. Staying with Alice was like taking part in a soap opera. We had to listen to the story of everyone who lived in the village. Over and over again. Charlie Elliot was infatuated with Maggie Kerr and had dropped out of the army when he found out she'd separated from her husband. Then he and Tom Kerr had a fight and Tom punched him on the nose. That was a real scandal because Tom's a pillar of the church and it was supposed to be a deadly secret, though most of the village must have heard about it in the end. According to Alice, he felt so guilty that he didn't feel able to sack Charlie from the job in the garage

173

although he was being such a pain in the arse and making Maggie's life hell. It was quite romantic, but very tedious.''

"Did Alice have any idea how the situation between Elliot and Maggie could be resolved?" Ramsay asked.

"Endless ideas," Stella said. "All totally impractical and rather interfering. She wasn't the saint the others have made her out to be, you know, just a nosy old woman. She even talked at one time of having Maggie and the boys to stay as lodgers at the Tower, though goodness knows what damage that would have done.''

"Did she ever talk to Charlie about Maggie?"

"Probably, though she never said. She wouldn't have told me, anyway. She'd know I'd not approve. Charlie would have told her to mind her own bloody business. And quite right, too.''

Again, as she finished talking, she glanced at the clock.

Ramsay paused and changed the subject of the conversation. "I must ask you some questions about yesterday morning," he said. "Charlie Elliot was killed between five and six-thirty. I have to know where everyone involved in Mrs. Parry's case was at that time. It's a matter of elimination. I'm sure you understand.''

"I don't know where James was," she said. "Asleep, I presume. We slept in separate rooms on Monday night. He was very sweet about it but said I was so restless I kept him awake. I was in rather a state on Tuesday morning—I have trouble sometimes with my nerves and it was a bad day. He was there when I woke up.''

"Were you in your room all night?" Ramsay asked.

"No," she said. "If you must know, I find it so damned hard to sleep I got up in the early hours and went for a drive. I thought the speed might relax me and help me sleep. It usually does.''

"But it didn't work?"

"No," she said. "It didn't work.''

"What time did you go out and when did you get back?"

"I don't know," she said. "And I don't know where I went, either. I just drove.''

174

"Do you and your husband each have a car?" Ramsay asked.

She nodded.

"And you took your car?"

"Yes, of course. It was parked outside the house. James keeps his in the garage."

"So you didn't notice whether your husband's car was there or not when you left the house?"

"Of course it was there. Why wouldn't it be there? What would James be doing driving round in the middle of the night?"

"But you didn't see it?" Ramsay asked.

"No," she agreed. "I didn't see it."

"Do you have any social contact with your husband's colleagues?" Ramsay asked.

"As little as possible," she said.

"You don't get on with them?"

"Oh," she said. "I get on with them. I get on with most people. But when they're all together they just talk about work and I find that tiresome. James is almost obsessive about the *Express*. I tell him he should delegate more and that he cares more about the bloody paper than he does about me, but it doesn't make any difference. It still takes up all his time."

"Does James discuss his staff with you?"

"He discusses everything with me," she said angrily, but he doubted if she stopped thinking about herself long enough to listen.

"There's a young reporter," he said. "Mary Raven. We'd like to talk to her, but she's proving a little elusive. You have no idea where she might be?"

Stella smiled and seemed pleased with herself. There was little indication that she was jealous of the woman or that she resented her.

"No," she said. "I don't know where she is. She's got something of a reputation, you know. She drinks a lot and I'm afraid she might be a bit promiscuous. James can be rather pompous and doesn't like it. I tell him it does him good to have someone young in the place. It stops him getting boring."

She looked at the clock again and this time Ramsay had no excuse to stay. He felt frustrated. He felt he had achieved nothing from the interview. He knew that Stella had been performing for him and that he could trust nothing she had said. At the door she stood with the same fixed smile on her face and waited until he had driven into the street. Then she shut the door behind her.

Just after Ramsay had turned into the road, he had to stop at a pedestrian crossing to allow an elderly lady across the road. It was only because of the delay that he saw Max Laidlaw's car drive through the gates and park outside the Laidlaws' house. The inspector turned into a side street so that he had a view of the front of the house. He saw Max knock on the door and Stella answer it. She was obviously furious and in her anger she was very tall, very regal. She took something from Max's hand and there was an exchange, possibly, thought Ramsay, an argument. Max turned and strode back to his car. He reversed it into the street at great speed, almost causing an accident, then drove off without noticing Ramsay's car at all. Stella Laidlaw stood in the doorway watching the incident with a degree of satisfaction, posed as if for a photograph, framed by the buds of forsythia that grew on either side of it. Then she disappeared back into the house.

Before Ramsay could start his car, Stella ran out into the street, tying the belt of the full-length beige mackintosh as she went. She began to hurry towards the centre of the town. Ramsay waited for a few minutes, but she was walking so quickly that he was afraid he would lose her. He locked his car and began to follow her.

18

M*ax* Laidlaw waited for two days after the phone call before making a decision to see Stella. It was a gesture of pride and independence, although he knew he would do what she wanted in the end. Even on Wednesday he waited until he had completed all of his house calls before driving to her house. Let her stew, he thought. She had caused him anxiety enough. He had hardly slept for two days. Judy's endless questions, her reassurance, her persistence to know "the truth," was wearing him out. You don't really want the truth, he felt like saying. You want comfortable words, security, a well-behaved husband. The impulse to tell her everything had long gone.

On Tuesday the publicity surrounding Charlie Elliot's death irritated him beyond reason. Everyone was talking about it; colleagues and patients regarded him as a source of gossip. Several times he tried to phone Mary Raven, but there was no reply, and he almost wept with frustration. He had come to believe that only in Mary's company could he find peace. On Tuesday night, when Judy was asleep, he tried to phone Mary again, but although it was almost midnight there was still no reply, and he imagined her with another man, in terrible danger, arrested by the police.

The next day, Wednesday, his helplessness turned to aggression. From his weakness and his lack of power, which was illustrated by Stella's ability to use him, grew a violent anger that acted like a drug. It stopped him from thinking clearly and prevented him from considering the options that had seemed to provide a way out earlier in the week. He wanted revenge for the sleepless nights of worry, the disruption to his family life, even for his own sense of guilt. Someone had to pay.

The first person to pay had been Judy. At her insistence, he had returned home for lunch and at first it was pleasant. The kitchen door into the garden was open and the twins were playing happily outside. The children's voices and the birdsong and the mild spring sunshine relaxed him and he thought his worry had been unnecessary. He would help Stella once more, he thought, just once more, then it would all be over. But Judy began again to question him about his conversation with Alice on the evening of her death and he lost his temper.

"It's none of your business," he shouted. "None of your bloody business."

The twins stopped their game and stared through the open door, fascinated by his anger. Judy cried and there was a humiliating scene as she put her arms around him, dripping tears all over his face.

"Please, Max," she said. "I don't care what you've done. I can handle anything. But I can't take this silence. I want you to trust me."

Then he turned on her. "You think I killed Alice," he shouted. "Don't you? How can I trust you when you think me capable of that? What about Charlie Elliot? Do you think I murdered him, too?"

"I don't know," she cried. "I really don't know. I want to know where you were on Tuesday morning. I got up to see to the twins and you weren't there. What am I supposed to think?"

"I'm a doctor," he yelled. "I get called out in the middle of the night. You should be used to that by now."

Then he left the house, only half hearing the voice behind him calling him to come back, begging him to talk to her. He was pleased that he was hurting her.

He had one house call to do, and to his surprise he completed it calmly and efficiently. It was only as he drove to the other side of Otterbridge that the sense of imminent violence returned and grew. He drove automatically because he knew the road well, and when he arrived at the Laidlaws' house, it was with surprise, because he could not remember how he got there. He walked across the gravel, past the pool of crocuses, purple against the green of the lawn, and thumped on the door with his fist.

Stella opened the door immediately and he did not realise at first how angry she was. She looked quite cool and elegant, dressed in primrose yellow—a linen skirt and a fine woollen cardigan buttoned to her neck. Playing the part of the country lady again, he thought bitterly. If only her posh friends knew.

"Max!" she said, but her surprise was an affectation. She had been waiting for him for two days. She added, tight-lipped: "I was expecting you this morning. Or yesterday."

Yet despite her temper she was beginning to relax and grow more confident. He was here now and the agony of waiting was over.

"I had a surgery this morning," he said. Her imperious performance had put him off his stride. He knew he sounded defensive. "I'm a doctor with real patients. I've more important things to do than run after you."

"But, Max," she said, "I am a real patient. A private patient."

She looked at him greedily, but the well-bred voice did not change. "Have you brought my prescription? How kind!"

Her delicate fingers, as fine as claws, reached out for the envelope Max was holding.

"Thank you," she said. "How much do I owe you?"

It was as if he were a tradesman. He tried to show his disgust.

"I wouldn't take your money," he said.

She shrugged. "Well," she said. "That's very generous."

With the envelope in her hand, her tension and ill temper had disappeared. She had lost the edge of desperation in her voice and could tease him. She smiled. "Don't look so cross, Max," she said. "I won't be bothering you again. Not for a while."

179

"You won't be bothering me again at all," Max said. "You can do what you like. You'll get nothing more out of me."

"Max," she said. "Darling. Don't be so petulant. We've always been such good friends. You help me and I'll help you."

"Not anymore!" He was shouting. "I don't need your help. I can look after myself."

He was aware suddenly that he sounded childish, just like Peter in a temper, and he fell silent. She looked at him triumphantly, pleased because she had roused him to temper, aware of her power. She reached out and, with one long finger, stroked his cheek from the corner of his eye to his chin. He flushed and for a moment she thought she had provoked him too far and he would hit her. She waited, still smiling because such a reaction would have been a kind of victory, but, horrified, he turned quickly and walked down the drive. He drove away, the need for violence unfulfilled.

Stella watched Max storm away. Poor Max, she thought. He had always been so weak. Hardly a man at all!

She went back into the living room and looked at the pretty little clock on the mantelpiece. It was half-past four. Her mind was very clear, emptied of everything except a determination to get her own way and her plans to achieve it. Carolyn had a violin lesson after school but would be home soon. Stella went into the kitchen and left a note for her daughter. She was in a hurry. She wanted to get into town and back before James returned from work.

On the way out of the house there was a moment of indecision, of self-disgust. After all James has done for you, she thought. You go behind his back and behave like this. But even as she paused on the doorstep, she knew that however disappointed James might be in her, he would never desert her. His admiration gave her the freedom to do as she pleased. This secrecy acted in the same way as the drugs Max had prescribed—it gave her confidence and power—but she was not afraid of what James would do if he found out. She would have liked to be the sort of wife he wanted, but the need for self-preservation was stronger and she hurried out of the house without looking back.

180

In the town the shops were beginning to close. Not far from home, Stella's attention was caught briefly by the clothes in an expensive dress shop. She turned her head to look at a model in the window but moved on, hardly faltering. Ramsay thought at first that she was heading for the *Express* office. She walked through the abbey ruins and along the riverbank to the town centre. The breeze that blew over the water detached a strand of hair from the clip at the back of her head, but she fixed it without stopping. She came to the market square, which was now quite empty apart from a pile of trestles and tarpaulins in one corner, and even over the cobbles she maintained her pace. By the time she came to Front Street she was almost running with her black handbag held firmly under her arm and the slim black shoes tapping on the pavement. The other people in the street moved to let her pass, then stared after her, at the slender ankles under the expensive coat. She seemed preoccupied and did not thank them for allowing her to move without interruption.

Once, just as she was crossing the road, a middle-aged woman called after her: "Stella, my dear! How are you?" But Stella ignored her and slipped across the congested road behind a lorry full of sheep.

At the far end of Front Street Stella began to move more slowly. She looked about her. Ramsay had to take care not to be seen. As he hid in doorways and stooped to tie already fastened shoelaces, he felt uncomfortable, ridiculous. How could he justify this wasted time? He should be looking for Mary Raven. What would he do if Stella ended up in the smart wine bar in the High Street, sharing a bottle of claret with her husband or one of her friends? Yet as he came closer to her he saw a desperation and an increasing lack of control in her movements that made him think she might be dangerous.

At a street corner she stopped suddenly and looked all around her. She must have seen Ramsay but, in her haste and agitation, seemed not to recognise him. Perhaps she was looking for someone else. He stood, thinking she was on the verge of some crisis as the pale blue eyes searched both sides of the street, then she set off again with her jerky, unpredictable walk.

181

She's mad, he thought. She's quite crazy.

She disappeared then down an alley into a street of small shops. Ramsay's way was blocked by a group of schoolgirls in the old-fashioned brown uniforms of an expensive Otterbridge day school, and when he pushed through into the street, there was no sign of Stella. Most of the shops were closed. The sun was low and the street was peaceful. A newsagent was bringing papers from a rack outside in preparation for closing and on the far corner a couple of men were sitting on the steps of a pub waiting for it to open. It seemed as if Stella Laidlaw had vanished into thin air. He ran down the pavement, pushing at locked doors, peering into shop windows. When he came to the chemist shop, he thought that it, too, had closed. The window was unlit and only a sign on the door saying that the pharmacist was on the out-of-hours duty rota made him look inside. Stella was there, the only customer. She was talking to a respectable elderly gentleman in a suit, who stood behind a counter where the dispensing took place. It was hard for Ramsay to see what was going on. The shop was disorganised and dusty, and the window was cluttered with bottles of shampoos and boxes of food supplements and milk drinks. A normal exchange seemed to be taking place. The chemist disappeared into a little room behind the counter and Stella waited, pacing between a pile of disposable nappies and a tray of lipsticks. The chemist returned; she took a wallet from her handbag, paid him, and then almost ran out of the shop, although the man called after her that he owed her some change.

Then suddenly the street was full of brown-uniformed schoolgirls tunnelling through the narrow alley, no longer prim and pompous but with all the ambiguity of adolescence. At one moment they were posing, loose-tied and tarty, then they were children again, throwing a schoolbag from one to another, jumping to catch it and showing regulation-brown knickers. Then they were racing to the newsagent before it closed, hoping to buy . . . What? Ramsay wondered. Cigarettes? Romantic magazines? Gum? They pushed into the shop and the street was empty again, except for Stella Laid-

182

law hurrying away. In the narrowest part of the alley, framed on each side by high walls, another schoolgirl stood. She was younger than the rest. Her arms were straight beside her, one of them weighed down by a violin case, the other, as if for balance, by a briefcase full of books.

"Mummy!" she called, and if she had not spoken Stella would have walked right up to her without realising who it was. "What are you doing here?"

Stella stopped and smiled at her daughter, as if waking slowly from a dream.

"Why," she said, "I thought it would be nice to come and meet you so we can walk home together."

She slipped her arm through Carolyn's arm without offering to carry the bag or the violin, her attention fixed on the shops in the main street. The girl hung back, staring down the alley after her friends. She saw Ramsay, who was still standing outside the chemist shop. Their eyes met, but the child gave no sign that she had seen him and did not mention him to her mother.

In the shop the chemist was back in his dispensary. The doorbell brought him out into the shop to the counter.

"Yes," he said. "Can I help you?"

"Who was the woman who was here just now?"

"Oh, I'm sorry," the chemist said. "I can't tell you that, you know."

Ramsay showed his identification card. "What did she want?" he asked.

"She was bringing a prescription," the chemist said rather defensively. "There was nothing unusual about it. Tranquilisers. She seemed rather neurotic, didn't she. It was written by Dr. Laidlaw."

"His surgery's on the other side of town," Ramsay said. "Why did she bring it here to have it made up?"

"I don't know. Perhaps it was more convenient."

"Is it legal for a doctor to prescribe for his own relative?"

"But she wasn't a relative," the chemist said impatiently. "At least I had no indication that she was. The prescription was in the name of Raven. Mary Raven."

183

On her walk home with her mother Carolyn felt the same panic that she had had some years ago when she had been pushed into the deep end of the swimming pool before she could swim. There was the same gasping breathlessness, the same sense of inevitable pain. Then, she had fought to the side of the pool and saved herself. Now she felt helpless. The sight of Ramsay close to her mother had confirmed all her worst fears. He must know everything.

In the house her mother suddenly became kind and solicitous. Carolyn wasn't looking well, she said. There was a lot of flu about. Perhaps she should go to bed. But Carolyn was frightened to leave her mother alone and sat with her in the kitchen. Stella's apparent concern for her well-being made her feel sick and angry, but it was better to put up with that than to be in bed, not knowing what Stella was up to.

"When will Dad be home?" she asked at last. Her mother was frying onions and mushrooms in a pan, and there was a smell of garlic.

"I don't know," Stella said. "He should be here by now. Perhaps he's working late." She seemed quite unconcerned and Carolyn marvelled at adults' capacity for deceit. She was desperate for her father's return.

"Haven't you any homework to do, darling?" Stella asked. "Or violin practise?"

But Carolyn shook her head. She knew she could not concentrate on anything until she had spoken to her father.

Stella began to chop parsley with a wide-bladed knife, holding the handle with one hand and hitting the blade quickly with the palm of the other. Carolyn watched, fascinated, and when the phone rang, she was unable to move. Stella set the knife down on the chopping board and went out to answer the phone.

"That was Daddy," she said when she returned. "He's got a meeting and will be working late tonight, so it'll just be us for supper."

She smiled, and Carolyn, faint and exhausted, thought, This must be what it's like to drown.

19

In the days of waiting for Max to make a decision, Mary became obsessed with the idea of her story. She had never, she supposed, been a person with a highly developed sense of proportion. She smoked too much, drank too much, loved too much. Now she wanted to see the story through to its conclusion, and even her desire for Max occupied less of her thoughts.

When Hunter and Ramsay were waiting outside her flat on Tuesday night, she was in Newcastle, wandering round the bars where reporters hung out, talking, picking up information, drinking whisky, buying drinks. Later she staggered to the students' house there, woke the neighbours up by banging on the door to be let in, and spent the night on the settee.

The next day she decided not to go into the office to work at all. Even the news of Charlie Elliot's murder could not distract her. Every other reporter in the northeast would be working on that. Her story would be exclusive, more important in the long run. If she went to the office, James would want to know what she was up to and she was not ready yet to discuss it with him. He would talk her round and send her to interview a housewife in Hexham whose first novel had been bought by Mills & Boon. In her obsession it no longer mattered whether or not she got the sack from the *Express*. Other papers would run her story, she thought. Better papers. She imagined it splashed over the front page of the *Journal*, sold

185

outside of the metro stations in Newcastle and Gateshead, bought by all the businessmen on their way to work. From the students' house she phoned the office to tell them she would not be there.

"I'm not coming in today, Marg," she said to the receptionist. "Make up some story for me, will you? You should be good at fiction by now."

"Oh, pet," Marjory said. "Do you think that's wise? You know what he's like."

"This is a big story, Marg. It'll make my fortune for me. Tell him I'm ill. Tell him I've got a hangover."

"The police are looking for you. That inspector's already phoned here twice."

"He'll have to wait then. I'm too busy to see him today."

"I don't think you're well, dear," the receptionist said. "You sound very highly strung. I'm worried about you. We all are. Why don't you see a doctor?"

And that, Mary thought, lighting a cigarette from the one she was about to put out, is the last thing I need.

Mary spent the day in the library in Newcastle looking up old press reports, feverishly taking notes, stopping only to take the lift to the gloomy cafeteria in the basement to drink black coffee or to go to the lavatory. When she left the place, she had no idea what time it was—her watch had stopped—but it was dark and she was very hungry. She drove back to Otterbridge, stopping on the way to collect fish and chips.

She was in the shower when Max arrived. There was a loud knock on the door and she thought it must be the police, tracking her down at last, so she dried off and made herself decent before she went to answer it.

When she saw Max standing there, she was astonished. Usually he came discreetly, slipping into the house when no-one was there to see him, tapping gently on the door so that he would not be heard by the other tenants. By the time she had got to the door, he was banging it with his fist and shouting.

"Mary Raven, let me in!"

She saw immediately that he had been drinking, and that

186

surprised her, too. Usually, when they went out, he drank little and then he ordered what she considered women's wimpish drinks: white wine and small glasses of lager. Now he was loudly and incoherently drunk. She let him in, glad to have the opportunity of looking after him, and switched on the fire because he seemed very cold. Then she made coffee for him. When she returned from the kitchen, she found him weeping. There was more wrong with him than just the drink, she thought. She, after all, was an expert in these things.

"Max," she said. "What's the matter?"

She sat on his lap and put her arms around his neck, thinking that she might distract him from his misery with sex. But he seemed only to want her for comfort and clung to her, his head against her shoulder, still crying. At any other time she might have tried to laugh him out or it, but he seemed quite distraught and she began to be frightened.

"Max," she said. "What have you done?"

But that seemed only to distress him more.

"I'll find somewhere else to go," he said. "You don't want me here."

"Don't be silly," she said. "Of course I want you. I always want you. Why don't you spend the night here? You can't go back to your wife like this."

She took his hand as if he were a big and backward child and took him to the bedroom. There she undressed him gently, wishing he was more himself so that he could appreciate the care she was taking of him. She sat him in a chair while she made the bed, smoothing biscuit crumbs from the sheets onto the carpet, shaking pillows so that he would be comfortable. Then she kissed him gently and left him to sleep.

In the morning, she thought, when he's sober, we'll talk about this and make love slowly. And at least when he was in trouble he came to me and not to his wife.

She made more coffee for herself and sat in front of the gas fire to drink it, satisfied because Max was under her roof again.

She was still there when Hunter arrived to invite her to the police station for a few questions.

"What questions?" she demanded. "I've told you everything I know." But she did not make too much fuss because she was afraid Max would wake, and she knew that at all costs Max must be protected from the police.

Ramsay saw Mary Raven in his office instead of in the interview room next to the cells. He thought she was stubborn and would react to confrontation with rudeness or awkward silence. He needed to persuade her that he did not suspect her of either murder and that he needed her help. Yet throughout the interview he was surprised by her determination to give nothing away. She seemed to be trying to be obstructive and he could not understand it. He grew frustrated by her attitude. She was an intelligent woman, wasn't she? Couldn't she see that she would land herself in trouble if she did not tell the truth? He could not tell that she did not care what happened to her—she had a naïve belief in English justice and knew she was innocent. But she had Max to protect, and as the questioning progressed his alcoholic agitation seemed more significant and sinister.

"Miss Raven," Ramsay said. "We have evidence that you remained in Brinkbonnie last Saturday after seeing Mrs. Parry. Why didn't you tell me before?"

It was not what she had been expecting and she looked at him before answering. She could not tell whether or not he was bluffing. He was cleverer than she had realised. She decided that the only thing to do was to stick to her story.

"Sorry," she said. "I don't know where your information's come from, but you've made a mistake."

"I don't think so," he said.

"I heard that your mate went and spoke to Sophie in Newcastle," she said. "You know I can't have murdered Mrs. Parry. I was at her birthday party."

"But you might have seen something," Ramsay said. "You could be an important witness."

"Sorry," she said again, implying that she was not sorry at all. "I can't help you."

"Someone saw you," he insisted. "I think I explained

before. Charlie Elliot saw you. Do you not think it's something of a coincidence that now he's dead?''

She shrugged, as if the death of Charlie Elliot was a matter of total indifference to her, yet she was remembering with a sudden clarity the look on Max Laidlaw's face when she had told him that Charlie had seen her in the churchyard.

"That had nothing to do with me.''

"How well do you know Dr. Laidlaw, Miss Raven?''

She feigned anger. "Look," she said. "You've asked me that before. It's late. I want to go home.''

"Could you answer the questions," he said. "Humour me.''

"Dr. Laidlaw isn't my doctor, but I go to his practise and see him sometimes. I know his wife.''

"Has he written any prescriptions for you lately?''

This time the question genuinely surprised her.

"No," she said. "Can't you tell? I'm the picture of health.''

"A prescription with your name on it was taken to a pharmacist in the middle of Otterbridge today.''

"It must be a coincidence," she said. "Really, I haven't been to the doctor for years.''

"It was a fictional prescription," he said. "Made out for someone else entirely. But Dr. Laidlaw chose your name. Why was that, do you think? Why, of all the patients in the practise, was yours the first to come into his mind?''

"I don't bloody know!" she said, but she was secretly delighted.

"When did you last see Dr. Laidlaw?''

"I can't remember.''

There was a pause. Mary lit another cigarette. It was very late and she had not slept well on Sophie's sofa. She yawned.

"We've had some difficulty in finding you during the last few days," Ramsay said. "Can you give me some idea of where you've been?''

"Be more specific," Mary said, playing for time.

"What about Tuesday morning?" Ramsay said. "That's when Charlie Elliot was murdered.''

But if he hoped to frighten her he did not succeed. She seemd to take a keen interest in the questions. She was wary. But she did not feel under any personal threat.

"I talked to you," she said. "You came into the café in town and I saw you there."

What about earlier that morning?" he asked. "Between five and six-thirty. Where were you then?"

"I was at home," she said. "I was restless and couldn't sleep. I started to do some work."

What's wrong with all these women? Ramsay thought, remembering that Stella Laidlaw, too, had complained of being restless. Do they all suffer from insomnia?

"Can anyone confirm that you were at home?" he asked.

"I was typing," she said. "Someone else in the house might have heard it."

"Why have you spent so little time in the office?" he asked. It was a final question. He expected to get nothing else out of her. He was profoundly disappointed.

So she told Ramsay a little about her story. It was a relief to have something to tell him without pretence, and as she spoke with immense enthusiasm he became more interested.

"If it comes to anything," he said, "you should let me know. It might be a police matter."

"Yes," she said. Perhaps he wasn't such a bad policeman after all. She was tempted just for a moment to trust him. Then she remembered Max, sobbing and overwrought, and knew that this was just another trick to put her off her guard.

Ramsay told Hunter to take Mary home, and as he had just started eating a bacon sandwich in the canteen, she had a long wait for him. It was half-past one and the town was quite quiet. Hunter said nothing as he drove through the empty streets. Mary Raven wasn't his type.

"Do you want me to come in with you?" he asked when he parked outside.

"No," she said. "I can manage fine." And he put her independence down to the sort of woman she was. He almost expected a lecture on feminism.

She waited until the car had pulled away before she went

into her flat. She moved quietly because she did not want to draw attention to herself and she did not want to disturb Max. She pushed open the door into the bedroom, expecting to hear his drunken heavy breathing. But Max had gone and the only sign that he had been there was the crumpled bed.

Her first impulse was to rush out into the street to look for him, but she realised that he had probably been gone for hours. She climbed into the bed and fell asleep, exhausted.

When she woke, she switched on the radio immediately, half expecting to hear that Max Laidlaw had been arrested for murder. There was nothing. She phoned his home, but Judy answered the phone in a tight and tearful voice, and she replaced the receiver without speaking. It was too early for him to be at the surgery. Again, to escape her growing anxiety, she returned to her story. She looked back in her shorthand notebook for the name and address of the man she had seen in the magistrates court who had been convicted for a second time of drunk driving, then went out intending to find him.

In the street outside her flat she thought at first that the Mini would refuse to start. It spluttered and choked and she explained to it, more loudly and obscenely with every twist of the key in the ignition, that she needed this story, she really needed it. At last the engine turned over. As she looked in the mirror before driving off, she thought she saw the back of someone in the front garden of the house where she had her bedsit. She thought for an instant that it was Max, but when she looked again behind her, the figure had gone. Then she told herself that she was losing her mind. She was tired and she had made the image up. It was the postman or that strange man who lived on the ground floor who always went into the garden to clean his shoes. But all day as she drove around the region following her story, asking her questions, becoming more alarmed and triumphant about the answers she received, she had the sense of a shadow behind her. She never saw anyone. She did not even think that she was being followed. It was that someone knew where she was going and arrived there first, that he was following the workings,

191

the logic of her mind. You're imagining things, she thought. You're so desperate to have this story to yourself that you're imagining the competition.

The drunk driver had his own business in a new glass-and-plastic factory on the industrial estate to the west of Otter-bridge. He made valves, he told her. She gathered it was something to do with the oil trade, deep-sea diving. He sat in his cluttered office and explained it all in detail, hoping, she supposed, for a feature that would give him free adver-tisement, but she did not take it in. He offered to take her round the workshop and she went because she thought it would please him. He had a daughter, he said, not much younger than her, a student. She seemed to remind him of his daughter, and when he offered to take her out for lunch, she accepted, thinking she might get more out of him when he had drunk a couple of pints.

"Only the pub over the road," he said, grinning. "I can't take you into town. Not now. I have to get a taxi home and back." Then, suddenly and lonely: "My wife's left me, you know. She said the publicity was the last straw. I hope my daughter will keep in touch all the same."

And there, in the pub over Scotch and scampi, he told her everything she wanted and more, and she came away with a list of contacts. As she went to the ladies' halfway through lunch, she looked carefully around the lounge bar, sensing again the shadow behind her, but she saw no-one she recog-nised. When she drove away from the factory, the Mini start-ing this time as sweetly as anything, it was probably only coincidence that a large grey saloon parked along the road pulled out, too, and kept far enough away from her that it was impossible for her to see the driver.

She arrived home just as the children were coming out of the school on the corner of her street and the pavement was full of mothers. In her flat the curtains were still drawn from the day before and there was a bottle of sour milk on the table. Mary Raven opened the curtains and opened the win-dow to let out the smell, but the noise of the children dis-tracted her and she shut it again. She tried to phone Colin

Henshaw, as she had tried several times over the previous days, but again his wife answered. Mary pretended to be an estate agent phoning on behalf of a client who wanted to buy one of the new houses in Brinkbonnie, but Mrs. Henshaw still said he would be out all day.

"*Who* are you?" Rosemary Henshaw repeated suspiciously when Mary gave her fictitious name, as if she recognised the voice on the telephone and did not believe the fiction.

"Perhaps you could tell me where I can get hold of him," Mary persisted.

"No," Rosemary Henshaw said shortly. "I'm sorry. I've no idea."

So Mary went back to the list of contacts, and encouraging the Mini with soft words and endearments, she set off round the region again, feeling the shape of the story growing more solid with every interview she did, already seeing her name on the front page of the London dailies.

When she got back to the flat late that night, triumphant, needing coffee, whisky, the biggest Chinese take-away in the world, there was a note from James Laidlaw asking her to make sure she reported to the office the next day.

Sod you, she thought. One more day and I'll have this cracked. Then I won't need you anymore. You'll be finished.

Of Max there was no word.

20

R*amsay* was in his kitchen, drinking coffee, spreading some of his mother's homemade marmalade on a piece of toast when Jack Robson appeared at the cottage. The interview with Mary Raven the night before had depressed and frustrated him. He had expected more from her. He had thought she would provide all the answers he needed. If she had not killed Alice Parry, why was she being so obstructive? Ramsay was sure Max Laidlaw was her secret lover and his failure to persuade her to tell him that had left him feeling incompetent. She was hardly the sort to be coy about sex. He could not help feeling that Hunter would have made a better job of it.

When the knock came on the front door, it was still early, before eight o'clock, and Ramsay supposed it was probably the postman with a circular too big to fit through the letter box. Instead it was Jack Robson, his face glowing after the walk from the other end of the village. He stood, his hands in his pockets, waiting to be let in.

"Hey, man," Robson said. "You're a hard person to get hold of. I was here several times yesterday evening and I couldn't catch you in."

"No," Ramsay said. "I was working late." He did not know what to make of Robson's appearance. In a serious investigation there was always the pressure of time, and once he let the old man into the house it might be hard to get rid of him. Yet there was always the possibility that he had useful information.

"Come in," he said. "I'll make you some tea."

"Well," Robson said. "If you're sure you've time." He scrubbed his boots on the doormat and stepped in, looking around him with unembarrassed curiosity. "You've a nice place here. And a canny view."

"Aye," Ramsay said. "Unless Henshaw gets planning permission and there's a new estate built at the end of the garden. There'll not be much of a view then."

"You don't want to worry about that," Robson said. "Building out there would extend the boundary of the village and that's not in the structure plan."

"The structure plan didn't count for much in Brinkbonnie."

"No," Robson said. "Well, I'm here to talk about that."

Ramsay took Robson into the kitchen and made strong, sweet tea the way Jack liked it.

"Have you come up with anything?" he asked. He felt suddenly optimistic. Surely Jack would not be here so early in the morning if he did not think he could help.

Robson sat on a painted wooden chair. "I've no evidence," he said. "Nothing I can lay my finger on. But I've got a theory."

Ramsay was disappointed. He wanted something more concrete than theories.

"Go on," he said.

"I've been through all the records," Robson said. "I've gone back five years. I'm sure Henshaw's found some way of manipulating the system. He even managed to get planning permission for sites where other developers had previously been turned down."

"So how's he doing it?"

"It's nothing to do with the council," Robson said. "I've already told you I'm certain of that."

"Is it one of the officials then? Someone in the planning department?"

"No," Robson said. "I think the corruption is more grassroots than that. You can have a village with a well-organised

195

community group that successfully fights off any development, then along comes Henshaw and miraculously all the opposition disappears. It seems to happen again and again.''

Ramsay was listening impassively. "Tell me your theory," he said.

Robson paused and poured out more tea.

"Most protest groups have one or two activists who do all the work," he said. "The rest turn up at the meetings—if the weather's not too bad and there's nothing good on the telly. It's the same in any political organisation, and in most places you find the same people running everything—they're school governors, on the parish council, even running the WI. If Henshaw managed to threaten, bribe, or blackmail the activists in each group, there would be no real opposition left. The organisation would fall apart. Then the Department of the Environment inspector would think that no-one cared sufficiently about the development to make a fuss and he would let it go through.''

"But to prevent your activists from being effective, Henshaw would have to have detailed information on people all over Northumberland. It hardly seems likely.''

"He's got a lot of contacts," Robson said. "A lot of people owe him favours. And we know he's used dirty tactics in the past. Besides, he wouldn't have to do it in every case. Only when it seemed likely that other methods wouldn't work.''

Ramsay had been standing throughout the conversation and moved to the window to look down the dene. His mind was working very quickly and he felt suddenly light-headed. For the first time he had a plausible motive for Alice Parry's murder. She had the confidence of everyone in the village. If Henshaw had chosen leading members of the Save Brinkbonnie group as victims of his persuasion, it was quite possible that Alice would have heard about it. Perhaps, when she went to see Henshaw in an attempt to buy back the land, she had tried some gentle blackmail of her own. Ramsay imagined her standing up to the developer: "Sell me the land

196

or I'll tell everyone what methods you've used to get your own way. My nephew's a newspaper editor. He'll be glad of the story."

Rosemary Henshaw had said that Alice was angry when she came to the house. Nothing could be more daunting, Ramsay thought, than a middle-class lady spurred on by righteous indignation. But perhaps Henshaw had called her bluff. Perhaps he had pointed out to her that the people most likely to suffer from exposure were the people whose indiscretions had made them potential victims of blackmail. That would explain her distress in the pub after she had left him. Then perhaps he had decided that her knowledge was too dangerous, and he had followed her and murdered her before she reached home. There was a lot of conjecture in the theory, but it fitted the facts. Ramsay was attracted to it, too, because it made Henshaw the most likely suspect. If he were convicted of murder, Ramsay's view would be safe.

"Well?" Robson demanded, breaking in on his thoughts. "What do you think?"

Ramsay turned back slowly to face the room. "It's very interesting," he said noncommittally. "I'm grateful for all your help."

"I don't want your gratitude, man. I want to know if you think I'm right."

"I think it might be worth following up," Ramsay said.

Jack was thrilled. "What do you want me to do? I'm a well-known man in this county. I could speak to a few people."

"No," Ramsay said. The last thing he wanted was Jack Robson frightening off Henshaw before they had proof. "We have to be discreet, you know, and it's a police matter now. But you can help all the same."

"How?" Robson asked. "Just tell me, man. I'll do anything I can."

"I'll need a list of names," Ramsay said. "Members of residents' associations or community groups living in areas where Henshaw's recently won a planning appeal. The ac-

197

tivists you were talking about. The people who do all the work. Can you do that?"

Robson was disappointed. He had expected something more exciting. He wanted a challenge.

"Aye," he said. "I can do that for you. I can think of someone now who led the group in Wytham before those houses went up. Her name's Jane Massie. She's involved in everything that goes on in Wytham. I'll write down the address for you. She lives in that big house opposite the new estate. You can have a longer list later if you need it."

Ramsay nodded gravely. He stood on the front step and watched Robson walk quickly down the road on his way to work in the school.

In the kitchen Ramsay emptied the teapot and rinsed the mugs. He preferred to have things tidy to return home to. He was determined in his new home not to descend into bachelor squalor. As he tidied the room, he was testing Robson's theory against the facts. It might work, he thought. It might just work. But who would Henshaw have approached in Brinkbonnie to influence the opposition? Charlie Elliot? Fred Elliot? Tom Kerr? All were prominent members of the Save Brinkbonnie group and possible candidates. He felt he needed to spend more time in Brinkbonnie, listening to the gossip, getting a feel for the place, before he could make a sensible judgement.

But that would have to wait. The most immediate concern was to talk to Max Laidlaw. Ramsay thought that the doctor would be less able to stand up to questioning than Mary Raven. He was weak and indecisive. Besides, the police had the illegal prescription given to Stella, and faced with that evidence he might be persuaded to admit his relationship with Mary. An affair with one of the practise's patients would provide another motive for murder, Ramsay thought, if Alice Parry had found out about it, and as he was always telling Hunter, it was important to keep his options open.

Ramsay drove to the Health Centre in Otterbridge, thinking that it might be more tactful to talk to the doctor there than at home. He waited patiently behind an old woman

198

whose joints were swollen with arthritis while she collected a repeat prescription, then asked to see Dr. Laidlaw.

"I'm sorry," the receptionist said, hardly looking up. "Dr. Laidlaw's taken a few days off for his aunt's funeral."

When the inspector arrived at the Laidlaws' house, he thought at first that no-one was there. It was a sunny, breezy day and he had expected children in the garden, washing on the line, but the house was quiet and in shadow. He was about to give up and turn away when Judy Laidlaw came to the door.

"Inspector!" she said. His presence frightened her. "What is it? Come in."

"I was looking for your husband," Ramsay said. Then, in an attempt to put her at ease: "It's very quiet here today. Has he taken the children out?"

"No," she said. "The children are with a friend for the morning. Max is out, I'm afraid."

She led him automatically down the bare wooden stairs to the basement kitchen.

"Could you tell me when he'll be back?" Ramsay asked. "It's quite important."

She hesitated, turning away from him so he could not see her face. "No," she said quietly. "I don't know where he is. We had an argument yesterday at lunchtime and I've not seen him since."

Then she turned back to face him and he saw she was crying, her body heaving with frightened, silent sobs. "I'm so worried about him," she said. "I think something dreadful has happened to him. It's not like him to stay out all night without telling me."

Ramsay stood awkwardly, not sure what to do, how to comfort her. He would have liked to put his arm around her but was frightened the gesture would be misinterpreted. She seemed so desperate for affection.

"Shall I make some tea?" he said. "Then you can tell me all about it. Or perhaps you'd prefer me to leave you alone. I could come back later with a policewoman."

"No," she said. Her eyes were raw from crying and he

realised she must have been sobbing all night. "Don't go! Don't leave me alone! I'll make the tea."

"There've been no accidents, you know," he said, trying to reassure her. "Nothing serious. I would have heard about anything like that."

"Oh, well," she said, trying to smile. "I'm just being silly. He'll come back, I expect, when he's stopped being angry. It was my fault for asking all those questions. When you're on your own, you imagine all sorts of dreadful things."

"Yes," he said. "I suppose you do. What questions were you asking?"

"It was about Alice," she said. "She and Max had a private conversation on the night of her death. I wanted to know what it was about."

"And he wouldn't tell you?"

She shook her head. "It upset him. He said it showed I didn't trust him. He accused me of thinking he killed her. But it wasn't that."

"Can you tell me what you thought the conversation between Alice and your husband was about? I don't want to upset you, and I'll treat it as confidential unless it's important, but it might help me find out who *did* kill her."

"It wasn't Max," she said, the hysteria returning. "He wouldn't have done a thing like that."

"Tell me now," Ramsay said firmly. "Why do you think Mrs. Parry wanted to talk to Max?"

"I think she'd found out that Max was having an affair," Judy said quickly. She was blushing.

"And was he? Having an affair?"

"I think so. I didn't want to believe it at first. I found a letter in his jacket pocket once. It was beautiful, very tender, very loving, very lyrical. I've never written anything like that to him. I suppose I've always taken our relationship for granted. He told me it was from a patient, an elderly, neurotic patient who was infatuated with him. All of the doctors in the practise had received love letters at one time or another from her, he said. Now it was his turn."

200

"And you believed him?"

"Because I wanted to."

"Was the letter signed?"

She shook her head. "It didn't even start 'Dear Max,' " she said. "It was set out more like a poem."

"Did you recognise the handwriting?"

She shook her head again.

"Could it have been written by Stella Laidlaw?" he asked. It was an explanation for the scene he had witnessed yesterday, which he could not ignore.

"Stella!" She seemed astonished. "No, of course not. Stella wouldn't write love letters to Max. She has hardly enough warmth to give to her husband and daughter. She wouldn't have any affection left over for a lover."

"You're certain the handwriting wasn't hers?"

"No," she said. "I couldn't say that. It never occurred to me that it could be Stella. I was in a state when I found it. I made a big scene. I didn't look at it very rationally. Why do you think it might have been written by Stella?"

"Dr. Laidlaw went to her house yesterday afternoon," Ramsay said. "Have you any idea why he should go to visit her?"

"No," Judy said. "None at all. He always seemed to dislike her."

"She wasn't a patient of your husband?"

"No," Judy said. "Of course not. James and Stella have their own doctor with a practise on that side of town. He's much more their type, a friend of James's. They went to school together."

"Has Stella been ill?"

"She had nervous trouble," Judy said. "She was very depressed after Carolyn was born. Not just the normal baby blues a lot of mothers experience, but a real psychosis. She went to hospital for a while. She seemed well enough when she first came out, but she still has bouts of depression. She's not very easy to live with. James never complains—he seems to adore her whatever she does. On bad days she can be rude and aggressive, and he has to go round apologising and explaining for her. I feel rather sorry for him. There doesn't seem to be a lot that anyone can do."

"James has never asked Max to treat her?"

"No, of course not. It's not something Max is specially qualified in. James would be more likely to consult a specialist."

There was a pause. Judy Laidlaw poured out tea, then hunted in a cupboard for biscuits. Ramsay waited until she was sitting down again.

"Yesterday afternoon your husband delivered a prescription to Mrs. Laidlaw. It was made out for a course of tranquilisers. Have you any explanation for his doing that?"

She shook her head. All the crying had dulled her, left her with a headache. She could not think clearly.

"I know Stella's doctor doesn't like her taking tranquilisers," she said. "I think she may have become dependent on them when she first came out of hospital. The dangers of dependence weren't so well documented then. She's complained to me sometimes that they're the only things that help. She asked me if there was any equivalent she could buy over the counter. Of course, there isn't."

"So Max might have given Mrs. Laidlaw the prescription to help her, because he felt sorry for her?"

"No," she said sharply. "He wouldn't do that. He's a good doctor. He knows the rules. I can't imagine why he would prescribe for her unless . . ." Her voice dropped.

"Unless?" he prompted.

"Unless she had put him under some sort of pressure. Max is weak. In some situations he might be prepared to take the easy way out."

"And what might Mrs. Laidlaw be using to put pressure on your husband?"

"I don't know!" she cried, and he realised he had pressed her too far, too quickly. "I just don't know."

"Perhaps," he said gently, more the doctor himself now than the policeman, "perhaps we have come back again to Max's affair."

"I don't know what you mean," Judy said. "Stella wasn't

202

capable of loving anyone. I've explained already. She certainly wasn't capable of writing that letter."

"But perhaps," he said more gently, still reassuring her with his voice, telling her that he knew how hard all this was for her, "perhaps she knew who did write it."

"Blackmail!" Judy said. "You think Stella was blackmailing him about his lover."

"Is that possible?"

The speed and certainty of her answer surprised him. "Yes," Judy said. "She's a bitch. I'd believe anything of her."

She thought then that he was through, but he stayed on, pouring more tea for himself and for her, so that she knew his questions had not finished and she must brace herself again for another shock, more unpleasantness.

"You know who it is," she said suddenly, as if the thing would be easier to bear if it were she who took the initiative. "You know whom he's been having an affair with."

"I've an idea," he said. "I've no certainty."

"Well," she demanded. "Tell me!"

"There's a young reporter on the *Express*," he said, "called Mary Raven. She spoke to Alice Parry on the afternoon of her death. It's possible, don't you think, that she might have confided in the old lady about her love affair with Mrs. Parry's nephew. Especially if the affair was at an end, going badly. Then Mrs. Parry asked to speak to Max in private. Don't you think she might have been telling him to sort himself out, to come to a decision one way or another, that he wasn't being fair to either of you? All evening Mary Raven waited in the churchyard outside the Tower. Don't you think she was waiting for her secret lover, hoping that he would leave his wife, and then there would be no need to keep him secret anymore?"

"I know Mary," Judy said, almost to herself. "She comes here sometimes. I like her." Then she turned to Ramsay, her voice hoarse and shrill with distress. "What are you saying?" she asked. "Are you saying that Max and Mary *did* murder Alice? To stop their secret coming out? That's no

203

reason. I wouldn't have made a scene about the affair. We would have sorted something out. Tell me! What do you think happened?''

"I don't know," Ramsay said, aware that she needed the definite answer he was unable to give. "Perhaps nothing happened. Perhaps Max stayed in the Tower watching television and eventually Mary went away. We know she can't have killed Mrs. Parry herself. She was at a party in Newcastle when the murder was committed. Did Max tell you anything about what happened that night when you'd gone to bed?''

"No," she said. She looked sadly at Ramsay. "I've told you. He won't tell me anything at all.''

She turned to the policeman, suddenly angry and upset. "Max didn't kill Alice," she cried. "I know he wouldn't do anything like that. But I'll tell you something you should know. Do you know why Stella Laidlaw was taken into hospital, finally, after Carolyn was born? Because the health visitor turned up at the house one day and found her standing over the cot with a bread knife! If you ask James, he'll have to tell you. Or her doctor. If you're looking for a culprit, why don't you talk to her?''

But later, when Ramsay tried to telephone James at the *Express* office, Marjory told him that James was out all day. She was so skilled at protecting her boss that he could not tell whether she was telling the truth or not.

21

Brinkbonnie was quiet, its people shocked and in mourning. There had been tragedies in the village before—many years before a young boy, the son of a fisherman, had been swept from the beach by a freak wave and, more recently, the teacher's wife had been killed in a car crash on the Otterbridge Road—but on those occasions the grief was shared. People came together to remember the dead and fight off the sense of their own mortality. After the murders of Alice Parry and Charlie Elliot, that was impossible. There was nothing left to hold people together and households turned in on themselves, sometimes regarding members of their own family with doubt and mistrust. They spoke of Alice Parry and Charlie Elliot as little as possible and regarded the press and the police, who insisted on prying with questions, with equal hostility. Only the very old men, who saw the death of people younger than themselves as some sort of victory, continued to go to the pub and talk about the case with a grim humour.

On the farm on the hill Robert Grey worked as normal until the late afternoon, when he, too, went to the pub and got thoroughly drunk. At home he seemed preoccupied by some secret trouble of his own and he hardly talked to his wife and son. Ian was still at home from school and watched his father with curiosity, as if expecting some sudden, unpredictable outburst. He would have liked to go up to his father and offer him comfort, support, one man to another, but he knew that might offend his mother and he loved her too much for that. So Ian sat in the kitchen and watched his father across the farmyard.

Celia Grey was in the kitchen making bread. She stood at the table pushing and tearing at the dough while the smell of yeast filled the house. Ian was reminded of his grandmother, who had lived with them for as long as he could remember, but who had recently died. When he was younger, the old lady had baked every week. It occurred to Ian then that for generations women who looked like his mother had stood in the kitchen running the farm. In the only sense that mattered, the farm belonged to her. His father's name, scratched on the five-bar gate, was only a gesture of possession and independence. When the bread came out of the oven and Celia Grey knocked it out of the tins, it was, as he knew it would be, perfect. She was incapable of doing anything badly. She moved the kettle onto the hot part of the range.

"Go and fetch your father," she said. "Tell him I'm making some tea."

He nodded, pulled on Wellingtons, and went outside.

Robert Grey was in the far end of the tractor shed, in the shadow. He stood quite still, with his back to the boy.

"Dad," Ian said. "Mum said you're to come in for tea."

The farmer turned quickly. He was holding a wide screwdriver that looked like a knife.

"No," he said. "I'll not come in. I'll just finish this, then I'll be out of her way."

"Dad," Ian said. "What are you going to do? Things can't go on like this."

The farmer moved towards him, the screwdriver still in his hand.

"No," he said slowly. "Things can't go on like this."

He threw the screwdriver onto a grubby workbench and walked out across the yard towards the village.

Since Charlie Elliot's death the post office had been closed, and one of the major talking points in the pub among the old men was their inability to collect their pensions.

"Of course old Fred has had a bad time," they grumbled, "but it's about time he started thinking about other folk."

Even the news that a relief postmistress would be sent out from Otterbridge the following week did nothing to console them. It wouldn't be the same, they said. Nothing in the village would be the same.

Fred Elliot would not talk to anybody except his widowed sister who had come down from Berwick to look after him and to her he spoke only in monosyllables. He could not explain to her his sense of responsibility, but he went over it again and again in his mind. He knew it was all his fault. If he had told the policeman about Charlie leaving the house again on Saturday night, his son might still be alive.

"I only did what I thought best," he repeated to his sister, who clucked about him not listening, not understanding.

"Of course you did, pet," she said. "Of course you did."

Sometimes when his sister was busy, he would escape to the shed in the backyard to count and tidy the piles of waste-paper, which he intended to sell to provide funds for the hospital where his wife had died. That gave him some comfort, but his sister always found him there and dragged him back to the fire as if he were a naughty child.

"It won't do you any good," she said, "brooding on your own out there." She sat him in his favourite armchair and made him tea and pretended not to notice that he was crying.

In the house behind the garage Maggie sometimes found the tension almost unbearable. Work was no relief with the old men gloatingly reconstructing the crimes as they slurped their beer. Often, when the boys came home from school, she ran away with them and the dogs to the beach. There they would chase together into the wind, shouting to each other, laughing, trying to forget the solemn silence in the house, the sound of Olive crying to herself in her bedroom when she thought no-one was listening. The boys made death-defying leaps from the highest dunes to the beach and ran along the water's edge until the water splashed over their Wellingtons.

Despite the secret sobbing, Maggie was more concerned

207

about her father than her mother. It was natural that her mother should be upset. She and Alice Parry had been friends. But in a week her father seemed to have aged so that she hardly recognised him. He had always been the stern one, the one to insist on discipline when the boys misbehaved at table, to supervise their schoolwork. Now he was hardly aware of their presence. The boys sensed it and stole unusual privileges—late television, sweets before meals, rudeness to their mother—but still they failed to provoke him to any reaction.

On Friday morning, almost a week after Alice Parry's death, Tom Kerr had arranged to meet the vicar in the church to discuss the music for Easter. Kerr was also sacristan and he felt a major responsibility for preparing the church for the festival, but throughout the conversation his mind wandered and he saw the priest looking at him strangely.

"I'm sorry," he said. "This terrible business has upset me. I can't concentrate on anything."

"No," the vicar said. "Of course."

Let me talk to you, Kerr wanted to say. I need help. But the moment was lost and the vicar looked at his watch and then hurried away to a mothers' union meeting in the neighbouring parish. Kerr lingered in the church.

Maggie found him there, sitting on one of the pews close to the aisle, not praying but staring at the light coming through the stained-glass window above the altar.

"Dad," she said. "What's the matter? Mam's worried about you. She saw the vicar leave half an hour ago."

She squeezed past and sat beside him on the polished pew. It was Lent and the church was bare. Maggie wished her father would stand up and walk out into the fresh air. Churches made her uncomfortable.

"I don't know what to do," Tom Kerr said. "I've been foolish. I'm in terrible trouble and I don't know what to do to put it right."

"Tell me," she said. "Perhaps I can help."

"No," he said sharply. "This is my business. No-one else must get involved. I'll have to sort it out for myself."

208

"It's my fault, isn't it?" she cried. "It's something to do with Charlie. What have you done?"

He turned to face her and the warm light from the stained glass reflected on his spectacles so that she could not see his eyes.

"You'll have to leave it to me," he said. "Now go away. I want to be on my own to think."

She left him, trying to tell herself that he was a stubborn man with too many principles. His imagined crimes would be trivial compared with the things she could dream up. But she remembered his terrifying and merciless temper and her anxiety grew.

When Ramsay arrived in Brinkbonnie at midday, he went to the garage first. If Henshaw were blackmailing or threatening one of the leaders of the village, Ramsay thought, Tom Kerr would know. He seemed to have assumed responsibility for the place's moral welfare. The workshop was unlocked and Ramsay went inside, but it was empty, and when he knocked at the door of the house, there was no reply. He walked on past the row of cottages and crossed the road towards the pub. In the Tower field the surveyors were back, sitting close to the hedge to eat their sandwiches so that they could not be easily seen from the street.

In the Castle Hotel Maggie Kerr was behind the bar and the same old men sat staring at their beer and the dominoes board. There Ramsay made himself popular. He bought them all drinks and sat down with them and encouraged them to gossip. There must be scandal in a village like this, he said. There must be secrets, skeletons in cupboards. The old men chuckled and said he was right. "Man, you could write a book about the things that go on in this village." But their scandals had happened years before. They talked about the American soldiers based in Otterbridge and children born out of wedlock during the war. They talked of family feuds and grievances stored for twenty years. None of it helped Ramsay at all, and he was about to leave when they started talking about Robert and Celia Grey. Again they began their story many years before. It had all started with the old lady, they

209

said, Celia's mother. She was the cause of all their problems, sitting in the corner of the kitchen like a poisonous old spider, giving out her orders. No wonder Celia went a bit wild when the old cow died.

"Wild?" Ramsay said. "I wouldn't call Celia Grey wild."

"No," they said. "Well, strong-willed then. She knows what she wants and nothing will stop her getting it."

"Tell me about it," Ramsay said, buying more drinks, hoping for details.

The old men accepted the drinks but became coy when he pressed them to be more specific about the Greys' problems. They were happier talking about the past.

Ramsay became impatient and left the pub for the post office. Under the watchful eye of Elliot's sister, he talked to the postmaster.

"Mr. Elliot," he said carefully. "When you first got involved with the Save Brinkbonnie campaign, did Henshaw ever approach you with money to stop your objections?"

Elliot looked up at him in wonder. "No," he said. "Even Henshaw knows me well enough to realise I'd not be taken in by anything like that."

That was true, Ramsay thought. Fred Elliot was the last person Henshaw would approach to sabotage the campaign. He was too obviously incorruptible.

"What about Charlie?" Ramsay asked. "Did Henshaw put any pressure on Charlie?"

But at the name of his son Fred Elliot went to pieces. He began to cry and his sister stood between them, holding her apron wide as if she were protecting a child from a dangerous animal. She made strange shooing noises.

"Go away," she said. "Can't you see he's no use to you? Leave him to grieve in peace."

So Ramsay went back onto the street to continue his search for information.

In the churchyard preparations were beginning for Alice Parry's funeral. An old man leaned on a spade, pressing it against the turf as if testing to see how hard a job he would have in digging the grave. He seemed daunted by the task

210

because he laid the spade on the grass and began to walk away towards the back of the church.

"Excuse me!" Ramsay shouted, and the old man turned slowly to stare at him. "Have you seen Mr. Kerr?"

The gravedigger looked at him, giving no sign that he had heard the question.

"You must know Mr. Kerr," Ramsay said. "He's the choirmaster."

"No," the old man said. "I've not seen him today." He walked off.

On the church porch, emerging at last to go back to the garage to work, Tom Kerr heard the exchange. He leaned against the closed door and waited until he heard the policeman move on before he scuttled home across the green, but he knew it would be impossible to hide from Ramsay for ever.

Ramsay moved up the Otterbridge Road towards the Henshaws' bungalow. It was likely, he thought, that Colin Henshaw would be out during the day. Perhaps Rosemary Henshaw would speak to him more freely if he saw her alone. He turned into the drive and was relieved to see that the garage was empty. The Renault was parked on the gravel, but Henshaw's Rover had gone.

Rosemary Henshaw looked more comfortable, more approachable than when Ramsay had last seen her. She still wore makeup, but she was not so shiny or impenetrable as she had been that Sunday night. She was dressed in a pale green jogging suit that was stretched across her stomach. Ramsay thought he had disturbed her in the middle of her lunch. When she opened the door, she was brushing crumbs from the front of her sweatshirt.

"Yes?" she said. Then: "You're the policeman, aren't you. You were here the other night."

Ramsay smiled at her. "You were kind enough to tell me to drop in if I thought you could help," he said.

Hunter isn't the only one who can turn on the charm, he thought. But Hunter's so much better at it than I am.

"Of course," she said. She seemed pleased to have the

company. "Come into the kitchen. I was just having a sandwich. Perhaps you'd like something."

"You're not expecting your husband?" Ramsay said.

She giggled as if the questions were a proposition. "He's always busy," she said. "He's working on different developments all over the country. I never know where he's working, but he lets me know if he's going to be back early and he's said nothing today."

She took him through the house, which was as glossy and dust-free as her face, to the kitchen, which seemed full of electrical gadgets. There was a portable television on a work top and an earnest young woman with a shrill Scottish accent gave consumer advice. Rosemary Henshaw switched it off.

"What would you like to eat?" she asked. "I could pop something from the freezer into the microwave. It wouldn't take a minute. Or a sandwich. I could do you a sandwich."

Ramsay said that a sandwich would be very nice. She sliced a stottie deftly and began to fill it with ham and tomato.

"What time did your husband go out this morning?" Ramsay asked.

"I don't know," she said, giggling again. "He was gone when I got up. I'm dreadful in the mornings. He sees himself out."

"What about Tuesday morning?" Ramsay asked. "Did he go out early then?"

"Why?" she asked, suddenly suspicious. "What's this all about?"

Ramsay answered the question though he knew she must already know why he was asking. She was no fool.

"Charlie Elliot was murdered on Tuesday morning, very early," Ramsay said. "You must have heard that."

"I heard he was dead," she said. "I didn't ask for any details. I don't want to know."

"He was stabbed," Ramsay said. "Just like Alice Parry."

"I don't understand what's going on," she cried. "Everyone said he killed the old lady."

"Well," Ramsay said. "Now he's dead."

There was a silence and then she turned to him.

"Why are you here?" she asked. "I don't understand what it has to do with us."

"It's to do with everybody," he said, suddenly angry. "Everyone in Brinkbonnie. Alice Parry and Charlie Elliot lived here. Elliot's body was found in the small stone barn on the hill behind your house. The land is owned by your neighbours, the Greys. You all have an interest in getting the thing resolved."

"Yes," she said, though he could not tell if she understood. "Yes, I see that."

"So," he said gently. "Will you tell me where your husband was on Tuesday morning?" He watched her face, saw her prepare to lie then change her mind.

"I don't know," she said. "He did go out very early. I heard him go and it was still dark. I presumed it was work."

"Did you ask him why he left so early?"

"No," she said. She gave no explanation for the lack of communication between them. "No."

"And what about Saturday night?" Ramsay asked softly. "He did go out, didn't he, after Alice Parry left your house?"

"Yes," she said, and began to cry. Tears were her usual weapon against confrontation. "I don't know where he was. He won't tell me."

"What happened when Mrs. Parry was here on Saturday night?" Ramsay asked. She was so distraught that he hoped she would answer without thinking, under the spell of his sympathy. "It wasn't a cosy little chat after all, was it?"

But if he expected her to be honest, he was disappointed. She looked up sharply and he knew she was preparing to lie.

"It was!" she said. She seemed terrified. "It happened just like Colin told you."

"There's no reason to be frightened, you know," he said. "We can give you all the protection you need."

"No!" she cried. "I don't need protection from Colin. He's my husband. You're mad."

She was almost hysterical and seemed not to care that he did not believe her. He sat in silence, hoping that she might

213

grow calmer and volunteer to change her story, but she got up and fetched a packet of cigarettes from her handbag.

She lit one, her hands shaking. Eventually she did regain her composure, but her story did not change.

"You must understand," she said at last, "that Colin and Mrs. Parry got on very well that evening. She was angry when she arrived, but by the time she left, things had been sorted out between them."

"How had things been sorted out?" Ramsay asked. "What did your husband say to Mrs. Parry to make her change her mind?"

"Nothing," she said awkwardly, but she would not meet his eyes. "There was nothing to tell. She realised, I suppose, that the battle had been lost. There was nothing she could do to make him change his mind."

There was a silence. Through the kitchen window Ramsay saw the elderly gardener push a barrow of dead leaves over the patio towards the compost heap.

"I'm sorry to have upset you," Ramsay said. "It's been a difficult time for everyone. Could you answer a few more questions?"

She nodded.

"It's about your husband's business," Ramsay said. "I'm a layman and there are some points in the planning procedure that I don't quite understand. Quite often the local council rejects his plans, but Mr. Henshaw always seems to win an appeal. Can you explain how he does that?"

She looked at him suspiciously, thinking that the question had some deeper significance.

"He's clever," she said. "He knows what the planning inspector will accept." Then she smiled. "Besides, he's a lot of important contacts."

"Yes," Ramsay said. "I'm sure he has. I wanted to ask you about that. Did he ever discuss his contacts with you? In Brinkbonnie, for example, did he have someone to help him here?"

She shook her head. "I can't help you," she said quickly.

214

"You'll have to talk to Colin. I don't know anything about his business. I told that reporter the same."

"Oh," Ramsay said. "Has Mary Raven been bothering you again?"

"Yes," Rosemary Henshaw said, glad of the change of subject. "Nosy little madam. She was here today calling for Colin. I told her he didn't want to talk to her. She said it would be good publicity for his business. I told her he was doing well enough. He didn't need her sort of publicity."

"When was she here?" Ramsay asked.

"Not very long ago," she said. "Just before I started my lunch. I'm surprised you didn't see her on the road."

She stood up and began to fuss with coffee, searching in a tin for biscuits. But Ramsay did not want to prolong the interview. He had learned enough.

"Will you tell Mr. Henshaw that I'll be in the police house in the village until this evening," he said as he left. "There might be something he wants to tell me."

Then he went out, striding down the drive and the Otterbridge Road through Brinkbonnie, walking in the middle of the street so that the people hiding behind their net curtains would not miss him. He wanted everyone to see him make his way to the police house. He was convinced that someone in the village had information for him.

22

In the police house Hunter was coordinating the search for Max Laidlaw.

"We should find Mary Raven," Ramsay said. "I'm sure he was having an affair with her. She'll lead you to him. She's been in Brinkbonnie today."

"What has she been doing here?" Hunter was hardly interested. That bloody woman, he thought. Ramsay's obsessed with her.

She wants to speak to Henshaw. Something to do with a story."

"Bloody reporters," Hunter said.

"I want you to go to Wytham," Ramsay said, "to talk to a woman there." He was torn. He would have liked to go to Wytham himself to see the woman Robson had suggested. He was still committed to the theory that Henshaw was a blackmailer. But it was more important, he thought, to stay in Brinkbonnie, to be accessible if one of the community leaders there wanted to speak to him. He explained Robson's idea to Hunter and was aware immediately of the sergeant's scepticism.

"Talk to her," he said. "Be discreet. Just ask how she planned the campaign against Henshaw and why it came to nothing in the end. Find out if she was really active all the way through. You might need to talk to other people in the place, too. If she makes some excuse for having dropped out

of the fight, press her. Be sympathetic. Give her the chance
to tell you. Ask if Henshaw made any contact with her.''

Go teach your grandmother to suck eggs, Hunter thought,
but he said nothing. He was glad of the excuse to get out of
Brinkbonnie. He hated the lack of activity and the constant
wind. A few new houses would be an improvement, he
thought. They might even liven the place up.

He found Jane Massie's house very easily. It was, as Jack
Robson had said, close to the new housing estate on the
opposite side of the main road, backing onto open countryside. As he parked, Hunter looked at the development with
some envy. If he won the pools, he thought, he wouldn't
mind living in a place like that. Somewhere with a bit of
class and style. In contrast, the Massies' house was not to
his taste. It was built of grey stone, square and solid. The
window frames needed a lick of paint.

When Hunter knocked at the door, there was no reply, and
he found Jane Massie in the long back garden feeding hens.
She was a short woman, rather overweight, probably in her
early thirties. He was surprised. From Ramsay's description,
he had expected someone older. She was wearing a calf-
length dress in a patterned corduroy and the sort of shoes
with buckles he had only seen on children. He dismissed her
in his mind as an aging hippie, but all the same he found her
attractive. Her face was young and very pretty. When she
saw him, she hitched up her skirt and climbed out of the hen
run to meet him. Two small boys in dungarees appeared from
the hen house and clambered after her.

She did not seem shocked to see a stranger wandering
through the back garden. She seemed, to Hunter, to have
great self-confidence. He knew few women like her and was
nervous.

"Hello," she said. "Can I help you?" She came, as he
had expected, from the south.

The boys hid behind her.

"Mrs. Massie," he said, "I'm Sergeant Hunter from the
Northumbria police. Could I have a few words with you?"

"Yes," she said. "What's wrong? There's not been an accident?"

"No," he said. "It's nothing like that."

She took him into the house through a back door into a kitchen that smelled of lentils and garlic. She rinsed her hands under the tap.

"I'm sorry I panicked," she said. "My husband's away on business. I hate the thought of him driving down the A1. You hear of so many accidents. Would you like some tea? We don't drink coffee, I'm afraid."

He nodded.

"How can I help you?" she asked. In the garden the boys were splashing each other from muddy puddles, but she made no attempt to stop them. He thought his mother would have skinned him alive if he'd dirtied his clothes like that.

"We're conducting an investigation into certain planning irregularities that might have taken place when the estate over the road was built," he said. "I understand you were involved in opposing the development."

"I certainly was," she said. "It's a dreadful eyesore. It's about time someone put a stop to Henshaw. It's too late for us, but it might stop some other village from being ruined."

"Were you aware while you were running the campaign that some of Henshaw's tactics might be dishonest?" he asked.

"No," she said. "Not exactly. Everything seemed to be going as we had expected until the builder appealed to the Department of the Environment inspector. It was a terrible surprise then when Henshaw won."

"Were you involved in the campaign all the way through?"

"Oh, yes," she said angrily. "Even when everyone all around me seemed to be losing interest. I kept going to the bitter end."

"What do you mean that the people around you lost interest?"

She shrugged. "I don't know," she said. "The village just seemed to give up and accept its fate."

218

"It wasn't that one or two prominent members of your committee dropped out?"

She shook her head. "No," she said. "It was nothing like that. The committee remained remarkably united. They were very supportive."

There was a pause. Hunter drank his tea.

"It couldn't have been that at the end of the campaign you all got"—he hesitated, searching for the word he wanted—"complacent? You thought you would win so you didn't bother to put up much of a fight?"

"No," she said. "Really, I've thought about it and I'm sure our tactics were just right. My husband's in public relations and he advised us. Look, if you're interested, I can show you a file of letters I sent asking for support—to councillors, the local M.P., the media. I kept copies of them all. We had a concerted attack in the last couple of weeks just before the appeal was heard."

She disappeared into another room and returned with a yellow envelope file bursting with typewritten notes and letters. She sorted through them and took out a handful to show Hunter.

"Look," she said. "All these are dated in the month before the appeal. I really don't think we could have done any more. We just didn't get the response from the public that we could have hoped for. Perhaps the campaign had just been going on for too long and they had a sort of protest fatigue. This sort of development had happened so often in the county that it just didn't seem exciting anymore."

"Do you know Henshaw?" Hunter asked. "Personally?"

She laughed. "No," she said. "We don't move in the same social circles."

"Did he ever approach you during the campaign?"

"Not during the campaign," she said. "He came here afterwards, when the inspector's decision was finally made public, to gloat. He stood on the doorstep and shook my hand and said that now that the due process of law had been completed he hoped we could be good neighbours."

"What did you say?"

She shrugged. "What could I say? As far as I knew he was right. Everything was legal and aboveboard. I was as gracious as I could manage, wished him luck for the future, and asked him for a donation for playgroup equipment. As he was so keen to be a good neighbour. I'm on the playgroup committee and we're always short of money."

"Did you get your donation?" Hunter asked.

She smiled wryly. "Oh, yes, we got it. And just as the bulldozers were moving in, there was a picture in the local paper of Henshaw surrounded by grateful toddlers and piles of new toys. He knows more about public relations than my husband."

"Yes," Hunter said. "I see." So Ramsay was wrong again, he thought. He should have more sense than to believe Jack Robson's fairy stories.

She looked at her watch. "I haven't been a lot of help, have I?" she asked. "If there's nothing else you want to know, I'll have to be out soon to collect my older boys from school. I should avoid that while you've got the chance. There'll be no peace then."

She let him out of the back door and into the garden again. As he left he saw her rounding up her sons, scolding them halfheartedly for the state they were in, laughing as she gathered them to her.

In the police house Ramsay sat alone and waited for something to happen. He was not sure what he was expecting but sensed that they were close to some resolution. He put out a general call that he should be notified of Mary Raven's whereabouts, but he did not want to apprehend her. If they found Max Laidlaw, he should be brought in for questioning immediately.

He telephoned Judy, who answered the phone very quickly.

"Yes," she said. "Who's there?" He could sense her holding her breath, praying that it was her husband.

"I'm sorry," he said. "It's Inspector Ramsay. I was calling to find out if you've heard from your husband."

220

"No," she said. "I've heard nothing. No-one seems to know where he is."

The children must have been returned to her because in the background he heard one of the children calling for a drink.

"Try not to worry," he said. "If Max does get in touch, perhaps you could let me know."

"Yes," she said. She sounded exhausted. "Of course." She seemed not even to have the energy to replace the receiver because as he pressed the cradle to cut off the call he heard the toddler talking again.

The afternoon wore on and he waited for a knock at the door, for the message that someone in the village wanted to talk to him. He switched on the light to make the place more welcoming and phoned the Otterbridge Incident Room again. Mary Raven had been seen in Otterbridge, they said. They were keeping an eye on her.

"Don't lose her!" Ramsay said. "And don't pick her up unless she takes you to Max Laidlaw."

He settled down to wait again.

He welcomed Hunter's return at least as a break from the tension, but he was disappointed that it was the policeman and not one of the locals who stood outside waiting to be let in.

"Well?" he demanded as soon as Hunter was inside. "How did you get on?"

Hunter shook his head. "I'm sorry," he said. "Robson's theory won't work. Jane Massie was really committed to the campaign to stop the houses being built. I believed her. She showed me evidence, too. She wrote lots of letters all the way through. There's no way that the campaign collapsed because she dropped out, and she says that the same committee ran the thing all the way through. No-one made any excuses to leave or not pull their weight."

Ramsay was listening intently. "Did Henshaw make any approaches to her while the planning process was going through?" he asked.

Hunter shook his head again. "Not until it was all over,"

he said, "and then he gave a donation to the village playgroup. Jane Massie runs that, too."

Then Ramsay lost patience. He had been waiting long enough. He wanted to talk to Henshaw again, to confront him with his wife's statement that he had left the house on Saturday night after Alice Parry's visit. He felt that the builder was mocking him.

"Stay here," he said to Hunter. "I'm expecting someone from the village to make an approach. Be gentle with them. I don't want them frightened off."

He slammed the door behind him and walked quickly across the green to the Otterbridge Road. Perhaps it was because he was so angry and preoccupied that he made the same mistake as he had on the night after Alice Parry's murder and walked into the Greys' farmyard instead of the Henshaws' drive. The place was quiet. He felt rather ridiculous, standing in the muddy farmyard looking round him absentmindedly, and the embarrassment of his previous mistake returned. He imagined Celia Grey looking down on him from one of the upstairs windows, sneering at his indecision. It would be impossible now to turn round and go away. Charlie Elliot's body had been found on Grey's land, so he had a perfectly good excuse for being there. So, still imagining that he was being watched, trying to present an air of purpose, he walked towards the back door. If it had not been for his pride, he would never have seen Henshaw's Rover tucked into one of the machinery sheds. Only the bumper was showing.

The back door was slightly open and the kitchen was empty. He knocked and called, but no-one answered. He waited, still thinking that his approach had been seen, then pushed open the door and went inside. The farmyard had been full of late-afternoon sunshine and long, warm shadows. When he entered the shadow of the kitchen, he shivered. He put his hand on the top of the range, but it was cold. The kitchen was much tidier than it had been on his previous visit, the sink and draining board empty, the work surfaces clear except for a bowl of rather mucky, recently collected eggs. The tile floor had been washed and in one corner it was still damp. He moved on through the door that led into the rest of the house, into the entrance hall where he had stood with Celia Grey on his last visit, trying to persuade her to allow him to talk to her son. The sun came in from an upstairs window and lit the specks of dust in the stairwell. There were two other doors leading from the hall. Both were huge and heavy and must have blocked out all sound. Both were shut tight. He called out and his voice echoed over the stone flags: "Mrs. Grey! Are you there?" Immediately after speaking he opened the nearest of the doors.

They were sitting together in a small living room. Ramsay guessed that Celia Grey would consider it her own room. It would not be used by the rest of the family. It had no television and he could not imagine a teenage boy in here. The windows were small and it was still in shadow. There was a brick fireplace with a bowl of dried flowers on the grate. On a small sofa Henshaw and Celia sat close to each other. Henshaw was turned towards her, holding one of her hands in both of his. When he saw Ramsay, standing just inside the room, he jumped to his feet.

"What the hell do you think you're doing here?" he demanded. "I thought you needed a search warrant before you did this sort of thing."

"I did knock," Ramsay said mildly. "I was hoping to talk to Mrs. Grey, but it's convenient that you're here, too."

"You can't talk to her now," Henshaw blustered. "Can't you see that she's upset? You know what they found on their land earlier this week. It's been a terrible shock."

"Did Mrs. Grey have a shock on the evening of Alice Parry's death?" Ramsay asked.

"What do you mean?"

"You came here, didn't you, on Saturday night?" Ramsay asked. Without waiting for an answer, he turned to Celia Grey. "I think your husband was away," he said, "and you sent your son out into the village. But Mr. Henshaw was late. He had an unexpected visitor. Someone it was hard to

223

get rid of. Was Mr. Henshaw still here when Ian came home? Perhaps we should ask your son.''

"What are you saying?'' It was Henshaw again, red-faced with anger and concern. "Bob and Celia are neighbours, friends. I'm here because I heard that Charlie Elliot had been found in the barn. I wanted to offer my help. He's a good chap, Bob, but not very imaginative. I thought she might need some support.''

"Do you always park your car in the shed so it can't be seen from the road?'' Ramsay asked reasonably, and Henshaw's outburst seemed unbalanced and irrational.

"I don't know what you mean,'' Henshaw said. "You should watch what you're saying.''

Celia Grey stood up and both men fell silent. "It's no good, Colin,'' she said. "He knows. I told you it would all come out in the end.''

"It's none of their business,'' Henshaw muttered. He gazed at her sentimentally. "How could anyone else understand?''

"I'm afraid it is my business,'' Ramsay said. "Do you realise that you're a suspect in a murder enquiry, Mr. Henshaw? We believe that Charlie Elliot was murdered by the same person as Alice Parry. We're still looking for her killer. If you have any information that would eliminate you from our enquiries, it would be in your interest to give it.''

"Colin was here when Alice Parry was killed,'' Celia Grey said. "You were right. My husband was visiting his mother in hospital in the Lake District. I'd rather you didn't ask my son, but you were right about that, too. Colin was still here when he arrived home.''

"What about Monday evening?'' Ramsay asked. "Was Mr. Henshaw here then, too? Is that why you didn't notice any noise in the farmyard?''

She nodded.

"Thank you,'' Ramsay said. They were a strangely matched couple, he thought. She seemed so upright and cold. He could picture her dressed in Puritan black and white as one of the New England settlers, motivated by principle and guilt.

Henshaw, in contrast, was driven by greed and ambition and seemed to have no sense of morality at all. Yet he looked at her now with tenderness and admiration and he had done everything in his power to protect her. "It would have been easier," Ramsay said, "if you'd told me straightaway."

"I couldn't have Celia bothered," Henshaw muttered. "I had to consider her reputation. She has her position in the village to think about. Don't you know she's chairwoman of the WI?"

There was no irony in his voice. It seemed to Ramsay then that Henshaw was the innocent and Celia Grey was the corrupter of souls. He wondered when and how the relationship had started. He thought it could have no future.

"Now I know all about your affair," he said. "Perhaps you could tell me what *really* happened in your conversation with Alice Parry."

"Nothing," Henshaw said rudely. "I've told you everything that happened. There's nothing more to say."

Ramsay did not believe him, but time was slipping past and he was no nearer to reaching a solution. He left them, closeted in the half darkness, sharing their secret, frightened affection.

23

*B*y early evening of the same day, Mary Raven had her story. It was complex. She would have preferred to talk to Henshaw, of course. She was convinced that he played a part in it somewhere. But she had evidence enough without him, and she had not tried too hard to find him. She had rattled into Brinkbonnie in the morning, staying long enough to annoy Rosemary Henshaw, then driven on to talk to other people in different places. At the back of her mind all the time there was her concern for Max, and as she drove along, she stared out as if she might see him by chance walking down the pavement towards her. Perhaps the anxiety clouded her judgement because she had no sense of danger.

She had gone to the west of Newcastle to a converted warehouse where an ex-councillor had set up a charitable trust for alcoholics. She talked to the man and all of the residents, as well as an old lady who had lived rough for years, walking from the Scottish borders to the Tees every summer, and who had been persuaded to make her home in this building off the Scotswood Road with its view of the Tyne. Then Mary drove back to Otterbridge to the geriatric hospital and talked to another old lady, her body as fine and frail as a pipe-cleaner doll, her mind as bright and clear as a child's, her memory perfect. By this time Mary was pushed on not only by ambition but by anger.

When she got to her flat, Mary saw her landlady, who

lived in the house next door, staring at her curiously through the living-room window. When Mary moved she disappeared guiltily, so Mary thought: She's planning to put the rent up again. But the landlady had promised to phone the police as soon as Mary got home. She thought Mary was a nice girl and had never liked the police, so it was a difficult and awkward thing to do.

Inside the flat Mary boiled the kettle, made a mug of coffee, and started in her mind to write her story. Absent-mindedly she went to collect her mail from the front door. There was a leaflet about the poll tax, and hand-delivered, still stuck in the flap of the letter box, a note.

"Meet me," it said. "Brinkbonnie dunes. Eight o'clock."

He had signed it with the incomprehensible scribble that could only be deciphered by colleagues and pharmacists.

She stood for a moment in the grimy, ill-lit hall holding the note and staring at it. The coffee mug in the other hand tilted and tipped hot liquid over the carpet and her foot. There was none of the elation she might have expected. She was glad he was safe and had apparently so far avoided arrest, but she was not even sure if she wanted to see him.

I'm tired, she thought. I can't handle this. Not now. I need a drink.

The day before, she would have been overjoyed to receive such a summons from Max. Now it was just something else to worry about.

She walked into the living room and propped the note in the typewriter her parents had given her as an eighteenth-birthday present. She stared at it anxiously as if it were a bomb. She looked at her watch. It was seven-thirty already. She went to the window to draw the curtains to put off making a decision. The street was empty. Whatever shadow she had imagined had been following her had disappeared. It was all hallucination, she thought. I'm losing my mind. She finished her coffee and took the empty mug into the kitchen. The phone began to ring, disturbing and insistent. Suddenly, just to avoid answering it, she picked up her jacket and car

227

keys and went outside, leaving the light on in the living room and the note in the typewriter.

Carolyn Laidlaw arrived home from school on Friday evening to find the house empty. She had her own key and let herself in, apprehensive about what she might find there. She switched on the radio to Metro, almost expecting to hear on the local news that someone had been arrested for the Brinkbonnie murders, but there was only a bland announcement that the police were following a number of leads.

In her parents' bedroom she found signs that her mother had left the house in a hurry. There were the clothes that she had been wearing that morning flung on the floor and in the bathroom a tap had been left running. Carolyn was tempted to search through the dressing-table drawers while she had the house to herself, but while she would have welcomed certainty she was frightened about what she might find there.

Her father had said he would be working late and she wondered if she should contact him at the office to find out where her mother was, but she knew that would worry him, so she kept her fear to herself, listening all the time to the radio, until she heard the key in the door. Then she could not stop crying.

The discovery that Colin Henshaw could not have killed Alice Parry left Ramsay with a sense of panic. At first he could not think clearly. Perhaps Henshaw had hired someone to commit the murder, he thought, because his commitment to Robson's theory was so great that he was reluctant to let it go. But that would not work. If Henshaw had not killed Mrs. Parry, Charlie Elliot could have had nothing to blackmail the builder about, and the motive for the second murder disappeared, too. Ramsay had been certain that this evening would mark the end of the investigation, and now it seemed they would have to start at the beginning again and reconsider all the old evidence. Hunter had been right all along, Ramsay thought. This case was about more than a few houses.

In the police house Hunter was almost asleep. His chair

228

was tilted backwards and his feet were on the desk. When Ramsay came into the room, he sat up slowly and stretched.

"Well?" he said. "How did you get on?"

"Henshaw is having an affair with Celia Grey at the farm," Ramsay said. "He was there on Saturday night, so he couldn't have killed Alice Parry. He might have murdered Charlie Elliot, but I can't see what motive he would have had."

Hunter knew better than to gloat. "At least we've eliminated Henshaw from our enquiries then," he said. "That's a positive move."

"Yes," Ramsay said. He did not feel positive. "I suppose so."

"Someone came to talk to you while you were out," Hunter said. "He wouldn't speak to me. Tom Kerr. From the garage." He looked at the desk where he had scribbled notes on an envelope. "He said he'll be in all evening. On his own. The rest of the family will be out. He seemed to think that was important."

Ramsay listened absent-mindedly. Now that Robson's theory of local activists having been put under pressure by Henshaw seemed impossible, he was not sure what useful information Tom Kerr could have.

"He seemed very keen to talk to you," Hunter said. "A bit tense and strung-up."

"All right," Ramsay said. "I'll go and see him now. Is there anything from the Incident Room?"

"Yes," Hunter said. "Some bright P.C. thought he saw Mary Raven's Mini outside the old Cottage Hospital in Otterbridge. God knows what she was doing there."

"Well, you won't know," Ramsay said, "unless you ask. Go to the hospital and find out. Max Laidlaw is a doctor. Perhaps he's hiding out there. I'll meet you in the Incident Room later."

At first Ramsay thought that the house behind the garage was empty. Although it was nearly dark, there were no lights on and everything was quiet. When the sun went down, the temperature had suddenly dropped and he waited impatiently

229

on the doorstep to be let in. At last he heard footsteps on the other side of the door and then Tom Kerr opened it and waited silently for Ramsay to follow him into the house.

He must have been sitting, Ramsay thought, just by the light of the fire, but now he switched on a small lamp that revealed the tension in his face. His cheeks were drawn and behind his glasses his eyelids seemed grey and heavy.

"Inspector," he said. "It was good of you to come. Sit by the fire. You'll be cold."

Ramsay sat and waited for an explanation, but the words when they came still surprised him.

"Inspector," Kerr said. "My conscience has been troubling me. There's something you should know. . . ."

Ramsay said nothing but waited for the man to speak again.

Kerr stared into the fire. "I have a temper," he said. "A terrible temper. Since I was a child it's got me into trouble."

Still Ramsay remained silent. The man needed to talk. Interruption would only distract him.

"Even when Charlie and Maggie were children I found it hard to like him," Tom Kerr said. "I was not sorry when Maggie broke off that first engagement. I found Charlie moody, unstable. I thought such an attachment was unnatural at that age. They shouldn't have been taking things so seriously."

He paused, apparently in deep thought, perhaps remembering his daughter when she was a girl.

"It wasn't any easier when he left the army and came back. I told myself that Margaret was partly responsible and the the boy had been genuinely misled about the way she felt, but it was hard to find any sympathy for him. Perhaps that's why I took him on in the garage. I thought that if I could not find any charity for him in my heart, I could at least go some way to meet his practical needs. It was a mistake, a form of pride. I suppose I wanted the village to see that I was not lacking in duty. Even though he was a reasonable worker, he annoyed me. I dreaded going to work. Then things came to a head and there was a fight in

230

the street. I lost my temper. If I'd had the chance, I would have killed him.''

''Mr. Kerr,'' Ramsay said. ''Is this why you wanted to talk to me? To tell me about the fight? I had already heard about it. It really shouldn't cause you any anxiety. There's no question that the police would prosecute after all this time.'' He felt a sense of anticlimax.

''No!'' Tom Kerr cried. ''I'm trying to explain. That's how it all started. But the real wickedness came later.''

''I think,'' Ramsay said, ''you should tell me all about it.''

The man started speaking, bending towards Ramsay across the fire in an attempt to explain his actions, pleading indirectly for understanding. When Ramsay stood up half an hour later to drive into Otterbridge, he thought he knew why Alice Parry had been murdered. He left Tom Kerr still sitting by the fire. The confession seemed to have brought him little relief and Ramsay was not sure if it was wise to leave him alone.

''You can go,'' Kerr said. ''Olive will be back soon. I'll talk to her then.''

In the car Ramsay spoke to Otterbridge control on the radio. ''If you see Mary Raven, I want her stopped and brought in for questioning,'' he said, almost shouting in his jubiliation. ''Find her for me now.''

Hunter thought that the visit to the old Cottage Hospital would be a waste of time. There must be dozens of orange Minis in Otterbridge, he thought. The policeman on the beat must have made a mistake. Why would Mary Raven want to go there? The place had been changed to specialise in the care of geriatrics about ten years previously when a big, new district hospital had been built just outside the town. He had been there once before to visit an elderly aunt who was dying and he had hoped never to step inside the place again.

He found it easy enough to find out who Mary had been talking to. The arrival of a reporter in the unit had caused something of a stir among the people who could find little to

231

change the routine of their days. Those who were well enough to communicate were still talking about it as they sat in their beds to eat the evening meal. There was the smell of vegetables and milk pudding.

They brought the old lady to him in a wheelchair and he sat in the sweltering day room with its dying potted plants and ancient magazines and listened while she repeated her story. Outside it was dark and eventually the woman slipped into sleep, almost in midsentence. A brisk and cheerful nursing sister who had heard it all before filled in the gaps. It made little sense to Hunter, but he had the intelligence to realise how it might be important. When he emerged from the hospital into the quiet, tree-lined street, he thought that Ramsay would be pleased.

He and Ramsay arrived at the police station at the same time, both excited, both wanting to share their discoveries, so they had to sit in the office and make time to listen before they could make sense of it all.

"It works," Ramsay said, and thought that Jack Robson had almost been right.

Then they heard that a call had been received from Mary Raven's landlady saying that the reporter had returned to her flat.

"Send someone to bring her in," Ramsay said, and then they had to wait. Despite the friction that had been there between them during the course of the investigation, they seemed very close as they shared the anticipation.

The constable sent to fetch Mary Raven came onto the radio in the Incident Room.

"The lights are on," the constable said, "but I can't get any reply."

"Get in!" Ramsay shouted. "Get hold of the landlady and get in. I'll be there."

So he and Hunter drove to Mary's flat. Hunter was driving, overtaking cars on the main street, jumping traffic lights, enjoying himself. When they arrived at the flat, there was a group of people on the pavement staring inside. The landlady had been found in the local pub and had brought all her

232

friends with her. Some still held glasses. Ramsay tried to send them all home, but the big car with its screeching brakes and Hunter posing like a detective from *Miami Vice* only increased their curiosity and excitement.

The sight of the crowd troubled Ramsay. He was worried about what he might find inside. The last thing he needed was another tragedy. But the constable who was holding his ground by the front door of the flat shook his head.

"Sorry," he said. "I can't have got here in time. She's not here. She must have left in a hurry, though."

Ramsay made a quick search of the bedroom and kitchen before he saw the note in the typewriter. Then he ordered Hunter into the car and they drove away without explaining to the police constable or the watchers, leaving the doors wide open and the landlady complaining about her interrupted evening.

24

It was already eight o'clock when Mary began the drive down the lane from Brinkbonnie village. It led behind the sand dunes to the Wildlife Trust carpark at the north of the bay where she and Max had parked on the night of their first meeting. She had been held up by an accident on the road outside Otterbridge where the young policeman in charge of controlling the traffic had seemed out of his depth, and she sped through Brinkbonnie, noticing nothing unusual there. The sky was clear and there was a moon. From the lane she saw the Tower and the mass of woodland behind it and the high moors spread beyond. Nearer the track was a pool and flat, grassy fields. She came to the hut where in summer the Wildlife Trust warden stood to collect money for the carpark. She could not see Max's car but knew it was there. The carpark went on for half a mile, broken into sections by the dunes and the thickets of blackthorn and bramble. He would have parked farther along, she thought, and for a moment she was worried why he thought such secrecy necessary. There was also a feeling of satisfaction that when he was in trouble he had come to her. She drove the Mini only a short distance from the carpark's entrance and left it in full view, so that if by any chance Max had not yet arrived he would know she was there.

These things—the Mini parked at the entrance to the links,

the accident on the Otterbridge Road, which made her late—were to contribute to the outcome of the case.

When she got out of the car, she shivered. She was wearing trousers and a sweater, but there was already a frost in the air and she had been expecting perhaps the same warmth of the night of the Wildlife Trust barbecue. She was very tired and the evening had a dreamlike quality. She was light-headed and imagined that here, in the same place, she and Max could regain the romantic intensity that had begun the affair. She was already anticipating the elation that followed any contact with Max.

If he's here, she thought, he'll be waiting on the shore, at the edge of the water, where I waited for him the last time. She began to climb through the soft sand of the dunes to reach the beach. The silence was impressive. The tide must have been out because there was no sound of water. Uusually at Brinkbonnie, even on the quietest days, there were dogs barking, gulls crying, the noise of a tractor in a distant field. Now there was only the sound of her own breathing and the sand shifting under her feet as she walked. Occasionally she put out her hand to steady herself. The sand was cold and the grains were sharp as ice.

When she reached the highest dune in the system she climbed it and stood there, her arms raised above her head so that her silhouette would stand out against the skyline and wherever Max was he would see her and come to find her. She would have called out to him, shouted over the empty folds of sand, but the silence was daunting and she did not have the courage to break it. From there, for the first time, she saw the sea, the soft, seven-mile waves breaking noise-lessly. She had thought he might be waiting on the hard sand by the edge of the tide where she had waited the first time. It would be such a romantic thing to do. She imagined him looking up at her with the same challenge as she had given him. But as far as she could see the beach was empty, broken only by the square chunks of concrete that had been set on the beach in the last war, separating the dunes from the flat sand, to stop enemy tanks from driving inland.

She sat down, holding her knees, grateful after the frenzy of the previous two days for the space and quiet. Suddenly, farther below and behind her, she heard the noise of shifting sand that had marked her own progress.

"Max!" she called. She wanted to see him very much. "Is that you, Max?" But there was no reply and she thought she must have caused the sand to slide when she sat down. Or perhaps a small animal had made its home there and been disturbed. Even then she was not frightened. She did not know that there was anything to be afraid of, except the possibility that Max had deserted her again. The fear came later.

She stood up and ran down the sand hill to the beach, stopping short this time of the incoming tide. It was too cold for bare feet and she was wearing leather boots that would be damaged by the water. She walked along the tide line where wood and straw, pieces of glass and seacoal, had been washed up with the pebbles and shells. Occasionally she crouched to pick up a smooth stone or a piece of patterned pottery, but she kept her eyes on the dunes, hoping eventually to see Max's silhouette against the horizon coming to meet her.

After half an hour she told herself he would not be coming. This is ridiculous, she thought, a repeat of that farce in the churchyard. Why do I allow myself to be humiliated by him? I've more important things to do tonight. But still, in a way, she was grateful to him, because he had brought her out into the fresh air and when she returned home she would be ready to write the story with a clear head. She turned and began to walk south along the beach, back towards the car.

When the man appeared in front of her, she could not imagine, at first, where he had come from. It was as if he had appeared by magic from the sand.

"Max," she cried. "Max. How did you get here? I didn't see you." And she began to run towards him, tears streaming down her face.

It was only when she saw the blade of the wide, triangular kitchen knife, shining in the moonlight, that she began to feel afraid. It was that and his failure to answer, his stillness and silence. She realised then that he had been waiting for her crouched behind one of the blocks of concrete. He had known all the time where she was. He had seen her on the high dune, watched her walk along the tide line, and waited patiently for her return. She screamed and began to run away from him. She knew instinctively that she would have no chance against him on the flat sand. He was stronger than she and much faster. Her only hope was to get back to the car.

She began to scramble up the dunes on all fours, pulling with her hands and kicking with her feet. He seemed surprised by her sudden movement and could not use both hands because he was still holding the knife, blade outstretched. But he seemed to have power in his legs to compensate, and when she slipped, gulping for air, exhausted, he almost caught her. She kicked back with one foot, sending a shower of fine sand over his face and into his eyes. He swore and lunged foward with the knife towards her, but he could not see and missed her. She ran on. She could not hear him behind her. She slowed down for a moment and listened, but there was no sound of movement. He must have followed a different path, she thought. He would hope to trick her by getting ahead of her and cutting her off from the car. She stood quite still and listened again, but there was silence.

She was more frightened then than she had been when he was right behind her, tearing at her trouser leg with his knife. From the dune where she stood, catching her breath, she could see her car, ordinary and familiar on the grass. It seemed such a short distance away. She supposed she should creep towards it, keeping below the skyline, playing the same game as he was, so he would not know where she was either. But suddenly panic took over and she ran towards the orange car at full-tilt. She might even have started screaming again. She wanted only to be away from the place and the man who was following her. She thought when she reached the short, cropped grass of the carpark that the nightmare was over. There was nothing then between her and safety. It was only when she was nearly at the car, with several yards to go, already feeling in her pocket for her keys, that a man stepped out of the shadow of the Mini. He caught her in his arms and her screams echoed over the quiet and empty landscape.

On the way to Brinkbonnie Ramsay said nothing. After the shared elation of the Incident Room he seemed to close in on himself and shut Hunter off. He was deep in concentrated thought and Hunter sensed a lack of confidence.

He's losing his nerve, Hunter thought. He's not up to the job. That was the trouble with these small-town men. So little happened in the rural divisions that when there was some action they didn't have a clue how to do the thing properly. Perhaps it was time to put in for a transfer to Newcastle Central before he turned into one of them.

Just outside Brinkbonnie they were given the information that a young policeman had seen Mary's car at an accident on the Otterbridge Road, and they knew they were going in the right direction. Hunter cheered under his breath, but Ramsay would not allow himself to be optimistic. On the edge of the village he made Hunter slow down. He did not want the people there frightened by speeding cars and sirens. On the lane they went faster again and saw the Mini immediately, parked just beyond the carpark attendant's hut.

"No sign of Laidlaw," Hunter said. Ramsay's silence was irritating him. What was the matter with the man? The thing was nearly over. Still Ramsay said nothing.

"Shall I drive on up the track and look for his car?" Hunter asked.

"Yes," Ramsay said. "Drive on. But if we don't find it soon, park. We must find the woman. That's the important thing."

The track was dry and rutted and Hunter was driving slowly. There was no sign of a car and he could sense his superior's tension and impatience.

"This is impossible," Ramsay said irritably. "The car could be anywhere behind those bushes. We'll need to look on foot."

238

Hunter drove on, unsure of what the inspector wanted him to do.

"Stop," Ramsay said suddenly. "Stop here. Something's wrong. We must find Mary Raven." He felt that they had been deceived.

They got out of the car and stood in the frosty silence. Hunter shut the car doors and the noise was loud and shocking.

"Where do we start?" Hunter asked. He had none of Ramsay's sense of foreboding. "They could be anywhere." He imagined them lying together in some hollow in the dunes, a pornographic fantasy of sex in the open air. He stood in the moonlight and grinned at the idea.

"You cross the dunes to the beach," Ramsay said. "I'll walk back to her car."

"What do you want me to do if I see her?"

"Nothing," Ramsay said sharply. "Not if she's on her own. Wait until he finds her."

"Shall I radio for help?"

"No," Ramsay said. "I'll do it. But by the time they all get here it'll be too late."

The first scream surprised them both. Hunter was only a few yards from the car. He began to run through the dunes towards the beach, swearing at the spikes of marram grass that scratched his hands and the sand that filled his shoes. Ramsay stood and listened, then walked quickly towards the carpark entrance, his shadow long behind him.

When Mary Raven hurtled down the sand bank and into his arms, he felt only relief. He held her, trying to calm her as she sobbed, awkward at first, then remembering what it was like to hold a woman in his arms. At first she was hysterical in her terror. She tried to pull away from him, tearing at his face with her fingernails and kicking his legs with her heavy boots. Then she recognised him.

"He tried to kill me," she sobbed. "He had a knife and he tried to kill me. It couldn't have been Max. Max would never have done a thing like that."

239

"No," Ramsay said, his arms still around her shoulder, trying to stop her trembling. "It wasn't Max."

From the main road they heard the sirens of police cars coming to assist them, and as they came to the end of the track, Hunter emerged from the nearest dune, his hand bleeding, his face triumphant, with his prisoner.

"Too late as usual," he said, nodding towards the flashing blue lights. It would do no harm, this, he thought. It might mean a promotion if Ramsay didn't take all the credit.

"Where's the knife?" Ramsay asked.

"He dropped it in the dunes." He looked towards the reinforcements. "They'll find it."

"Well, then," Ramsay said. "You'd better get him back to Otterbridge."

James Laidlaw looked strangely young without his spectacles. In the half light on the dunes Mary had mistaken him for Max and Ramsay could see how that was possible. James had lost all desire to fight. When they opened the back door of the police car for him, he got in without a word. He sat upright, a respectable figure. He was still wearing a suit. A policewoman who had taken Mary to her car was wrapping her in a rug, pouring tea from a flask.

Hunter was about to drive away when Ramsay tapped on the window. Hunter opened it with hostility, expecting another command or rebuke.

"Well done," Ramsay said. "That was a good arrest."

25

Ramsay would have liked to take Mary Raven to his cottage in Heppleburn to talk to her. He would have been more comfortable there, without interruptions and telephone calls. He could have made her coffee and waited until she was ready to talk. But he knew it would not do and the interview would have to take place in the police station in Otterbridge, with its institutional furniture and the knowledge that somewhere in the same building James Laidlaw was being questioned, too.

At first she refused to go with him.

"It's *my* story," she said. "I need a phone and a typewriter. No other bugger's going to get the glory after all this work."

"It will be your story," he said, coaxing her with his attention and his gratitude. "There'll be no press release tonight. All the papers will know is that James Laidlaw has been arrested. They'll be desperate to talk to you tomorrow. And, you know, I might be able to give you some useful information."

So she allowed herself to be helped into the back of his car, complaining only when he drove past the Castle Hotel without stopping to buy her a drink. At the police station he left her for a while in the company of a policewoman, but she seemed not to mind and from the corridor he saw her scribbling intensely in her notebook. He went to talk to

241

Hunter. Laidlaw, it seemed, had started talking as soon as the car left Brinkbonnie and nothing could stop him.

"He asked to write a statement," Hunter said. "He's doing that now. He refused to see a solicitor. We'll have no problem with a conviction."

So when Ramsay returned to begin his interview with Mary, he knew most of the details of the case. But he gave nothing away. He was diffident, unsure, so she thought he needed her. He let her believe that it was her story after all.

"How did you find out about James Laidlaw's racket?" Ramsay asked. They drank tea with a little whisky in it. They were at the top of the building and there were no blinds on the windows. Outside spotlights lit up the old walls that surrounded the town and the ruins of the abbey.

"It was just really a wild guess at first," she said. She was more herself, excitable, proud. She was showing off. "His decisions about which stories to run were so arbitrary. The Brinkbonnie development was just an example. When the plans first went before the council, he wrote an editorial about the destruction of rural communities. It didn't bother him that Alice Parry was his aunt. Then, when the village started its own campaign, he began to talk about objectivity and ordered me off. I thought it was just some weird autocracy—that he wanted to show me who was boss—until I did court duty on the morning after Mrs. Parry died."

She paused to catch her breath. He waited patiently and smiled to encourage her.

"People who appear in court are often much more worried about being in the paper than they are about the fine they receive from the magistrates," she said. "James usually did the monthly magistrates court and that was strange in itself. Most editors think themselves too superior to mix with petty criminals—they're more likely to be taking the magistrates out to lunch. James said it was his way of keeping his finger on the pulse of the town, but of course it wasn't that at all."

Ramsay interrupted gently, reluctantly, showing her that he was entertained by her conversation, but that he needed all the details.

"What did happen when you were in the court that Monday?" he asked.

"There was this drunk driver," she said, making the most of the drama, playing up to him, watching his reaction. "He'd been in court before and he was disqualified for twelve months. But he had his own business and was much more worried about the bad publicity than about losing his licence. He came up to me in the waiting room and asked if there was any way of keeping his name out of the paper. Of course I said it was impossible. He got quite cross and said he had heard it was possible to come to an arrangement about it. He was a wealthy man, he said. Money was no object. At first I thought he was just an isolated loony who was trying it on, but when I considered it later he seemed indignant, almost self-righteous, as if I was treating him unfairly."

"So James was taking bribes from people who had appeared in court and wanted the fact kept secret?"

"Yes," she said, and her eyes sparkled because he was listening to her so carefully and following her line of thought so well. "But that wasn't all he was doing."

She paused dramatically while he poured her more whisky, then, although he already knew what was coming, he waited, attentive for her next revelation.

"The odd twenty quid to keep a bank manager's name out of the paper was only chicken feed," she said. "That wouldn't keep our Stella in designer frocks and fancy kitchens. So James got more ambitious and the racket with local businesses started."

"When was that, Mary?" Ramsay asked, quiet and apologetic. "When did the local business racket first start?"

"Years ago," she said. "Perhaps even before I started on the paper."

"Tell me," he said. "How did it work?"

"Well," she said, tantalising him, the perfect performer. "Of course I don't know all the details . . ."

"But it's your story, Mary. You know how it worked."

"Oh, yes," she said. "I know how it worked. James Laidlaw, the great investigative journalist, threatened to put people out of business if they didn't pay him lots of money. That's how it worked."

"How could he do that, Mary? I need to know."

"He snooped," she said. "He was a bloody good reporter. He followed leads, listened to rumours. He found out all the things that people wanted to hide. And if they were clean as the driven snow, he started the rumours himself."

"What about evidence?" Ramsay asked. "You'll need evidence for your story."

"There are some people willing to talk," Mary said. "There's May Smith in the cottage hospital. She'll talk to you."

"May Smith?" Ramsay said, although Hunter had been visiting her only hours before. "Who's she, Mary?"

"She's an old lady. She was a resident in the White Gates old people's home. She liked it there. She was happy. But the place had to close because James ran a campaign about it in the *Express*. Relatives of the old folks who lived there took them away because they thought everything you read in the papers is true."

"Why did he run the campaign, Mary?"

"Because the matron refused to pay him protection money."

"Why didn't she go to the police?"

"Would you have believed her?" Mary demanded. "After all the publicity there's been about the ill treatment of old people in nursing homes? Or would you have thought she was making the whole thing up to protect her business?"

"Perhaps," Ramsay said. "But we would have looked into the complaint."

"And you would have found nothing!" she said. "No witnesses, nothing. None of the other old people's homes in the area would admit to paying up in case the same thing happened to them. James Laidlaw was a powerful man, and married to a Rutherford. They were frightened of him. They thought he was worth a fortune."

She paused again, went to the window, and looked down on the street.

244

"Someone did tell the police what James was doing," she said. "Joe West, the county councillor. Do you remember him? But you were too busy investigating the allegations of fraud James was making in the *Express* to take any notice."

Ramsay thought. He remembered Joe West, though he had not dealt with the investigation personally, and he could recall no connection in the case with the *Express*. It was something about fraudulent expense claims for his council work. And he had had his house painted, Ramsay remembered, by council workmen using materials paid for by Northumberland County. In the end they had decided not to prosecute. How many other councillors, after all, could claim total honesty if there was a major investigation? Joe West had resigned and they had considered the matter at an end.

"What happened to him?" Ramsay asked.

"He's great," she said. "Really amazing. It's the best thing that ever happened to him. He's running a project for the homeless in Newcastle down by the river. But he hates James Laidlaw. He'll talk to you and you should go to see the centre."

It wasn't only the wealthy businessmen and powerful councillors in the area who had been blackmailed by Laidlaw, Ramsay thought. It must have become almost a habit. He had made the same threat to Tom Kerr about his brawl in the street with Charlie Elliot. Ramsay remembered his conversation with the choirmaster in the dimly lit room earlier that evening.

"I could never have gone into the church again," Tom Kerr had cried. "Not with a story like that splashed all over the paper. How could people have any respect for me?"

"So what did you do?" Ramsay had asked.

"What do you think I did? I paid him and I've been paying him ever since."

Ramsay drew his thoughts back to the office and to the woman who sat with him.

"Now, Mary," he said. "What has all this to do with Alice Parry?"

"Don't you know?" she cried, immensely pleased because she thought she still had the power to surprise him. "Do you mean you really haven't guessed?"

245

He did not answer directly. He had never enjoyed lying.

"It's your story," he said again. I want you to tell it, I want to know what Alice Parry said to you on the afternoon of her death."

"Oh, that," she said. "That's almost irrelevant."

"All the same," he said. "For completeness. Out of interest. I want to know."

"We talked about Max," she said. "We were having an affair."

"Yes," he said gently. He did not want to hurt her. He paused. "Did you realise Stella Laidlaw was blackmailing him about it?"

She looked up sharply. "No," she said. "I hadn't realised even that she knew about us. She must have guessed. Blackmail must run in the family."

"Do you know where Max is?" he asked. "We need to find him to tell him what's happened. Besides, his wife is very worried about him."

"No," she said. "I haven't seen him since the night you took me in for questioning." She grinned briefly. "He was there in the flat when the policeman came to fetch me."

She paused. "He'll be hiding," she said. "Poor Max."

"You must have thought the note arranging to meet you at Brinkbonnie was from Max," he said. "And you went to meet him."

"Yes," she said. "It looked like Max's writing. James must be an expert in forgery, too."

She looked up at him. "How could James know about Max and me. I suppose he guessed."

"Apparently," Ramsay said, "when he realized you suspected him of blackmail, he searched your desk at work. There was an old letter from Max. It was rather explicit. It even mentioned where you met."

She sat, deflated and very sad, so he felt sorry for her. To cheer her up, he said, pleading: "Tell me the rest of it then. Tell my why James Laidlaw murdered Alice Parry."

She brightened immediately. "Henshaw had bought James off," she said. "You must have worked that out."

Ramsay remained impassive. He did not want to disappoint her and spoil her story. But he had worked it out. After the discussion with Tom Kerr, the explanation was inevitable. Henshaw hadn't bribed community activists as Jack Robson had thought, he hadn't needed to. Any village event is considered entirely unimportant until it is reported in the local newspaper. The story gives it credibility. With James Laidlaw in his pocket Henshaw could dictate the image the public received of his development. And of the developer, Ramsay thought, remembering the picture in the *Express* of Henshaw surrounded by adoring toddlers. Then he remembered the evening he had gone to the Laidlaws' house and the interview being interrupted by an angry visitor. He realised now that the visitor was Colin Henshaw, furious because he thought James Laidlaw would break their deal.

Mary seemed encouraged by Ramsay's silence and continued: "Henshaw wouldn't talk to me, but I think he started paying James after the first editorial about the Brinkbonnie development. He had lots of other plans waiting to be approved by the planning department and he wouldn't want bad publicity at that stage."

"Tell me Mary," he said, "exactly what you think happened." He said it to humour her because she needed to feel clever and in control after the assault on the sand dunes. James Laidlaw had already admitted the whole thing to Hunter. But he said it, too, because she was lively and funny and he did not want the conversation to end.

"Mrs. Parry felt guilty about selling her land to Henshaw," Mary said, "and after I'd spoken to her that afternoon she decided to try to buy the field back. Of course Henshaw refused to sell. There must have been an argument and Henshaw told Mrs. Parry about James. You can imagine him, can't you, blurting it out in the middle of the row: "You won't get any support, you know, from that nephew of yours. I'm paying him off. You've no chance without the publicity of getting the support for your campaign." Then Mrs. Parry not wanting to believe it but seeing in the end that it was

247

probably true. Poor Mrs. Parry. How upset she must have been.''

"James Laidlaw was waiting for her in the garden when she got back from the pub,'' Ramsay said, taking the initiative for the first time. The pretence that he was the passive recipient of her knowledge was over. After all, he had promised Mary some useful information. "Stella had taken a sleeping pill and it was easy enough for him to leave the room without anyone noticing. He went out through the kitchen door. Max was watching television and didn't hear anything.''

He pictured James in the windy garden with its smell of ivy and salt in the black shadow of the Tower, waiting for Alice, wondering what Henshaw had told her. Then she had come back, angry and disappointed, threatening to expose him. He had killed her, stabbing her from behind with a knife he had taken from the kitchen as he had followed her into the house.

"I didn't see James,'' Mary said, breaking into his thoughts. She was embarrassed. It was a sort of confession. "I was in the churchyard waiting for Max. He didn't turn up. I supposed, of course, that it meant that he'd decided to stay with Judy. I was upset. I thought he didn't care about me. I left soon after eleven and I saw no-one in the Tower garden then. But perhaps James was hiding.''

"No,'' Ramsay said. "He couldn't have been hiding. He was seen by someone in the village.''

"Who?'' she demanded. "Who saw him?''

It was his turn to tease her. "Can't you guess?'' he asked.

"Charlie Elliot!'' she said, delighted because she had worked it out after all. "It must have been Charlie Elliot, but you said he was home before Mrs. Parry died.''

"He was,'' Ramsay said. "But he came out again. He was drunk, a little amorous. He'd always been obsessed with Maggie Kerr and he stood in the street and stared up at her window. On his way home he must have seen James Laidlaw standing in the moonlight in the middle of the Tower lawn waiting for Mrs. Parry. It wouldn't have meant anything to him until the next day when he heard about Mrs. Parry's death.''

''But why didn't Charlie tell you about James?'' She had taken a notebook from her pocket and was scribbling details in shorthand. The door opened and Hunter slipped quietly into the room, but she took no notice of him.

''Because it would have meant admitting that he was out of the house at about the time Mrs. Parry died,'' Ramsay said. ''Besides, he hoped to use the information against Laidlaw.''

''And that's why he died,'' she said.

He nodded.

''Charlie phoned Laidlaw the day he disappeared,'' Hunter said. ''Laidlaw promised to come to his hideout the next day with enough money for Charlie to go abroad, start again. Instead he came up early in the morning and killed him.''

He spoke with great satisfaction and she looked at him with distaste. She seemed small and very tired. The euphoria of her story and the pleasure in the completeness of all the details had gone. She was realising, Ramsay thought, how close she had been to becoming the third victim.

''I didn't realise about Charlie Elliot,'' she said. ''I thought he was the murderer. It never occurred to me that James might have killed his aunt. I thought it was just about money.'' She paused. ''Why did he do it?'' she asked. ''Why was he so desperate for money? The paper can't have been doing badly.''

Ramsay looked at Hunter to check his facts. ''It was Stella,'' he said. ''As you said, she has expensive tastes. Everyone thought her father paid for that big house by the river, but he'd had nothing to do with her since she went into hospital. James was afraid of losing her. He thought if he gave her everything she wanted he might keep her happy.''

''What will she do now?'' Mary asked.

Ramsay shook his head. ''I don't know.'' But it wasn't Stella who concerned him. It was the child with the white hair and the transparent skin who had lost the only adults she could trust. He never knew that Carolyn had realised almost

249

from the beginning that her father had killed Alice Parry. Peter, sleepless with excitement, had seen his uncle on the lawn, waiting. He had told Carolyn because he told her everything and he had kept the secret because she had wanted him to. Yet though Ramsay never knew of that terrible responsibility, he considered her the real victim of the case.

Ramsay heard from Mary again two months later. She phoned him at Otterbridge and offered to buy him lunch.

"To celebrate," she said. "I've just got a job on the *Journal*."

"I'm not surprised," he said. It had been impossible in the weeks after the Brinkbonnie murders to escape Mary's picture in the press and the articles of the "local intrepid reporter who finds solution to murder mystery." She had even been on national television. "They're lucky to have you."

"Let's go the Castle in Brinkbonnie," she said. "You can pick me up at the flat, then I can get drunk."

So he gave her a lift to Brinkbonnie. The sun was shining and there was a mild westerly wind. In the street where she lived the blossoms dropped from the trees like snow. In Brinkbonnie everything seemed much the same. As they drove down the Otterbridge Road he looked into the Greys' farmyard, but there was no blue Rover in view. Perhaps it was discreetly parked in the tractor shed. The post office was still shut for lunch and the same cars were for sale outside Kerr's garage. They stopped, for a moment, outside the field where the houses were planned, but there were no bulldozers. The council had decided to appeal against the inspector's decision to the high court, so building was delayed.

In the Castle they sat on the stage in the lounge bar and ordered steak. She drank beer and most of a bottle of overpriced red wine. She wore wide red dungarees and enormous earrings shaped like frogs.

Halfway through the meal when she was already loud and flushed she put down her knife and fork.

"Did you know that Max and Judy are moving into the

Tower?'' she asked. And he realised that he was only there because there was no-one else she could talk to about her secret lover.

"No," he said. "I didn't know."

"He resigned from the Health Centre after the business with Stella and the prescription," she said. "They're planning to open the Tower to the public, run courses in local crafts, folk music. You know the sort of thing."

He nodded.

"Have you seen Max?" he asked gently.

"No," she said. "I thought he might have been in touch, but it's probably just as well this way."

"Yes," he said. He could think of nothing more to say.

"I'm moving to Newcastle at the weekend," she said. "I'm not really a small-town girl."

He would have liked to ask her what had happened to Stella and the little girl, but decided in the end that he preferred not to know.

When he dropped her outside her flat, he thought she might ask him to come in for a drink, but she only waved like a child and beamed when he wished her good luck. He went home to the cottage in Heppleburn. In the woods in the dene there were bluebells and wood anemones and the trees were green with new leaves. He made a pot of coffee, so the smell of it filled the house, sat on the windowsill, and thought that he should appreciate the view while it was still there. Then the telephone rang and Hunter, at the other end, told him he was needed at work.

About the Author

The daughter of a village school teacher, Ann Cleeves lives in Nathumberland, England, where she spends her time with her two small children and writing.

Murder in My Backyard is her sixth novel. She is also the author of *A Bird in the Hand, Come Death and High Water, Murder in Paradise, A Prey to Murder*, and *A Lesson in Dying*.